Eliza Long

HEARTS OF THE OZARKS
BOOK 1

AVA MacKINNEY

Publishing Coordinator – Sharon Kizziah-Holmes
Cover Design – Jaycee DeLorenzo

Paperback-Press
an imprint of A & S Publishing
Paperback Press, LLC

ISBN -13: 978-1-956806-98-4

DEDICATION

I dedicate this book to the love of my life, my biggest supporter and most enthusiastic encourager; my husband, Steve. Back when I thought this might be a crazy dream and consume way too much of my (our) time, he gave me the green light. Thank you, Steve, for nourishing my dream and creating a haven to allow it to flourish.

ACKNOWLEDGMENTS

So many people deserve to be mentioned as encouragers and professional support as I journeyed down this path. Many friends helped me on my way as beta readers, editors, and with timely kicks in the seat of my pants when needed.

I want to mention one in particular; Dena Way. When I was young and insecure, she was the first person I dared to mention that I might want to write a novel. Lo and behold, she didn't laugh! Because she believed in me, I took those first baby steps into the writing world. I will be forever grateful. Also, a shout out to her husband, Dan, who is one of my best beta readers, with a sharp eye and great advice.

I also want to thank my publishing coordinator, Sharon Kizziah-Holmes at Paperback Press. She has patiently guided me through the publishing path, answering my endless questions and giving her expert advice.

Thanks also to my two editors, Kate Richards and Nanette Sipe, whose expertise has helped me craft a novel that is way better than the original.

PROLOGUE

Warrensburg, Missouri, April 25, 1848

Five-year-old Eliza Long gripped her father's hand and kept her eyes on her brother's casket as it was lowered into the hard Missouri ground. Her chin trembled, and she gasped for air, trying desperately to keep quiet so she wouldn't have to endure the sad, pitying stares from the others again.

Her grandparents, her neighbors, even people she didn't know stood in a tight group around her and her pa, trying in their own way to ease the awful pain and grief. It only made it worse, more real. She wanted them to leave, to go back to what they were doing before this awful monster of a tragedy fell upon their family. For three days now, she had somehow convinced herself it hadn't really happened, that her brother was still here. But no longer could she lie to herself. Sam was gone. Her only sibling gone forever. Nothing could bring him back.

A loud, gulping sob escaped her clenched lips. She

ripped her hand from her father's and ran toward the cemetery fence. She heard gasps and sad murmurings behind her then footsteps closing in. Her short legs propelled her the rest of the way then up onto a stump and over the fence.

"Eliza, stop!" came the voice of Jonathan Monroe, her brother's closest friend. He stopped at the fence, but Eliza was careening down the steep hill toward the woods behind the church, her bonnet on the ground and her dark braids streaming behind her.

An hour later, Jonathan found her sitting in the tree house he and Sam had built the previous summer. Three walls, a sturdy floor, and a roof had provided hours of companionship for the two boys and the tagalong five-year-old. Despite their age difference of eight years, Sam had included his little sister in most of his and Jonathan's escapades. Jonathan had never minded though. Eliza was a fun little tyke. Her mother had died giving birth to her, and, besides their father and grandparents, they only had each other.

Jonathan climbed up the tree silently and saw her sitting on the floor staring through the one open wall at her house down in the valley surrounded by giant oaks and several barns. He scooted across the splintered floor and took a seat beside her. He'd known he'd find her here. This was where she usually ran when things weren't going well.

Sam had always worried about her it seemed. Jonathan had never been sure why. Daniel Long, their pa, was a good man—a hardworking, very busy man but kind. Their grandparents were also good people. A little crotchety at times, perhaps, but that was to be expected at their age. Sam seemed to think it was his job to protect his little mite of a sister. For five years, since his ma died giving birth,

Sam had tended to Eliza every moment he was able, as if he were honoring a vow he'd given his ma. Consequently, Jonathan, too, had grown an almost paternal sense of protectiveness toward the child. He had held and cuddled her as a baby, encouraged her as she took her first steps and spoke her first words, laughed at her awkward baby speech when she started using full sentences. Together, to her grandmother's chagrin, they taught her to love the outdoors, to fish and hunt, to ride horses and camp.

He looked at her now, her face wet with tears, not moving a muscle or making a sound. His heart almost broke imagining what she must be feeling. It was hard for him losing his best friend, especially so suddenly, so unexpectedly. One minute Sam was riding Star, his horse, over a hill, beckoning Jon to hurry; the next minute, he lay on the ground, blood gushing from a wound on his head. He was gone before Jonathan could get to him. Something had spooked the horse and, apparently, Sam had struck his head on one of the sharp rocks jutting from the ground.

Jonathan put an arm around Eliza's skinny shoulders. Her body felt rigid but, as he gently pulled her toward him, she went limp and wailed. She clutched his shirt and buried her face against his chest. His other hand came up to caress her head. A lump formed in his throat as he made a silent vow to Sam to always be there for his beloved, little sister.

CHAPTER ONE

Springfield, Missouri, August 1861 – Thirteen years later

Daniel Long stood and reached out to shake the outstretched hand of the tall soldier that had just entered the parlor. "Jonathan Monroe! It is so good to see you again, my boy!"

"And you, sir!" Jonathan answered with a broad smile. They laughed and embraced.

Daniel was pleased to see what the years had done to his young friend. From the looks of his tan, chiseled face, and his broad, muscular build, it was easy to see Jon spent his hours doing manual labor under the sun.

"I'd never thought I'd be greeting you in these circumstances. War is a terrible thing, and I pray it will be done and over with in short order."

"Me, too, sir. I've got better things to do with my time than traipsing around these hills shooting at folks!" The older man laughed and motioned for Jonathan to sit in a chair at the far end of the room.

Jonathan sat, settled his hat on his knee, and ran his hand through his thick, dark hair. "So, has your family been well, sir? I haven't heard from any of you for years."

"My parents both died sometime after your family moved. I sold the property and bought a farm north of Springfield. I've been raising horses, a dream I've had for years. And yourself, Jon? Where have you been hiding all these years?"

"Actually, not that far from you. I have a spread down in Ozark. Raising horses, too." He grinned at Daniel. "Horses and beef cattle for over five years now."

"Good for you! How 'bout your family?"

"Pa and Ma sold the land, split the money six ways between all us boys then moved in with Roger and his wife."

"Still have your horses?"

"I sold about half to the US government. I'm hoping to work out a deal to sell the rest before they all get stolen by the Confederates. There's a few too many secessionists hanging around our neck of the woods. I'm getting nervous. I've got most of them hidden away, but you can't keep too many secrets around here anymore."

"You better get 'em sold quick. Even the government will be takin' what they want soon. You'll get nothing, except a thanks and a pat on the back. I sold mine three months ago and moved into Springfield. Into this boardinghouse, in fact. You are now sitting in my parlor." He chuckled.

Jonathan paused and studied his hands for a moment. "Uh, sir, you haven't mentioned Eliza. Is she..." A trace of fear flitted across his face.

"Eliza?" Daniel laughed. "Eliza's fine. In fact, she's the reason I invited you here today."

"She...she is?"

"When was the last time you saw her?"

"Ten years ago, when I was sixteen and she was eight. I

remember it like it was yesterday. She was so mad at me she wouldn't say goodbye, wouldn't even look at me."

"And why was that?"

"Because I was leaving."

Daniel shook his head sadly. "She lost some pretty important people in a short time. After Sam died, she never wanted to leave your side."

"I know. I'm sorry I left, sir. It's just that I had a chance to get this land cheap. It was my great-uncle's, and he made me an unbelievable offer. I had to do it."

"Don't apologize, Jon. You would have been a fool to pass up a good offer on land. And Eliza has survived. She moped around for a week or two then snapped out of it. She's a strong girl. We lived in the Fair Grove area for years, and she made a lot of good friends.

"But because it's just Eliza and me, now, I didn't think it would be safe for her alone on our farm. That's why we took up residence here. There's safety in numbers. I figured Springfield would be much safer than out in the countryside."

"You're right about that, sir. I just hope it's safe here, too."

"Well, with Lyon's 6000 soldiers here, it ought to be. Although I hear Generals Price and McCulloch are approaching with far more men than we have."

"We've beaten those scalawags several times already when we were outnumbered. We can do it again!"

Daniel Long slowly nodded his head. "Let's hope so, Jonathan, let's hope so." He raised his eyes and looked intently at the younger man. "I have a favor to ask of you, son."

"Anything, sir."

Daniel held up his hand and chuckled. "Not so fast. This is big. I want you to hear me out and then take some time to think about it. As you know, other than Eliza, I have no living relatives. If something should happen to me, Eliza

6

will be alone. I can't sleep at night thinking about her trying to survive this bloody war without someone to take care of her."

"Sir, the answer is yes!"

"I'm not finished. You are the closest thing to family she has, Jon, and, I'm convinced that you love her like she is your own sister, your own flesh and blood."

"That's true. I would die for her, if necessary."

Jonathan met Daniel's intense gaze with unwavering devotion.

"Jon, son, I need you to take her in as your own if I'm killed. I'm not sure how you can do this since you're a soldier as well. Would your family help out?"

"I have an aunt living here in Springfield, a strong Christian woman who moved here from Arkansas a few years ago. She's my ma's youngest sister, never been married. She lives in a big house over on Walnut Street. That's where I stay when I'm in town. Eliza could stay with her."

"Is she alone?"

"She has a couple of former slaves. She granted them their freedom a year or two ago, but they won't leave her. They're like family."

"Is she a secessionist or is she pro-union?"

Jonathan grinned. "You'll have to ask her. She won't talk about it. She's too busy loving everybody."

"I think I might like her."

"Come on over and meet her."

"I'd like that. It'll have to wait though. I have nothing but meetings and drills for the next couple of days then we'll be heading out to engage McCulloch and Price south of here. Perhaps there will be time after that. Are you marching with us, or are you and your men guarding Springfield?"

"Unfortunately, we're ordered to stay and guard the city. Not my choice. My men are ready to fight again."

"I've heard some good reports about you and your troops."

"Thank you, sir."

"And you've been promoted to lieutenant?"

"Not hard to accomplish in these times, sir. Most of my men are from the area. I've known them for years."

Several people sat around the large parlor, some alone and others engaged in conversation. Everyone raised their heads as a laughing young couple entered the room. The man was a smartly dressed officer, and the young woman clinging to his arm was startlingly beautiful, with her dark, cascading curls and sky-blue eyes.

Jonathan's jaw dropped. He would have recognized those eyes anywhere. But what happened to little Eliza? As the couple approached, Daniel rose to greet them, but Jonathan stayed glued to his seat.

"Henry, how have you been?" Daniel asked, his tone lacking warmth.

"Jonathan, I'd like you to meet Captain Henry Goodman, the nephew of one of my best friends."

Jonathan snapped to attention and stood. He extended his hand to Captain Goodman. Seeing disapproval on Goodman's face, he remembered his manners and saluted instead.

Eliza stared at him; her mouth open in surprise. She shook her head in disbelief.

"Jonathan? Jonathan Monroe? Is it really you?"

"Is this"—he gestured toward her with a sweep of his hand—"really you, Eliza? All grown up?"

Eliza laughed sweetly and twirled. "It's me, all grown up!" She stood for a moment with a huge smile on her face. Then she wrapped her arms around him in a long, tight embrace. "I thought I'd never see you again, Jon."

He, in turn, hugged her unashamedly and laughed with delight. When he saw Henry Goodman standing to the side with a scowl on his face, he twirled around with Eliza in his arms before he set her down.

"Have a seat, Eliza. We need to discuss something with you," Daniel said as he pulled another chair over. Captain Goodman quickly grabbed a chair and placed it next to Eliza's. Jonathan didn't miss the flash of irritation in Daniel's eyes.

Daniel reached over to take his daughter's hands in his own. "Dear, as you know, we are living in dangerous times."

Eliza squirmed and pulled free. "Don't, Pa. You're scaring me."

"It's certainly not my intention to scare you, Eliza. But I want to be honest with you about our circumstances."

"We've already had this talk, haven't we?"

"No, we haven't. Not this particular talk."

Eliza stood and stepped away. Daniel sat back in frustration. He looked at Jonathan and shook his head. Henry stood, walked over to Eliza, and placed his hands on her shoulders, only to have her shake free from him and walk to the other side of the room. After pacing back and forth, the width of the parlor, several times, she finally stopped, sighed loudly, and walked back to her chair.

She gently stroked her father's hands. "I'm sorry, Pa. Say what you have to say."

Daniel reached up and caressed her cheek. "Eliza, if anything should happen to me, if I'm killed or badly wounded...I've asked Jonathan to watch out for you, to..."

"Pshaw!" Henry interrupted. "Why this man here when you have me, old friend? Our families have been close for generations!"

Daniel, Jonathan, and Eliza all stared at Henry Goodman.

"Uh, Henry, would you please leave us alone to discuss

this?" Eliza asked politely.

"I think, under these extreme circumstances, it would be to your advantage that I stay," he answered.

"No, please. I need for you to leave us."

"Eliza, come outside with me for a moment, please," Henry said as he rose from his chair.

"No, Henry. I need to talk to my father."

"It won't take but a moment of your time. I insist."

Eliza stared at him again. "You insist?"

"Yes, it's for your own good."

Eliza shook her head in disbelief. Daniel winked at her.

"Leave, Henry," she asked again.

He stood rooted to the carpet.

"Now!"

He stared at her, breathing hard, his face aflame with indignation. Finally, he turned and marched out.

"Where did you find that boy?" Daniel asked.

"You introduced us, remember?" Eliza answered.

"I think I know him from somewhere," Jonathan said. "You said he's a friend of your family, sir?"

"Well, not exactly. I've never counted him among my friends. His father and uncle were two of my best friends since childhood. His father died a few years ago. His uncle is Abe Goodman, owner of the bank on Olive Street."

"I sense you're not too fond of him."

"Oh, you do, do you? Are you always this discerning, son?"

Jonathan chuckled. "It doesn't take a genius."

"He's right, you know, Pa. Why do you hate him?"

"Hate? I don't think I hate him. I just dislike him intensely. Can't you see why, after a display like that?" Daniel sat back and stretched his long legs out in front of him. "When his father died, Henry inherited a large sum of money. In a few short years, he squandered all of it with wild living: gambling, women, drink, you name it. It could have lasted him a lifetime if he'd been the man his father was. And furthermore, daughter of mine, when I introduced you to that rascal, I never intended for you to spend time with him."

"Sorry, he sort of…shows up and as you can see, he's a little hard to get rid of."

"Seems terribly possessive if you ask me," Jonathan said.

"Jonathan, I still can't believe it's you!"

"Wow, that's a quick change of subject."

"Time is too important to waste talking about him."

"I agree." Daniel leaned forward and kissed his daughter's cheek. "Back to more important matters. Jonathan has agreed to be your guardian if something should happen to me."

"Father, I don't need a guardian. I'm eighteen."

Jonathan quickly did some adding and realized Eliza was right. Eighteen? How did that happen so fast? After all, he was twenty-six and there was an eight-year difference in their age. Yup, she's eighteen. He shook his head in disbelief. Had it really been that long?

"Isn't that right, Jonathan?"

"Uh, I'm sorry, sir. You were saying?"

"Pay attention, son. I was telling Eliza you wouldn't be her legal guardian; you would simply fill the role of a family member, like a brother. Isn't that right?"

"Yes, exactly." He smiled at Eliza.

Her eyes had a curious twinkle.

"If anything happens, God forbid, you could come live with my aunt Mildred. She lives in a nice house just a couple of blocks from here."

"Is she really that bad?" Eliza asked.

"That bad? What are you talking about?"

"You said, 'God forbid' I could live with her. Or is it her you're worried about? God forbid your poor aunt ends up with me?"

Her eyes told Jonathan she hadn't changed much over

the years after all. He wrapped his arm around her neck and thumped her on the top of her pretty head with his knuckles. When he saw the looks passing between the other occupants of the room, he quickly let her go.

Eliza giggled and tried to push her unruly curls into place. "I almost forgot. I'm still mad at you for leaving."

"I'm sorry. I've been sorry all these years."

"He would have passed up an opportunity of a lifetime if he'd stayed. Besides, his folks had sold the place. Where would he have stayed?"

"I don't know. Back then, I figured he'd just move in with us."

"It's settled, then?" Daniel asked.

Jonathan and Eliza looked at him then at each other. They smiled and nodded.

"Good! Now maybe I can get some sleep!" He reached out and took Jonathan's hand in his left and Eliza's in his right. "Let's pray, shall we?" Three heads bowed together as they took the deep cry of Daniel's heart to their Lord.

CHAPTER TWO

"This may come across as treasonous if I were in the military, but I'm not, so I'll exercise my right to free speech and tell you I don't like and don't trust this General Lyon of yours," Abe Goodman said as he flicked the reins across the backs of the two old mules pulling his buckboard. Eliza gripped the side. She held great fondness for this friend of her father. Although Abe was a banker and successful businessman, he had humble roots and had no need or desire to flaunt his wealth.

"Lyon's been told by his superiors and his fellow officers, you included, Daniel, to retreat. Why isn't he? Doesn't he believe the reports coming in that we're outnumbered four to one?"

"Do you think this General McCulloch will be content to stay at Wilson's Creek? If we don't stop them, what's to keep him from marching on Springfield? He's ready to attack the city and secure southern Missouri and later the entire state for the Confederacy."

Abe snorted. "Let them try. We're ready to fight 'til the bitter end."

Daniel rode beside them on his beloved stallion, Napoleon, a powerfully built Morgan he had saved from his herd. He cleared his throat and nodded toward Eliza when Abe looked his way. Eliza heard and saw the entire exchange though.

Her father had allowed her to ride into camp with him that morning, along with his best friend Abe. He made it clear, though, she was to ride back to the boardinghouse with Abe and stay inside until she received word from Abe, Jonathan, or himself.

In spite of talk of "fighting to the bitter end," she managed to muster up a brave smile.

Daniel quickly added, "As Jonathan reminded me yesterday, this won't be the first time we've gone into battle when we were outnumbered. Lyon's pretty shrewd. He's known for his ability to lead his men to victory. And besides, it's closer to two to one, not four. These reports get more blown out of proportion every time a new one comes in."

Shots rang out ahead of them. The soldiers were in a huge encampment on an open prairie near Cave Springs, a city of tents with groups of soldiers drilling in various formations throughout the camp. Rifles and bayonets gleamed in the morning sunlight. Men barked orders; more gunshots rang out. She was strangely stirred to tears and tried to hide it from the two men she rode with.

It couldn't be ignored any longer. They were at war and quite possibly would be for months or years to come. Her dear father had sheltered her for too long from this encroaching monster, but, as they rode through the streets of Springfield, the mood of the city was unmistakable. Women and children stood in doorways, on porches, and in the streets waving at departing loved ones and weeping uncontrollably. Some were packing to leave, panic in their eyes. Several shopkeepers were nailing boards over their windows and hauling merchandise out to pile onto already full wagons. These were not citizens who were confident of victory; these were people filled with fear.

Her father greeted a fellow officer. Would this be the last time she saw him alive? The thought was quickly cut off and buried. She couldn't let herself think such things. She jumped from the seat of the buckboard to the ground and fussed with her dark curls again, trying to stuff them back into her bonnet. With her unruly mass, she was unable to wear her hair in the fashion of the day. She tried, but to no avail. Her hair did what it wanted to do, which was to go in a hundred directions at once. Her father always told her he loved her hair. She choked back a sob thinking about the way he playfully tugged at her curls, letting them wrap around his finger.

"Your mother had hair just like this you know," he had told her a thousand times over the years. "She passed her best traits on to you. And those eyes...those brilliant blue eyes! I've never in my life seen anything quite so pretty as your mother's eyes." He'd look off into the distance with a dreamy smile then back to Eliza and smile. "You've got the same eyes, my little princess."

Frustrated with the direction of her thoughts, Eliza feigned interest in the activity around her. She mustn't let her father see her sadness and her fear. He had to be able to ride into battle without worrying about her.

"Eliza, I have to leave you now," her father said from behind her. He dismounted. "I'm needed with my men now. Come over here, daughter."

He reached to her and, in spite of her resolve to be brave, she threw herself into his embrace, stifling a sob. He chuckled and hugged her long and hard. Then he took her by the shoulders and held her so he could look into her eyes. "Remember, stay put in your room until this is over. I'll come for you. If for some reason I can't, then Abe or Jon will. Do you understand me, girl?"

She nodded and drank in his kind, loving face, trying

desperately to convince herself he would be all right, that they would have many more moments like this. Tomorrow or the next day, they'd be sitting in the parlor laughing about how quickly the rebels turned tail and ran back to Arkansas.

He hugged her again quickly then released her. "I love you, girl," he said hoarsely then walked away.

Eliza was numb on the ride back to Springfield. Abe talked, but, later, she couldn't recall a single thing he said. When they arrived at the boardinghouse, he helped her down from the wagon, even offered to walk her inside, but she declined, partly because she needed to be alone and partly because it would be an effort for Abe to walk up and down the steps to the big front porch of the house.

Poor Abe had even less of a family than she did. He was her father's age but seemed so much older. He and his wife of twenty-five years had never been blessed with children. After Susan died, Abe stopped taking care of himself. He gained weight, smoked cigars nonstop, and worked from dawn to dusk. He only had his nephew, Henry, who was a constant thorn in the old man's side.

That night, Eliza lay in bed listening to the rain pour down. She tossed and turned throughout the night, praying, begging God to protect her father. Finally, sleep overtook her. When she woke, she jumped from her bed and ran to the window. It was still raining. Nothing about the view of the street below gave any hint of the result of the battle. Quickly, she dressed and ran downstairs to breakfast. The other boarders had tired, wary expressions.

"Has anyone heard?" she asked.

"Sorry, no news," an elderly gentleman answered.

"We expect to hear something soon though," a woman said.

Eliza tried to choke down a few bites and then returned to her room to pace.

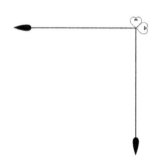

CHAPTER THREE

Eliza's eyes flew open when she heard someone holler her name. Had she been dreaming? How could she let herself fall asleep in the middle of the day at a time like this? She sat up, rubbed her eyes, and walked to the window to check the street below. A buckboard and mule sat in front of the house with a Negro man holding the reins. A loud pounding on her door caused her to jump.

"Miss Long! Open the door! Abe Goodman is here to see you!" The landlady, Mrs. Holden, stood in the hallway with fear in her eyes.

Eliza's feet flew down the stairs. She was unprepared for the expression on Abe's face. He stumbled into the parlor and shut the door behind him. Gasping for air, he said, "It's over! We've been beat!"

Eliza staggered to the closest chair and sat down. "Pa, where's Pa?"

Abe leaned wearily against the doorjamb, trying to catch his breath. "I haven't heard, Eliza. I just now got word that Lyon was killed, and his entire brigade is on the retreat back to Springfield."

"Then I should see him soon."

"No, Eliza, they're on the run. The Confederates are right behind them. We have to leave the city."

"I can't. My father will be expecting to find me here."

"Your father is expecting me to get you to safety, and this place will be swarming with Confederate soldiers in a matter of hours!" He pulled out a handkerchief and wiped his sweaty face.

"But, Abe, where will I find him? I have to find him," she pleaded.

"We'll find him, Eliza. It may be a few days, but we'll find him. He and his men will be traveling to Rolla, along with the rest of the city. We'll find him there if we don't meet up on the way." Abe gasped for air again and made his way to the chair in the corner. "But first, you need to pack quickly, only the essentials, and we need to leave. My man, Jim, will drive you. I have another wagon with my things."

He stood, walked over to the door, opened it, and looked out in the hallway. Then he closed the door and walked over to where Eliza sat. "Eliza," he said, his voice almost a whisper, "I have to move money out of the bank before the Confederates get their hands on it. I need you to help me. That buckboard out there has a false bottom. I built it months ago, suspecting this day would come. I have three other wagons with false bottoms. I'm sorry I didn't discuss this with you earlier, but I didn't want to give you more reason to fret. I have drivers for all my wagons, and you're the one I've selected for this one. You must tell no one. Do you understand?"

"Yes, yes, of course, Mr. Goodman. But, why me?"

"Because I trust you, Eliza. Jim's waiting out there. I trust him, too, but you're the one who will decide where to hide it. He's there for protection. Do you have a gun? And do you know how to use it?"

"Uh, yes, if Pa didn't take it."

She ran upstairs to her room and checked her dresser. Pushing her father's clothes aside, she reached to the back of the drawer and pulled out a Colt revolver and ammunition. Back downstairs, she showed it to Abe. "Good! Keep it with you at all times. Be ready to use it." Abe paused again to catch his breath and to wipe his beet-red face with his handkerchief. "Now pack and be downstairs in five minutes. Pack your pa's things, too. I'll meet you and Jim about five miles out on the Wire Road. Jim knows the place." He quickly gave her a fatherly pat on the head then left.

Her head reeling, Eliza grabbed her biggest satchel and started packing. What to take, what to leave; she couldn't think clearly enough to make decisions. She thought of what she might need to camp, which undoubtedly they'd be doing. Pots and pans? Matches? A bedroll? She managed to find them all, along with extra shoes, boots, a few toiletries, and a couple of her most practical dresses. She quickly added two pairs of her father's pants, a couple of extra shirts, and his farm boots. She ran down the stairs to find the rest of the household in various stages of panic and confusion. In the kitchen, she begged the landlady and cook to let her pack some food for the journey. The cook stood stubbornly, with arms folded, in the middle of her kitchen. Mrs. Holden, on the other hand, grabbed a sack and filled it with biscuits, cheese, and a loaf of bread and handed it to Eliza with tears in her eyes. "Blessings on you and your father, Eliza. I hope you return soon."

"So do I, Mrs. Holden. You take care of yourself, you hear?" She hugged her quickly and fled.

When Jim saw her appear at the top of the stairs loaded down with two large bags and the sack of food, he ran up, grabbed all three bags, and offered her his arm for support as they descended to the buckboard. Eliza examined it, amazed at Abe's workmanship. No one would ever suspect there was a false bottom.

Soon they were making their way through the city toward the Wire Road. They were surrounded by people doing the same, some openly wailing, others with fear-filled eyes, and others spewing their hatred toward their pursuers in outbursts of profanity. A line of wagons and livestock and people on foot formed. By the time they reached the road, their progress was impeded by the masses fleeing Springfield.

They plodded on, mile after mile, the heat of the sun bearing down on them. After the overnight rain, the humidity was high. Sweat trickled down Eliza's back. Jim kept wiping perspiration from his eyes so he could see. He seemed to be a gentle man. Eliza trusted Abe's judgment in sending this particular man along to assist her. Although she wasn't sure she trusted his judgment in selecting her for this errand of his. As important as it was, she had more important things to think about, such as finding her father. Then again, since Abe was going to help her with that, the least she could do was guard this treasure hidden beneath her.

Suddenly, Jim pulled the wagon over to the side, down a narrow winding road, and stopped under a giant sycamore tree on the bank of a small creek.

"This is where Mr. Abe wants to meet us. We're safe, miss, iffen ya'll wanna get out and freshen up."

"Thank you, Jim. I think I will."

They both walked to the edge of the creek and filled their tin cups with the cold, clear water. Eliza dipped a cloth in and wiped the dust and perspiration from her face then made herself as comfortable as possible on a flat rock jutting out over the water. She pulled out a biscuit and a chunk of cheese and offered it to Jim.

"No thanks, miss. Mr. Abe saw to it I had all the food I'd need for a few days. He packed some for you, too. I got some apples in here if you want one." Jim spoke in a deep, slow drawl and only occasionally made eye contact. When he did, Eliza couldn't help but notice how shy and gentle his eyes were. She liked him immensely.

"Mr. Abe is a good man."

"Yes, he is, Jim. How long have you worked for him?"

"I've been with him since I was a boy."

All of a sudden, it dawned on Eliza that she'd miss her father if he should pass by on the Wire Road while she sat down here and rested. She stood. "I have to go back up to the road and watch for my pa."

Jim stretched a hand out to motion for her to stop. "No, Miss Long. Mr. Abe made it clear we were to wait down here. He don't want no one to see us meetin' together. Said it's too dangerous."

"But, my pa!"

Jim stood and with compassion said, "The soldiers haven't started passing yet. We're a good ways ahead of them. You'll find your pa. Just give it time."

Eliza blinked back tears and forced herself to sit. She picked up small pebbles and threw them into the gurgling stream then drew her knees up to rest her head on. She kept her face turned to the opposite bank so Jim couldn't see the tears streaming down her cheeks.

After what seemed like hours, the two tired travelers heard the crunch of gravel as another wagon made its way down the little road toward them. Jim tucked his hand into his pocket where, Eliza guessed, he must be hiding a weapon of some sort.

Thankfully Abe rounded the corner. Desperate for news of her father, Eliza ran to greet him. He held a finger to his lips. When he climbed to the ground, he led his mule over to some grass and loosened the harness so the animal could graze while they talked.

"Eliza," he said after breathing deeply for a few minutes and mopping his brow. Jim handed him a tin cup full of water. "Eliza and Jim, come close. You both need to hear this." He coughed, wiped his mouth on his sleeve, and continued in a whisper. "This is for your ears only. Tell no one, and I mean no one! I know I can trust you, but what I need to know is that you're hearing me and taking this very seriously."

They both solemnly nodded.

"The load you're carrying is gold, pure gold. If certain people get even a hint that you have it, your lives could be in danger. I need for you to find a place to stash it, where no one could possibly find it. No one but the two of you should know where it is, do you understand?"

"I understand, but I can't for the life of me understand why you're giving me this job. Why don't you take it?"

"It gets complicated, but suffice it to say, my bank has had a generous amount of gold deposited there over the last several years. It's not common knowledge, and I'd like to keep it that way for security reasons. The few who know it's there will expect me to be the one transporting it out of Springfield. They might also expect my employees and close friends to help. I've divided it among several people I know and trust, people others might not suspect. You are one of those, Eliza. Because you are so new to Springfield, few people know you. And, Jim, although you've been with me for years, you seldom leave my farm.

"Believe me, I know this plan is not flawless. I had no other options, so I'm counting on you."

"I don't have any ideas about where to hide it though."

"Pray, Eliza. You believe in prayer, don't you? Until you get your answer, keep it here." He patted the side of the wagon.

She blinked and stared at him. He was serious. Yes, she believed in prayer, but for things like this? How would she know when God answered her?

"We mustn't be seen together after this. You leave, and I'll follow in an hour. If you make it to Rolla, I'll be staying with an old friend, Matt Taylor, on Maple Street. Contact me there."

CHAPTER FOUR

Eliza urged Jim to go slowly so the soldiers would have a chance to catch up. Late in the day, when they pulled over to eat, they heard hoofbeats of several horses approaching fast. It was a squadron of Missouri Volunteer Cavalry. Jonathan was a lieutenant in the Cavalry, so she stood and walked to the edge of the road, hoping to see him. Dust swirled through the air as they slowed from a canter to a trot, trying to ease past a small herd of dairy cows and wagons, two abreast on the road. Eliza shielded her eyes from the setting sun and strained to see the riders' faces.

Several riders rode past then one reined his horse to an abrupt stop. He turned and came back.

"Eliza!" Jonathan exclaimed with relief as he slid from his mount. "I've been searching for you!"

She grabbed his hand and squeezed it. "Jon, have you seen Pa?"

Jonathan immediately dropped his eyes to the ground.

Eliza gasped and covered her face with her hands, barely able to breathe.

"Eliza." He gently pried her hands loose. "Eliza, as far as I know he's still alive. I heard he was wounded though."

She dropped her hands and stared. "How badly?"

"I don't know."

"Where is he?"

"I'm not sure."

"We have to find him!" she almost shrieked.

Jonathan looked up at the thirty-six men from his squadron who were still astride their horses, waiting for him to join them. He signaled for his sergeant, who dismounted.

"Take the men on to Rolla and join up with the rest of the troop. Captain Harris said to meet on the northeast corner of the city near the Jones farm. I'll join you later."

"Will do, Lieutenant." With a wave, the sergeant swung into the saddle and signaled his men to follow.

Jonathan's tired face was covered with dirt. He ran his hand through his thick hair. "We can't try to find him yet, Eliza. I'm sorry."

"Jonathan, he needs me! He's out there somewhere hurt, bleeding, maybe dying! We have to go to him!"

"Eliza, an army of ten thousand or more Confederates is on our trail. They've most likely moved into Springfield by now and are probably following us to Rolla. This is not the time to go back."

"I can go back. I'm not a soldier. I can pretend to be a secessionist. They have no way of knowing."

"No, it's not safe! You're a woman alone. What are you thinking, Eliza?"

"Jim will go with me."

Jim's eyes immediately dropped to the ground.

"Where will you go? Do you have any idea where to start your search for him?"

"I'll ask around. Someone should know." Her tone was one of pleading desperation.

"Eliza." Jon's voice gentled as he took her shoulders in

his hands. "There are doctors assigned to the battlefield. Your pa is an officer. He will get the best treatment possible. We have people in place to get information to us. Wait until things settle down, and we have a better idea of what the situation in Springfield is. Then we can decide what to do."

Eliza stared into his pleading eyes. Then she covered her face with her hands again and walked away. She tried to compose herself. She prayed in desperation. Then it came to her in a flash. She was surprised at the intensity of the thoughts coursing through her mind. She knew it wouldn't be easy to convince Jon of her new plan. But, with or without him, she would do it.

"Jim, could I have a word with you?"

Jim glanced apologetically at Jonathan and walked to her.

In a whisper, Eliza asked, "Do you believe in prayer, Jim, like Abe asked?"

Jim nodded. "I sure do, Miss Long."

"Well, I prayed, and I know this may sound crazy, but I really think God has given me the answer."

His big, shy eyes tugged at her heart. "You mean about our load?"

"Yes, I wasn't even praying about that. It was the furthest thing from my mind. I was praying about my pa."

Jim nodded and waited.

"And then out of the blue, I got an answer to both my pa and the gold."

When she said the word, gold, Jim glanced quickly toward Jonathan. He gave Eliza an almost imperceptible shake of his head.

Jonathan watched them with obvious suspicion and slight annoyance. She lowered her voice.

"I'm sorry. I have a friend who lives on a big farm north of Springfield with her parents. There's a bluff way back in the woods where we used to play as kids. It's riddled with caves. She and I know them like the back of our hands. What better place to hide the...our 'load'?"

Jim nodded and grinned.

"And I can wait there for word about Pa. If we don't hear anything, at least we'll be close enough to ride into Springfield and try to find him." She quickly added, "I'll wait of course until we know it's safe."

"Sounds good to me, miss, but you're gonna hafta convince your friend over there."

"What? I'm sorry, Eliza, this is crazy. You can't just change course and head out over the open countryside." Jon was aghast when he heard her plan.

"I'm not going all the way to Rolla, Jonathan. It's too far. I'm sure Maddy's will be safe, at least for a while. Their farm is ten miles north of Springfield, near Fair Grove. If what you say is true, then the Rebels will be advancing east along this road toward Rolla, right? Not north. I want to be close enough to my pa that when I get word, I'll be able to go to him."

"I won't allow it. I'm sorry. I've given my word to your pa I'd take care of you and I can't very well do that now, can I, if I'm in Rolla and you're off somewhere else?"

Eliza laid her hand on Jon's arm and spoke slowly and confidently. "Might I remind you, Jonathan, that you are not my guardian? I am an adult and I will make this decision with or without your approval."

He wanted to shake some sense into her. What could he do short of abducting her? And this traitor Jim standing next to her, nodding his fool head; what had come over him? Jonathan sighed loudly with exasperation. He glared at both of them. Jim dropped his eyes, but Eliza's gaze never wavered.

"You are one stubborn woman! If you must go, I will

ride with you. Thank God Sergeant Harris is competent enough for me to trust my squadron to."

CHAPTER FIVE

The next morning, the three tired travelers pulled into the yard of the Malones. Maddy's elderly father, Frederick, appeared at his door with a rifle. Eliza waved before she took Jonathan's hand and stepped down.

"Mr. Malone, it's me, Eliza Long," she announced.

He propped the rifle against the railing and walked down the steps. "Eliza! How are you, girl?"

Mr. Malone looked questioningly at Jonathan.

"Mr. Malone, this is Lieutenant Jonathan Monroe of the…" She wasn't sure what to say.

"Company B, 2nd Battalion, 1st Regiment, Missouri Volunteer Cavalry at your service, sir."

"I'll bet you had to practice to get that right, didn't you, Lieutenant?" The old man laughed.

Jonathan good-naturedly joined him. "Yes, sir. And it wasn't easy, believe me."

"Well, come on in, you two, and tell me what's goin' on south of here. I keep hearin' rumors, and I'm not sure what to believe."

As they stepped through the door, Eliza was almost

attacked by a spindly girl with long blonde hair and freckles spread across her smiling face. "Eliza Long, what brings you here?"

"Maddy!" Eliza wrapped the girl up in her arms and laughed with delight at seeing her then, just as quickly, started bawling as she continued to cling to her. When they parted, Maddy wiped Eliza's tears with her hands and cooed comforting sounds to her. "What is it, Eliza?"

By then, Maddy's mother had joined them. She wrapped her soft, heavy arms around them both.

"My pa. He was wounded in the battle south of Springfield yesterday."

The women gasped. "How badly? Where is he?" they both asked at once.

"I don't know," she answered, brushing tears from her cheeks.

Jonathan proceeded to explain the outcome of the battle and the situation in Springfield to the best of his knowledge.

"Eliza wanted to come here and wait until she hears from Major Long and until it's safe to go to him."

"If you don't mind, that is," Eliza added.

"Of course, we don't mind, honey! You can stay as long as you like," Mrs. Malone said, rubbing her hand up and down Eliza's back.

Eliza had always loved being here with Maddy and her parents. All their other children were grown and gone. Maddy was the surprise baby Mrs. Malone had given birth to late in her life. What a blessing she was to her parents, though, with her sunny disposition and servant's heart. Maddy's tall, skinny father and short, plump mother had always reminded Eliza of the nursery rhyme, Jack Sprat. Maddy had obviously inherited her father's frame. Only two years younger than Eliza, she looked much younger with her straight, thin, wheat-colored hair and her pale waif-like face.

Yet she was strikingly beautiful, Eliza thought. Jon stared at Maddy as if she were some magical fairy in a storybook. Eliza was both surprised and ashamed at the slight tinge of jealousy she felt.

"May I impose on you and ask to spend a few hours in your hayloft for some much-needed rest before I return to my men?" Jon asked.

"We can do better than that! We have several unused bedrooms. Take your pick," Mrs. Malone said.

"I haven't slept in a real bed for over a month," Jon said. "I don't want to start getting used to one now. The barn will do fine. By the way, may Jim stay in the barn while Eliza is here?"

"Can he be trusted?" Frederick asked.

"Absolutely," Eliza answered. "I almost forgot about him! May we also keep the mule and wagon here?"

"I'll go out with Lieutenant Monroe to tend to things there, and Gertie and Maddy will take care of you, Liza," Frederick announced.

After Jon carried Eliza's bags upstairs, she got settled in and took a short nap. When she woke, she heard children's voices coming from downstairs. At reaching the bottom floor, she saw Maddy walk across the room holding a chubby baby girl with a little blonde boy following close behind.

"What have we here?" she asked.

"This," Maddy announced with her hand on the boy's head, "is Oliver MacGregor and his sister, Anabel. You remember their pa, don't you? Silas MacGregor? He has a big farm just to the north of us. He asked us to take the kids in while he's off at war. They were napping when you got here."

"I do remember. Their ma died giving birth to this little one, right?" She gently rested her hand on Anabel's head. "That's so sad. I never met little Anabel but I certainly remember Ollie. They're adorable."

Oliver stepped closer to Maddy and hid his face behind her skirt as Eliza approached him. Anabel just stared with her big blue eyes and sucked on her finger.

"How long have they been here?"

"About a month. Silas, their pa, hated to leave, but he figured he didn't have much choice. He's like the rest of us, hopin' he can do whatever it takes to end this craziness."

Maddy buried her nose in Anabel's soft baby neck and breathed deeply while keeping her hand protectively on Oliver's head.

"It appears you've grown attached," Eliza said.

Maddy blushed slightly. "I guess you could say that." She shrugged and admitted, "I'm afraid it's going to be hard to give them up."

Jon left after the noon meal. He met Eliza on the porch and warned her sternly to stay with the Malones unless she knew without a doubt that it was safe to venture into Springfield. "If you go to Springfield, you're to stay with my aunt Mildred Scott. She lives at 420 East Walnut in a big two-and-a-half-story yellow house." He gave her a slip of paper with the address. "She's expecting you." When Eliza looked doubtful, he quickly added, "She'll love you, Eliza, and you'll love her. Besides, that's where your pa wanted you to live."

"Why didn't she leave Springfield with the rest of us?"

"She's old and set in her ways. It would take more than a war to get her to move." He chuckled and shook his head. "She told me that as soon as the Union troops moved out, she would take down the American flag and string up a Confederate flag, just so the soldiers would leave her be!" He laughed.

Eliza stood in shock. "What? That's treasonous! How could anyone do such a thing?"

"Apparently, lots of folks in Springfield are doing that.

They've weighed their options. Taking their chances with the Rebels seemed better than leaving when they have no place to go. And in case you weren't aware," he warned, "not all Springfield citizens are pro-Union. You'd be wise to not spout your views too freely."

When he mounted to leave, Eliza stepped close and stroked his horse's neck. "Thank you, Jonathan, for everything. And please, please, stay safe. I couldn't bear it if something happened to you, too."

He reached down and took her hand. "You, too, little sister, you, too." With that, he left, hand held high in a goodbye wave.

That night, Eliza lay in bed plotting how she and Jim could get to the caves without arousing suspicion. If they traveled directly from the Malones', they would be seen and have to explain their actions. She could pretend to go visit a friend and circle around to the neighbors' property on the west and drive in the back way. But if she remembered correctly, the neighbors on that side were a bunch of scoundrels. She couldn't risk being seen by them. After tossing and turning all night, she came to the conclusion she'd have to trust Maddy with at least part of the plan.

At breakfast that morning, she suggested she and Maddy take the kids on a picnic out in the west pasture, near the bluff.

"That was one of my favorite places, growing up. It's been so long since I've been there."

"It's quite a long walk for their little legs," Maddy said.

"I didn't intend for us to walk. Jim can drive us in the buckboard."

"Well," Maddy said reluctantly, "if Ma can do without me for a while."

"I'll manage. Just be careful, girls. You never know these days who you might run into."

"We won't be long. Just long enough to eat and dangle our feet in the creek."

A couple of hours later, they were all headed for the bluff, Jim driving and the two young women riding in the back, each holding a child. Both Ollie and Anabel were warming up to Eliza. Ollie sat on her lap now, chattering away about how he was going to step on all the snakes and spiders they saw, so Eliza didn't need to be afraid. Anabel snuggled in Maddy's lap, smiling around her finger in her mouth.

Three times Maddy suggested they stop, but Eliza urged Jim to go a little farther. Finally, when they arrived at a place that suited Eliza, they climbed down from the wagon bed, spread a blanket on the grass near the creek, and unloaded the basket of food. Maddy kept sending perplexed glances in Eliza's direction.

After she took her first bite of cold chicken she said, "There's more to this than a simple picnic. Am I right, Eliza dear?"

Eliza put her chicken down and wiped her fingers on a napkin. "Yes, actually a lot more than you would ever guess." She scooted closer to Maddy and lowered her voice as if people were lurking behind every tree. "Maddy, I need to tell you something that you can't repeat to anyone, under any circumstances. Do you understand?"

"No, I don't understand. Just don't tell me. I hate keeping secrets."

Eliza noticed Jim's upraised eyebrow and shrugged. "Jim, I can't think of any other way to do this."

Jim motioned with his head for Eliza to step away and talk to him. She rose and followed him to the other side of the wagon. After she explained her plans to him, he agreed reluctantly and followed her back to Maddy.

"Maddy, please, I have to tell you because I need your help."

Maddy shook her head. "Can I tell my parents?" she

asked quietly.

"It's best they not know. It's actually safer for all of us."

"Safer? What is it, Eliza? Are you in some sort of trouble?"

"No, at least I hope not. If I can just carry out this one task, I think I'll be safe."

Maddy sighed. "I will do anything I need to do to help you. I won't tell anyone. What is it?"

Jim and I have some valuables that we need to find a safe hiding place for. I thought the caves up there on the bluff would be perfect. They're so isolated, and not many people know they're there."

"That's all?"

"Yes. If you could stay here with the kids, we'll drive up as close to the caves as we can get with the wagon. Then we'll carry the valuables from there."

"Valuables? Are they yours?"

"No. They belong to a friend. He asked us to hide them for him."

"What are they?"

Eliza smiled. "You don't like keeping secrets? The more I tell you, the bigger the secret gets. It's best you not know. But...this still needs to be kept absolutely quiet. Don't tell a soul! Please!"

"You know I won't, Eliza."

Jim and Eliza drove a short distance then crossed the creek and meandered between trees as they made their way up the hill to the base of the bluff. Eliza then left him with the wagon while she found the path that crisscrossed through the rocks up to the level of the caves. She remembered five caves of varying sizes in a row about halfway up the side of the steep, rocky hillside. All of them had entrances small enough she had to get on her hands and knees to be able to enter. Two of the caves she could enter only by crawling on her belly. She made her way along the rocks in front of the caves and noticed how much thicker the brush was than the last time she'd been here. In fact, the two small caves on the end were completely hidden.

She went back down to Jim. Together they ripped the boards up from the bed of the wagon. They pulled a large, heavy canvas sack out, opened it, and counted seven bags of gold coin. Jim slung the heavy bag over his shoulder. Eliza grabbed the lantern and they started back up the steep outcropping. When they reached the two hidden caves at the end, Jim offered to crawl in with the gold.

"No, I'll do it, Jim. I've been in there several times, and I have an idea where I want to hide it. Besides, when I come back here to get it, I need to know exactly where to find it."

"That makes sense, miss, but see how muddy it is in there. You'll ruin your dress."

Eliza looked down at one of only three dresses she'd packed and shrugged. "I have more in Springfield."

Jim chuckled softly and shook his head. "Here's the lantern. You can't carry all this at the same time, so I'll stand out here and hand the bags to you two at a time."

While Jim held the bushes out of the way, Eliza dropped to her stomach and inched her way forward, pushing the lantern and bags of gold ahead. This cave was way smaller than she remembered. There was no way Jim would fit.

Ten feet in, the tunnel opened up so she could get up on her knees. She held the lantern up and studied all sides of her cramped enclosure. It seemed as if the cave ended here, but if she remembered correctly and wasn't confusing this cave with another one, there was another tunnel leading away from here. She scooted around and ran her hands along the damp, slimy uneven wall of rock. There! She found it. It was perfect, she thought, better than she'd remembered! The entrance to the tunnel was completely hidden behind a rock. Again, she had to inch her way along on her stomach, using her elbows to drag her weight through. After crawling fifteen feet or more, she came to the end where the roof opened up and she was able to stand. She heard a flutter of wings over her and quickly squatted to the floor to wait for the bats to settle down. Cautiously she raised the lantern and studied the tall, narrow space. There were numerous crevices, some shallow, some deep. She stuffed the two bags in two separate holes then crawled back to get the rest.

After exiting the cave for the second time and stashing four bags of gold, Eliza sat down, completely exhausted. Jim offered her a drink from a canteen. She gratefully accepted.

"You know, Jim, I'm beginning to wonder if it's a mistake to hide all the gold in the same place. Maybe I should have scattered it among all the caves."

"I'm afraid if someone found some gold in one cave, they'd be sure to go diggin' in the others."

"You're right. But if I put it all in one place and someone finds it, then it will all be gone for sure."

"Did you say there's another cave hidden behind those bushes over there?"

"Yeah, but I'm afraid it's even smaller than this one. I'm not sure I'd fit, now that I'm older."

"Hmmm...the good thing 'bout that, Miss Long, is maybe it's too small for a man to get in. That's good, real good."

"You're right. If I climb in there, though, you may have to drag me out by my feet!"

He laughed and helped her to stand. "Let's hope not, miss!"

At first, they'd couldn't find the cave entrance, which was a good thing, they agreed, a very good thing. Then Eliza found she could get in if she carried a sack of gold in her teeth, kept her arms in front, wiggled a lot, and used her toes to propel herself forward. This cave also opened up to a space inside that might be large enough to turn around in. After inching forward five or six feet, the walls gave way to a room that was big enough to sit in. It also had various-sized crevices and bats, lots of bats. She let out a shriek as they swirled around her head and out the cave entrance toward Jim. He hollered. Then there was nothing but silence.

After several, long moments, she heard a faint voice. "Miss Long! Are you all right?"

She laughed. "I'm fine." After she stuffed the sack into a hole, she crawled out, took the last bag, inched her way back, and tucked the treasure snugly in a hole high up where she was sure the bats would be happy to guard it for her. She barely had enough energy to wiggle out of the cave, much less to walk down to the wagon.

When Maddy saw her, she gasped. "Eliza! You're filthy! And your dress! It's ruined!"

Eliza examined her mud-caked arms and dress and shoes.

"You can't go back to the house like this. What will my parents think?"

"I hadn't thought of that," she answered with a tired sigh.

"I know," Maddy said, taking her by the arm. She led her down to a place in the creek where the water was almost a foot deep. She walked into the deepest part and dragged Eliza with her. Then she splashed Eliza over and over again. Eliza squealed and sputtered and tried to fend off the onslaught of cold water, but Maddy wouldn't stop. Jim laughed, and Ollie shrieked with delight from the bank. Eliza finally splashed Maddy back. They kept at it until they were laughing hysterically and completely drenched. Eliza was almost clean but not enough for Maddy's taste. Whenever Maddy spotted mud, she'd send more water Eliza's way. Finally satisfied, they good-naturedly made their way to the bank. Unexpectedly, Eliza tripped and fell to her knees in the brown slime. She glared at Maddy.

"You tripped me! And I think you meant to!"

She reached back and grabbed Maddy by the foot and yanked. Maddy plopped down next to Eliza. "There! Now we're even!"

Maddy giggled and followed Eliza back into the water to wash the fresh mud off. When they came out, Maddy had a very satisfied smile on her innocent face.

"Ollie, when we get home, what are you going to tell Papa and Mama? That's what he calls my parents," Maddy said.

Ollie answered enthusiastically, "Papa, Mama! Maddy and, and, and the other lady spwashed and spwashed and got all wet! And, and, and then they fall down and got all dirty and spwashed some more!" He danced with joy at the anticipation of being the bearer of such exciting news.

Maddy winked at Eliza. "So now we don't have to tell any lies to try to cover up our secret."

"Smart girl. Thank you. So, you really did trip me on purpose?"

"Sorry, but you had to have an excuse for the mud we couldn't wash off."

"Ahh, that's why. You're pretty shrewd."

Maddy lowered her voice. "One of the reasons I hate secrets is because so often, you have to keep telling lies to cover it up. I don't want to lie if I can help it."

Eliza stopped and gave her a hug. "Thank you so much. You are a true friend. I feel like a big load has been lifted off my back." Then she grew sober. "Now, if I can figure out how to find my pa…"

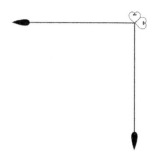

CHAPTER SIX

Several days later, word reached the Malones and Eliza that the Confederate soldiers had already left Springfield. Eliza reacted quickly, packing her belongings back into the buckboard with frenzied impatience directed at slow-moving Jim. Maddy and her mother stood on the porch and watched with concern. A stab of guilt flitted through Eliza's gut as she noticed Jim's sad, gentle eyes glance quickly at the Malones.

"Take care, Eliza. You hear?" Mrs. Malone called out. "Send us word about yer pa, all right?"

"I will, ma'am. Thank you so much for everything," Eliza called out as Jim guided the wagon down the drive.

Late in the afternoon, they reached the outskirts of Springfield. An old man standing on his porch gave directions to the field hospital south of town. "He might not be there anymore. It all depends..." the man said just after Jim and Eliza had thanked him and turned to leave.

"Why? What do you mean?" Eliza asked, panic rising in her chest.

"Well, there's so many wounded, they've got 'em spread out all over the place. Hospitals, churches, even some homes. I wouldn't be surpr—"

"He's an officer!" Eliza snapped. "Surely someone will know where to find him."

The man cocked an eyebrow and studied her for a moment. "Well, that depends. Is he a federal officer or a Confederate?"

"A federal officer. A major in the US Army," Eliza declared with stubborn pride in her tone.

"Well, then, that could be a problem."

"A problem? Why?"

"The Confederates might not feel like helping you none."

The color drained from Eliza's face as she reached out to hold onto the gatepost. "I...I thought they had left! We were told they'd left the city!"

The man chuckled.

Eliza wanted to run up the porch steps and slap him.

Jim stepped in front of her, hat in hands and eyes down, except for one brief imploring glance at the man. "Excuse me, sir. This is the young lady's pa we're talkin' about. She just wants to find him."

The man ran his fingers through his white hair. "I'm sorry, miss. I'm all riled up inside. Not thinkin' straight. The Confederates are still here. Make no mistake about that. Most of the soldiers rode out days ago, but they left plenty of those rats here to hold the city. And I wasn't pullin' your leg when I said they might not help you. Try the hospital at the courthouse; they might know something."

Eliza gripped the side of the buckboard as they wove their way through the eerily quiet streets. Images of her dear father flashed through her brain, of him alone and in agony, crying out for help, crying out for her. She let a moan escape and glanced to see if Jim had heard her. He kept staring straight ahead.

"Can we go any faster?" she asked.

"I'm afraid ol' Jemima couldn't handle goin' any faster, miss," he said gently, nodding toward the old mule that had faithfully hauled them all over the countryside.

Eliza started to complain then saw tears in the man's eyes. She quickly composed herself. Was it for her he cried? Or had he, too, lost someone precious? She had never thought to ask. She knotted her fingers in the folds of her skirt and tried to pray.

"There it is," Jim announced later as they drove into the square. He indicated the federal courthouse that had been used as Springfield's main hospital since the beginning of the war. Several Confederate soldiers stood guard around the square and at the entrance to the hospital. A few watched Jim and Eliza closely as they tied Jemima to a hitching post and climbed the steps to the imposing building. Two ragged soldiers stepped in front of them.

"No slaves allowed," one sneered, holding his rifle as a barrier.

"He's with me," Eliza announced with steel in her voice.

"I don't care, miss. We don't want his kind in here." His eyes raked up and down her body as he grinned.

"Private!" a welcome voice barked from the steps above them. "Let them pass!"

The two quickly stepped away and let Jim and Eliza continue up the stairs. Eliza could feel their eyes on her as she moved away. Glancing back when she reached the top, she was startled by the hatred she saw in the eyes of the soldier who had spoken to them.

Her world changed as soon as she stepped through the massive doors into a beehive of activity. Men on pallets lined the hallways. A stench that made her gag assailed her nostrils. A constant wailing and moaning came from every direction, occasionally punctuated by shrieks of pure agony. She clapped her hand over her nose and mouth, partly to keep the smell out but mostly to keep from adding her own cries to the chorus of suffering.

Where was her father in all this? Which cry was his? She whirled around in confusion, not knowing where to go next. A hand grabbed her elbow and steered her toward a door on the right, labeled "office."

"In here, miss. If you're trying to find someone, that is..." a woman said as she opened the door and ushered them both inside.

Another woman sitting at a desk, piled with uneven stacks of papers, asked, "May I help you?" Her eyes were tired yet kind.

"I'm trying to find my father. I got word he was wounded and might be here." Eliza choked back a sob.

"Which army?"

Eliza hesitated. Her answer could likely mean they'd be escorted out the door. "Uh...Federal Army, ma'am."

The woman grabbed a stack of papers to her left. "Rank?"

Immensely relieved, she answered, "A major, ma'am. Major Daniel Long."

For what seemed an eternity, the woman shuffled through the papers, read some notes then shuffled some more. She stopped, read more notes, looked up at Eliza and then back at the page she held in her hands.

After a long pause, she very quietly said, "I'm sorry, according to these reports, a Major Daniel Long died two days ago from wounds he received in battle."

A buzzing sensation started in the back of Eliza's head as the room dimmed. "What did you say?" her own voice asked from far away.

Strangely, the woman's mouth moved but Eliza heard nothing, except the long scream of anguish coming from her own throat, "*Nooooo*," as she backed against the wall and slumped to the floor.

Jim quickly gathered her in his arms and left, passing the two arrogant privates on the stairs. He carried her around the building and gently laid her down on a patch of grass. At first, she lay as still as death then she started thrashing from side to side and calling out to her pa. Jim took a rag from his pocket and wiped her tearstained face.

"There, there, little one," he cooed.

"Pa, Pa!" she hollered, louder each time. "I'm here, Pa!" she cried. "I found you! We can go home now, Pa!"

"Shhh, girl. Your pa's fine, now, don't ya know?"

Eliza stopped thrashing and gasped for breath, taking deep gulps of air as if she were drowning. Abruptly, she sat up and stared at Jim. "Where's Pa, Jim?"

He looked deeply into her eyes and answered, "He's with the good Lord, Miss Eliza."

She stared unblinking back at him. "No! No, he's, he's fine, Jim! He's fine. We just have to find him!"

Scrambling to her feet, she spun around, spotted the wagon, and marched for it. Jim caught up to her and gently grabbed her arm. "Miss Eliza, the lady done told us he died two days ago."

Eliza whirled around, shook free of his grip, and screamed, "No!"

"But, Miss, she had the report in front of her."

Eliza did the unthinkable. She stepped forward and slapped Jim across the face with all the strength and fury she could muster.

Soldiers ran to her defense, one of them cracking the butt of his rifle across Jim's skull. He crumpled at her feet.

"Stop!" she shrieked. "What have you done?"

"We saw him attack you, ma'am!"

"No! You're wrong!" Eliza stepped between them and Jim.

"We'll see to it he don't bother you no more!"

Eliza dropped to her knees next to Jim and gently touched the growing bump on his head.

"Men!" a voice above her barked. "Lock him up!"

"No! Don't you dare!" Eliza stood and faced the man in charge. His expression was kind. But nevertheless, he was a Confederate, and at the moment, she despised any and all Confederates. "He is mine, and we were just having a private discussion!"

"It sure didn't appear that way to my eyes," the lieutenant answered, as his men hauled Jim to his feet.

"He's a good man! He, he was only trying to help me!" she declared in a pleading tone.

The officer raised his eyebrow in doubt. "Why, then, did you slap him? Is this how you always treat your slaves when they're trying to help you?"

"No! No, please!" She reached out and grabbed Jim's sleeve. "I, I was reacting to some bad news. Jim's been nothing but kind to me! Please! Please, let him go!"

Two of the soldiers held Jim firmly and looked to the lieutenant for his answer. The officer studied Eliza's tear-streaked face for a moment then nodded at his men. "Release him." They did so, reluctantly, giving him a shove toward Eliza. "Go back to your posts. Leave these two alone." Turning toward Eliza, he introduced himself. "I'm Lt. Shaw. If any of my men give you trouble, let me know. Where do you live?"

"Uh…" Eliza glanced uncertainly at Jim. "Uh, over on Walnut Street."

The lieutenant narrowed his eyes.

"Actually, I live on Cherry St. in a boardinghouse, but a lady who lives on Walnut Street has invited me to live with her there until my father returns."

Again, the kind man tipped his hat and said, "Then you may go. Be careful."

Once they settled themselves in the wagon and made their way out of the square, Eliza said to Jim. "I am so sorry. I, I don't know what came over me."

He smiled. "It's all right, Miss Liza. I understand." He rubbed the side of his head. "What you did sure don't compare to this lump though."

Eliza buried her face in her hands to try to collect her thoughts. She straightened and said, "We need to go by the boardinghouse to get the rest of our things. Then we'll go to Jon's aunt's house."

Jim drove the mule south toward Cherry Street. When they arrived, she was surprised to find the house had been converted into a makeshift hospital. Agonizing moans and the smell of sweat greeted them at the door, along with Mrs. Holden, the landlady.

"Eliza! Dear! I didn't expect to see you for a while." She stepped out on the porch and closed the door behind her. Lowering her voice, she said, "I'm so sorry, but I'm afraid the whole place has been taken over by the secessionists. Including your room of course. They're using it for a hospital. They were going to kick me out, too, but I begged and begged, and they let me stay. I had to fly their flag though." She raised her eyes to the flagpole where she had so proudly flown the American flag only days earlier. "And, of course, cook for them and do whatever else they need. But at least I have food and a roof over my head, which is better than what most have."

"What about our things, Mrs. Holden? Are they still in our room?"

"No, dear. Follow me." She led them around to the back of the house to the cellar entrance. "I gathered up what I could before they moved the wounded in. I stashed it down here. It's not much. The rotten secesh took most of it for themselves." She led them down the stone steps into a dark, damp cellar. Climbing up on a stool, she reached way back on a high shelf and pulled out three tightly wrapped bundles and handed them down to Jim. "Be careful. They might steal them from you yet!"

Jim pulled the wagon to the alley behind the house, and the two let themselves out the back gate. Just before they left, Eliza thanked Mrs. Holden profusely for all the trouble she had gone through in the middle of the chaos. Then she grabbed her hand and asked, "Is it possible my father is in there with the other wounded?"

"No, dear. This is a Confederate hospital. Besides, I've gotten to know all these men, and your pa isn't one of them. There's lots of hospitals; you keep tryin'. You'll find him." They embraced and wept for each other.

"Thank you so, so much, Mrs. Holden. Pray for my pa, and God bless you."

Jim looked on and shook his head sadly.

CHAPTER SEVEN

Neither Jim nor Eliza could remember the address or the name of Jon's aunt. "Jon wrote it down for me," Eliza said as she opened her satchel and looked, "but I must have left it at the Malones'. I only remember she lived on Walnut Street in a two-story yellow house; and I'm not entirely certain of even that much."

The mule plodded down the wide, tree-lined street in the dusk. They had already stopped at one yellow house. It was boarded up and empty. They pulled up in front of a second one that had light coming from the front windows. Cautiously, they walked up the steps of a wide porch that wrapped around a beautiful two-and-a-half-story house. Soft voices drifted from an open window. Eliza knocked. The voices stopped and a curtain moved at the window. An old black man came to the door and greeted them warmly.

"I'm so sorry to bother you, but we're looking for the home of Jonathan Monroe's aunt."

The man's eyes opened in alarm as he stepped out onto the porch and shut the door. "Do you bring bad news of Jonny?"

"No, Jonathan is fine. He told me to come here to his aunt, that she'd be expecting me," Eliza said.

The man's face lit up. "And might you be the little lady, Eliza Long?"

Eliza smiled with relief, "Yes! Yes, that's me!"

"Come in, come in! Miss Scott, we have company!" he announced with great enthusiasm as he swung the door wide.

Mildred Scott's home seemed to be an oasis of light and cheer in the middle of misery. She was in her mid-fifties yet bustled about with the energy of youth. George, the man who had greeted them, and his wife, Sally, were former slaves of Miss Scott. After they had moved up from Arkansas, she'd granted them both their freedom, but they chose to remain with her and keep her family name. The house was well furnished and bursting with color. Flowers and potted plants brightened every corner. Eliza sat in a chair in the parlor, sipping on a glass of cold lemonade and marveled at her surroundings. Jim also sat there, lemonade in hand, which delighted her to no end.

After greetings and small talk, Mildred turned to Jim and kindly asked who he belonged to.

"The banker, Abe Goodman, ma'am. I work on his farm outside the city."

Her face saddened. "Have you heard about, Abe, Jim?"

Jim set his glass on the table and stared at her. "No, ma'am. Not since the day we ran from the city."

"I'm sorry to have to tell you this, Jim, but he died that day. We heard it was his heart. No one knows for sure. Abe wasn't a well man, and that day proved to be too much for the poor soul."

"But he was with us, that day. We, we talked to him," Eliza said.

"It must have happened later. Friends of ours saw him collapse on the road that evening. They took him to a nearby farm where they buried him. Under the circumstances, it was the best they could do."

Jim sat very still for a long time just staring at his hands. "I know Abe has no family other than his nephew, Henry. Will you belong to him now?" Mildred asked.

Jim's head came up quickly. "No ma'am. Not if I have any say. Mr. Goodman's nephew is not a man I want to be around. I'm sorry to be disrespectful, but it's the truth."

Mildred acknowledged George and Sally. They looked at each other then nodded approval at Mildred. "We want you to stay here with us, Jim. I'm not sure what the law will say about that, but for now, the law seems to be uncertain on lots of things. Besides, I assume Abe may have asked you to watch out for Eliza. So, we're only carrying out his orders. Does that suit the two of you?"

Eliza and Jim both agreed with gratitude toward their gracious hostess.

"And, Eliza, what have you heard about your father?"

Eliza froze. She couldn't answer. Jim looked sadly at her then up at their three hosts. Sally covered her face with her apron and turned away. Mildred clapped her hands over her mouth, eyes huge.

Finally, Eliza took a deep breath and shook her head. She stood and announced quite happily, "My father is alive. We just need to find him. So…first thing in the morning, Jim and I will…"

"Miss Eliza!" Jim stood also and stared at her in disbelief. "Miss Eliza, please. Try to remember. They told us he died," he said very softly.

Eliza's head snapped back in shock. "No! He's not dead. They're lying to us. Don't you know? They hate us. Of course, they'd lie about something like this."

Mildred asked, "Who told you he died, Eliza?"

"That awful woman in the office at the hospital. She's a Confederate like the rest of them. We have to find him and soon, before they kill him."

"The general hospital on the square?"

"Yes."

Mildred took Eliza's hand and pulled her to sit next to her on the settee. "I've been there, Eliza. Both Unionists and Confederate doctors and volunteers man that hospital. The woman you referred to might very well be a friend of mine. She's doing her best to keep accurate reports for both sides."

Eliza snatched her hand away. "He's alive. Until I see his dead body, I will not give up my search. He's out there somewhere in pain, not getting the care he needs. He's calling for me."

She stood again, this time with tears streaming down her face. Loudly, she declared, "He's calling for me. I can feel it in here!" She pounded her chest. "If he were dead, I wouldn't feel him calling my name over and over again." She dropped to her knees, weeping uncontrollably. "Over and over. He won't stop! And until I find him, I won't stop, either! Even if I have to go alone."

The next morning Eliza slept late. The other four adults sat around the kitchen table and plotted. "Unless we tie her up, there's no way we'll keep her here," Jim said. "I've watched her over the last couple of weeks. She's a fine young woman. Kind-hearted, smart, hardworking, but stubborn as all get out! If she sets her mind to something, nothin' nor no one will stop her."

"But we can't let her traipse all over Springfield searching for him. It's not safe. Furthermore, he's probably already been buried," Mildred said.

"It won't matter none. She'd just have him dug up. She has to see with her own eyes, his dead body, as gruesome as it'll be," said Jim with a shake of his head.

"With all the bodies out there, it's quite possible he's

not been buried yet," George said.

Sally shuddered. "It'll be three days today. I'd hate to have her see his body if it's been above the ground for three days."

They all nodded in agreement.

"As difficult as this will be for her, it may be necessary," Mildred said.

Again, they all nodded in agreement.

"George and Jim, take my buggy and go down and talk to Mrs. Kindle at the hospital. See if her records tell where he died. If so, do whatever you can to locate him. We'll keep Eliza occupied here."

"Ma'am, with all due respect, we might need you to go with us. I got this here lump on my head at that hospital and I'm a guessin' those rascals would like to put a matching one on the other side," Jim said with a shy grin. "Things have changed out there. Two slaves in a fancy buggy won't be safe."

Mildred narrowed her eyes then slapped the table. "Then I'll join you! We'll find that body or die trying!"

Eliza opened swollen eyes to find sunlight already streaming in through her window. She groaned, sat up, and rubbed her eyes. The bed creaked as she stood, and a gentle knock sounded on her door.

"Yes?"

Sally peeked around the door. "I have your bath drawn, Miss Eliza."

"I washed last night, Sally. I don't have time for a bath. I need to get going."

"But it's hot and, and sudsy. You'll feel so much better, Miss Eliza." She clasped her hands under her chin like a child begging for a favor.

Eliza smiled. "Fine, Sally. Where is it?"

"Follow me, child." Sally led her to Mildred's bedroom, where steam rose from a copper tub hidden behind a screen in the corner.

Eliza sighed as she sank down into the luxurious hot, soapy water. Sally was right; she instantly felt better. She scrubbed her tired, dirty body, washed her hair then just sat and breathed deeply, the steam rising up all around her.

At breakfast, the others were missing. Sally bustled about the kitchen, chattering happily while she prepared Eliza's meal. "Thank God we still have a cow and chickens. Not everyone does. Soldiers from both sides seem to think it's their right to help themselves to whatever they want. Tch, tch tch!" she clucked in annoyance. "If they need food, they should just ask. We'd be more than happy to help. In fact, we've done that from the very beginnin' of this fool war. Maybe that's why they've let us be. I dunno..." She rattled on about the weather and about Jonathan, what a good boy he was and what a big spread he had south of town. "I pray for his safety all day long. We sure do love that boy. He has five brothers, you know. I think he's the youngest. Mildred never sees those other boys. Maybe they live too far away. But that Jonathan, he's always been her favorite. She never had no chillins of her own. Law! She's never even been married. Never jumped the broomstick, bless her heart. But, oh what a fine woman! You'll never meet anyone as fine as Mildred Scott! Bless her dear sweet, lovin' soul. She's like a sister to me. Now I know that sounds disrespectful comin' from the lips of a blackie, but she's told me the same thing. Sisters, we are, just different colors. God made us both and put us both here in the same time and the same place just so we could be together and be sisters. George thinks we're funny. Now George, he's a good man. He—"

"Uh, Excuse me, Sally. Where's George now? And Mildred and Jim? I haven't seen them all morning."

"Oh, they're off runnin' errands, like most mornings. Do

you like your coffee black?" Sally plopped down in the chair across from Eliza and slid the coffee over to her, along with cream and a sugar bowl. "Now, Eliza, tell me how you know our Jonathan."

An hour passed as Eliza told of her and Jonathan's childhood. Sally kept asking question after question.

Finally, Eliza stood and said, "Sally, I'm sorry, but I have to go find Pa. I can't believe I've let the time slip by like this. Where is Jim? I need him." She marched to the door and opened it. "Is he in the barn?"

"I'm not sure where he is, Eliza. You could go check."

Jim wasn't there, but the mule and wagon were. She searched the garden and the shed. She walked around the perimeter of Mildred's property, looking over the fence at the neighbors' adjoining lot. She went back in the house and called down the cellar stairs. Went upstairs and called, called up the attic stairs. Nothing! No one! Not even a sign of George or Mildred.

She went back downstairs to confront Sally, but Sally was gone! Annoyed at this odd turn of events and with a rising panic in her chest as she imagined her father again calling to her, she hollered for Sally, as she frantically went from room to room. Finally, she spotted her digging in the garden.

"Sally," Eliza exclaimed, out of breath from her search, "where are they? Something strange is going on, and I want to know what it is. Please, Sally!"

Sally wiped her dirty hands on her apron and sighed. "Sit down, Eliza." She patted the ground next to her. "I'll tell you, dear."

Eliza sat and using her hand, shielded her eyes from the bright sunlight.

Sally, surprisingly, got straight to the point. "They're trying to find your father."

When Eliza protested, Sally soothed her with a hand on her arm. "They're doing it for you, Eliza. Because they care so much."

"But I wanted to go!"

"They'll take you to him after they find him. They felt it was no position for a young woman to be in, especially a woman grieving for her pa. You realize don't you, it may be necessary to see hundreds of wounded men and hundreds of dead bodies before they find him. It would kill you, honey, to have to see that. I know it would kill me and I'm not lookin' for my pa!"

"Hundreds?"

"I've heard reports that more than a thousand men on each side were killed or wounded in that one battle at Wilson's Creek. That's over two thousand men, and they were all brought to Springfield."

Eliza was stunned. She knew it had been bad and she knew they had lost, but she'd not imagined the toll was this high.

Late that afternoon, she ran down the stairs at the sounds of footsteps in the foyer. Jim and Mildred had returned, exhausted and very sad.

"We found him, Eliza," Mildred said.

Although deep in her soul, Eliza knew he was gone, she couldn't bear to give in to that knowledge until she saw him for herself. She walked to the door and down to the buggy and waited. They drove her to a cemetery on Grant Street, got out, and walked to where George waited beside a body, fanning constantly to keep the flies off. Rows of corpses lined the street to their left and it dawned on Eliza, even in her state of shock, that these dear friends must have searched through dozens and dozens of rotting, stinking bodies to locate her father's remains. She looked down at his shriveled, disfigured face, a piece of paper pinned to his shirt with his name and rank crudely written on it, his hair, his clothes, his belt, and knew. Slowly, she knelt by him and gently touched his cheek and smoothed his gray hair back from his precious forehead. She gazed longingly at the arms that had held her so tenderly all of her life and knew she'd never feel them around her again.

"Oh, Pa, I'm so sorry," she whispered. "I tried to come to you. I tried, Pa. I tried. But I'm too late. I'm so sorry." She wept bitterly, oblivious to the flies and the stench.

Mildred gently pulled her away. "We made arrangements for your pa's burial to take place after you got here, sweetheart."

Eliza wiped her eyes and stood. Rows of open graves stretched out before her. Markers made from wood stuck up from the ground.

Mildred stroked her back. "I paid the undertaker for a plot on the other side of the cemetery among the older gravestones, so he will be easier to locate later." She guided her in that direction while Jim and George carried the body on a tarp to the site. They laid him in a cedar casket and lowered him into the fresh hole. Prayers were said then the two men shoveled dirt over the casket. Eliza watched numbly from the side, not uttering a word. A wooden cross with his name written on it was driven deeply into the soil, with a promise from Mildred that she would see to it a proper gravestone would soon be in place.

They got back in the buggy, drove home, and Eliza walked silently into the house and up the stairs to her room.

CHAPTER EIGHT

As numb as she felt, Eliza still paid close attention to her new world.

Little of significance happened in Springfield, Missouri for the next two months, at least concerning the war. Confederate forces continued to hold the town, uncontested. People learned to survive. They continued to tend to the wounded. They buried more bodies. They listened to horrendous rumors coming in from all over the countryside, never certain what to believe nor who to blame. Several who had fled in August came back. Many others stayed away, finding safer refuge in Rolla and St. Louis.

The Scott household fared better than most, having two capable women and two able-bodied men to help. They kept their horse, cow, and chickens hidden and as quiet as possible. Jim managed to get out to Abe's farm several times and harvested vast stores of potatoes, turnips, apples, pumpkins, corn, and squash. Cleverly hiding them in the false bottom of Abe's old buckboard, he drove back to the Scott house and stored his treasure in the cellars.

Mildred declared her house must have been built "for such a time as this." There were two cellars under the house, each with a different entrance. The largest cellar had an entrance from the kitchen. The smaller one had a hidden entrance in a wall in an attached shed. Mildred had lived in the house for a year before she had discovered it. And George discovered a hidden entrance to a small cellar under the barn. The four of them agreed to divide the food up and store it in all three cellars.

Several times, Confederate soldiers appeared at their front door, but before they could blink an eye, Mildred swooped down on them as if they were long-lost sons, patting their backs and offering them food. Eliza fiercely resented Mildred's treatment of the hated enemy but soon realized Mildred had carefully considered her actions. As she had hoped, the Scott household had been spared the fate of most of their neighbors whose food stores had been raided and almost depleted.

Eliza watched and listened, but she seldom left her room. Sally took food to her, at first, but, at Mildred's insistence, Eliza joined the others downstairs for meals. She picked at her food and barely made eye contact. Unexpected noises caused her to jump and look around with fear. She refused to venture outside.

"Give her time," Mildred kept repeating to the others. "I've seen this before. It just takes time...and prayer. Keep praying for her."

"This is nothin', and I mean nothin' like the girl I met back in August!" Jim declared. "No matter what was goin' on, she could still find somethin' to laugh at! She had so much gumption, I didn't think anything could knock her down."

"She just lost her pa, Jim. Her pa!" Sally said, dabbing

at the corners of her eyes. "He was the only family she had."

"She has us, now," George offered.

"Well, remember, we were complete strangers just two months ago," Mildred said.

"Jon's not a stranger, is he? Ain't he like a brother or somethin'?" asked Jim.

"I guess they were pretty close," Mildred answered, "but Jon can't do her any good. He's not here. Heaven knows when we'll see him again. He can't just waltz into Springfield and pay us a friendly visit, not as long as we're occupied by the South."

George stood up and started pacing the floor. "I'm still waitin' for the Union forces to swoop down and take this city back from those Confederates. What's takin' them so long?" he asked.

George didn't have to wait much longer. On October 25th, Union General Fremont approached Springfield from the North. His bodyguard, consisting of three companies of cavalrymen, led by Major Zagonyi, and two companies of scouts marched into the city from the west side.

Approximately 1000 local Confederate militiamen hiding in the woods ambushed Major Zagonyi and his men as they rode into town. Although successful at surprising the men on horseback, the Rebels were chased from the woods and through the streets of Springfield before finally surrendering to Zagonyi. A deranged prisoner housed in the old courthouse in the center of the square panicked and set the thirty-year-old building on fire, burning it badly enough it had to be vacated. The Union forces finally moved in, captured the square, and freed Union prisoners from the jail. Union sympathizers gathered in the square to cheer the rescuing troops.

Eliza sat on Mildred's porch with the rest of the household when they heard the sound of gunfire and galloping horses. Before they could react, five mounted cavalrymen tore down their street and cut off three Rebel soldiers who had run between the houses. One was wounded before they gave themselves up to the men on horseback. Eliza and the others ran inside to watch from an upstairs window.

Although Eliza's heart was pounding with fear, she was very attentive to what was happening and asked endless questions.

"We're not sure what's happening yet, Eliza. We'll have to wait and see," Mildred said.

"I'll tell you what's happening," George said as he stood and danced an awkward jig. "We're being rescued! That's what's happening!" He let out a loud whoop of joy.

Eliza jumped up and grabbed his arm. "Is it true? Our men are here?"

"They're here all right, but we don't know what's happened yet. Or how long it will take," Mildred warned.

They heard more gunfire, farther away this time.

Eliza stood rigidly, staring out the window with her hands clasped under her chin and a passionate fire burning in her chest.

Soon, word reached them of Zagonyi's victory. Two days later, General Fremont marched through town with his troops and set up headquarters in Springfield. Pro-Union citizens were ecstatic. American flags went up all over the city. The following day, a funeral was held on the square for members of Fremont's Bodyguards who had lost their lives recapturing Springfield from the Confederates.

Eliza finally wanted to get out, so the day after the funeral George drove her and Mildred to the square to see for themselves the hustle and bustle of the new occupying army as they manned their posts and marched in the streets. The once beautiful city of Springfield already showed the sad signs of a city under siege. Many homes were abandoned, some destroyed or burned. Gardens were trampled, stores plundered, and taverns deserted.

The majority of troops set up camp about a mile west of the square. At Eliza's insistence, George took them there as well. Twenty thousand soldiers had marched across Missouri with Gen. Fremont. About half that number set up a temporary camp in Springfield. The sight was mind-boggling and immensely reassuring.

Eliza sat on the edge of her seat, watching the soldiers, intently searching for someone she knew. The officers' tents lined the east side of the encampment, with hundreds of smaller tents scattered across the trampled prairie grass. She and Mildred waved and greeted the soldiers.

"Oh, how I wish we'd thought to bring food to these poor men, something other than hardtack or jerky, something to remind them of home," Mildred said.

"There are so many, how could we even begin?" Eliza asked.

The following morning, Eliza ate a hearty breakfast then sat on the porch with the others. She took a short walk around the neighborhood that afternoon. The next day, she took a longer walk and returned with renewed energy.

"It's good to see you finally have some color in those cheeks of yours," Mildred said. "I think getting outside is doing you a world of good."

"That and knowing the seccesh are finally gone," laughed George.

The following morning after a long walk, she announced she was exhausted and planned to take a nap. "Please don't wake me. I'm fine. I just need to sleep."

As soon as she shut her door, she pulled a sack out from under the bed, dumped it on the floor, and quickly stripped down to her underwear. A pile of boy's clothes lay at her feet and, within five minutes, she managed to put them on and tuck the shirt into pants that were too loose to stay up. She pulled a belt from the pile, strung it through the belt loops, and cinched it tightly around her waist. Boots and a jacket came next. Finally, she pulled her long hair into a tight knot, twisted it into a bun, and tucked it all under a hat. Seeing her reflection, she realized she was still entirely too feminine. Buttoning her shirt all the way to the top helped hide her skinny neck. Then she experimented with her expression and her voice until she thought she might possibly be convincing.

Very carefully, Eliza opened her bedroom door and peeked into the hallway. She tiptoed toward the back of the house and down a narrow set of stairs seldom used by the family. It led to a storage room off the kitchen. A door led from there out to an attached shed then out to the yard beside the house. She grabbed a handful of dirt, rubbed it on her face then slipped through the gate in the back.

CHAPTER NINE

"**S**o, you want to sign up, I hear," Major McDonald asked. He studied the young lad from top to bottom and chuckled.

He'd walked by his lieutenant earlier and overheard the boy asking what he needed to do to enlist. Just as the major turned to go into his tent, he caught a glimpse of the boy's brilliant-blue eyes. He also noticed the appalling lack of respect the lad showed by not removing his hat when he spoke to an officer.

"Send the boy in here, Lieutenant," he'd ordered as he pushed through his tent flap. He settled himself behind his desk, a small folding table with a neat stack of papers on one side and a map spread across the middle. The scrawny lad entered and stood before him.

"So?" He looked intently into those blue eyes and waited for an answer.

"Uh, y...yes, sir, I do," the boy stammered.

"How old are you?"

"Uh...nineteen, sir."

"If you expect to be a soldier, you need to show respect to your commanding officers. Take off your hat, son."

The boy reached up and slowly removed the hat.

"Turn around," the major ordered.

The scrawny youth's eyes grew large.

"I told you to turn around," he growled.

Hesitating just a moment longer, the boy finally obeyed.

Major McDonald slapped his knee and started laughing. And kept laughing. He wiped his eyes and said, "Thank you, Miss Long! I haven't laughed like that in months. Good for the soul! I needed that!"

Dumbstruck, Eliza stood and watched him.

"If you want to pass yourself off as a boy, you're going to have to do a lot better than this!" he said, swooping his hand toward her.

Eliza was speechless. And mortified. She wished the ground would open up and swallow her. She gulped several times and tried to compose herself. The major's face was split with a huge smile. He shook his head as he watched her, as if he had a hard time believing what he was seeing.

"H...how do y...you know me?" she finally asked, trembling from head to toe and trying desperately to keep from crying.

"You don't remember me, Eliza?" he asked warmly.

She swallowed again. "No, sir. I don't."

"That's all right. Have a seat before you faint, lass." He stood and pulled out a chair for her.

"I'm Major George McDonald. I've been a friend of your father for years. I remember meeting you only once, and I think you were too occupied with other matters to give a middle-aged man any attention. You caught my attention for several reasons: your hair, your amazing blue eyes, and the simple fact that my oldest daughter is your age and my youngest daughter is also named Eliza. Thankfully they're safe in St. Louis with the rest of my family. I saw you briefly here in Springfield soon after you and your father moved here. He and I were in an officers' meeting, and he pointed you out to me as you walked by."

"Oh," she said dumbly.

"I'm so sorry about your father. He was a good man and a good soldier."

She swallowed and nodded, unable to speak.

"Do you have family in the area?"

Eliza shook her head and unsuccessfully fought her tears.

"Where is your family, Eliza?"

"There's no one left. Just me and Pa." She looked down, embarrassed. "Just me," she whispered.

Major McDonald waited for a moment before gently asking, "Eliza, lass, where are you living now?"

"On Walnut Street."

"By yourself?"

"No, sir."

He sat back and studied her for what seemed like an eternity to Eliza. Then he shook his head in puzzlement and stood.

"Tell me, Eliza, what possessed you to dress like this and come down here? Surely, you're not serious about enlisting."

"Yes, sir, I am." She lifted her chin and locked eyes with him.

McDonald let out a snort of disgust. "Just how long do you think this, this ridiculous disguise would have worked? What about your hair? Not to mention other things!"

"I was going to cut it if my plan worked."

"And you think that would work? Just cutting your hair?"

Eliza nodded with a trace of defiance creeping in, causing her to stand a little straighter.

"Excuse me for my bluntness, but this plan of yours is completely idiotic! Frankly, I'm appalled!"

"Other women have done this before and done it successfully! I've read about them! Lucy Brewer fought as a man in the War of 1812! Deborah Samson and Anne Bailey fought as men in the Revolutionary War! I'll even wager you have women out there right now in your camp!"

McDonald smiled and shook his head in disbelief. He walked back over to his chair and sat, still shaking his head. "You are a very remarkable and intelligent young lady, but my answer is still no! You've been found out, Eliza! On your first day, you were found out! What does that say to you?"

"You only recognized me because you knew me!" She paced then faced him again with desperation. "Please, please, Major McDonald, let me do this! Let me at least try. No one else knows but you. You could even help me!"

He put his hands up to stop her. "No! It's over, Eliza."

She felt like the air had been knocked out of her. Sitting, she buried her face in her hands and groaned.

McDonald leaned over his desk toward her. "Eliza, why is this so important to you?"

Eliza sat up and stared at him. Slowly and deliberately, she answered, "I want to kill the people who killed my father."

"Oh…" The major sat back. "I see…"

"My father lay for days, dying a slow agonizing death, and I wasn't there for him. I tried, but I was too slow. The people who did this to him have to pay. And I intend to make them pay in any and every way I can."

"This is war, Miss Long. There are good people on both sides."

"Our enemy has to be stopped."

"Yes, you are right." He sighed and ran his fingers through his hair. After a long pause, he asked, "To what lengths would you be willing to go to stop them?"

Her head snapped to attention. "Anything, sir. Anything at all!"

"Can you keep secrets?"

"Yes, of course!"

He hesitated then stood and walked to the entrance of his tent. "Stay here." He exited. She thought she heard his footsteps walk the perimeter of his tent before he came back in and sat behind his desk. "Pull your chair up close."

Eliza did as he instructed.

"Can you follow orders?" he asked very quietly, leaning over his desk.

"Yes, sir."

"Are you willing to die for this cause?"

"Gladly, if necessary."

"We've gotten word that possibly we'll move out. We're needed elsewhere. If our commanding officers don't leave enough men behind, this city could fall back into the hands of the Confederates."

Eliza gasped.

He steadied her with a stern look. "If you are to do the job I have in mind, you must rein in your emotions and every expression of your emotions. Do you think you are capable of that?"

She nodded very seriously, her breath bated.

"In essence, you must become an actress."

Again, she nodded.

"Because some of us anticipate leaving the city, we have recruited several civilian couriers and spies. We need eyes and ears everywhere, especially if the Confederates return. We want to know everything there is to know about them. The name of every officer, the location of every camp, every officer's tent, every movement of troops, every word out of every officer's mouth, anything and everything that seems suspicious. If you agree to help us, you will have to become an expert liar. Can you do this for our cause?"

"Yes, sir. I would be more than honored, sir."

"Good. Wait here." Again, he left the tent.

Much later, after endless minutes of biting her nails and

pacing, the major pushed his way past the canvas door, followed by another officer. McDonald put his finger to his lips to indicate silence just before he grabbed a third chair and added it to the other two at the tiny table.

"Miss Long, I'd like you to meet Captain Alcorn. He has a few questions for you."

Captain Alcorn was a small, very serious man, with keen eyes that seemed to take in everything. He reminded her of a schoolteacher she once had. Nodding toward Eliza, he began to interrogate her. Finally, he asked where she lived, who she lived with, who she knew in town, what her normal daily routine was, what horses and wagons were available for her use. Satisfied, he sat back and nodded to McDonald.

Major McDonald said, "Captain Alcorn is the officer in charge of organizing our civilian couriers and spies. That's why I've brought him here. We think we can use you."

"Miss Long, we have several others serving in this way. You may never know who they are. There will be times when you will have to work together. Don't approach them unless absolutely necessary. Can you sneak in and out of your house undetected?"

"Yes, I did today."

"Good. We have a plan for you, but we need to work out the details. Meet me at the mercantile on the square in two days at noon. That should give me enough time to put our plans together. Ask the owner, Mr. Mercer, if he has any red plaid fabric. He'll direct you to me. Furthermore, tell no one, absolutely no one, that you are working for us. We are suspicious of Miss Scott."

"Mildred Scott? But why?"

"Nothing more than she's from Arkansas, has relatives fighting for the South, and was quick to fly a Confederate flag. To do this right, you need to be suspicious of people. Always be on guard."

"H-how do you know this about her?"

"That's what we do," Captain Alcorn answered with a grin.

Both men stood. So, Eliza stood. Captain Alcorn slipped quietly out of the tent. Major McDonald told Eliza to put her hat on and hurry back to Walnut Street.

"Good luck. You'd better be ready with a believable story if they catch you sneaking in like that."

CHAPTER TEN

With great difficulty, Eliza managed to sneak back into the house and into her room hoping no one saw her. As soon as she shut her door, someone knocked. Eliza jumped and clutched her heart.

"Eliza? Is that you?" came Sally's worried voice.

"Yes, Sally. It's me."

"Where have you been, honey? You've had us scared to death! Are you all right?"

"Uh…when I woke up, I slipped out to take a walk."

"A walk? That was one long walk! Are you sure you're okay?"

"I'm fine, Sally. Don't worry."

"Well…supper's 'bout ready. Are you joining us?"

"I'll be right down."

With unbelievable speed, she ripped her clothes off, scrubbed the dirt from her face, dressed, and brushed her wild curls.

When she got downstairs the others were at the table waiting. They looked at her with puzzled expressions.

Still flustered by the rush to get home and by the

unforeseen turn of events, all Eliza could manage was a smile and a quick, "Have you prayed yet?"

The next two days seemed like an eternity to Eliza. She too became suspicious of poor Mildred Scott and her household. After all, as Captain Alcorn said, *to do this right, you need to be suspicious of people. Always be on guard.*

So, on guard, she was. Watching every move, listening to every conversation, trying to detect any sign of treason. She wandered around the yard, poking into every nook and cranny. Apparently, her odd behavior disturbed the others. They were obviously watching her. She had to be careful. Much more careful.

Eliza had a turmoil of mixed emotions when Jonathan showed up on his aunt Mildred's doorstep the evening before she was to report to the mercantile. They were eating supper when she heard heavy, firm steps on the porch. George swung the door open wide with a shout of joy. Mildred and Sally jumped up from the table and flew into Jonathan's outstretched arms. Jim respectfully rose and extended his hand shyly. Jonathan grasped it firmly and slapped him on the back.

"So good to see you! All of you! What a relief you made it safely! Thank you, Jim!" His gaze quickly moved to Eliza, still sitting at the table. He moved to her side and crouched down next to her chair.

"Eliza," Jonathan said gently and sorrowfully. "I heard about your pa." His voice choked as he cupped her face in his hand.

Everything in her fought against giving in to her grief again, but she couldn't hold back. Jon was family. Only Jon could understand. She sounded like a strangled animal as she threw herself into his arms and sobbed uncontrollably. He stood with her firmly locked in a brotherly embrace and tried to soothe her, but she cried harder. Finally, he walked to the parlor with her and shut the door. Setting her gently beside him on the settee, he smoothed her hair away from her face and handed her a handkerchief. Eliza blew her nose loudly and mopped her tear-stained face then buried her face and cried some more, leaning heavily on Jonathan's shoulder.

"I saw him," she hiccupped between her sobs. "It was really him. Oh, Jon, it was awful!"

"I'm so sorry, Eliza," he said as he stroked her head.

"They buried him in a cemetery over on Grant. I tried, Jon. I really tried, but I couldn't get to him in time. I...I couldn't find him." Curling into a ball, she started weeping loudly again, gasping to gain control.

Jonathan patted her back. "It's not your fault, Eliza. Even if you had found him, he would have died. I read the report of his injuries."

She sat and looked at him. "Oh, but, Jon, he died alone, surrounded by other dying men. I could have been there, holding his hand, giving him water, loving him. Don't you see?"

Jonathan pulled her face to his. "I see, Eliza, I see. I'm so sorry. But your pa died knowing how much you love him. He also died knowing how much he's loved by his Father in Heaven. That's what gave him the comfort he needed in those last hours."

Eliza nodded.

"This is war and war is hell on earth. But our God is still here. And our God still comforts His children in the middle of horrifying circumstances."

Eliza sat back and studied his face for a brief moment then leaned her head on him again and sighed. "Since when did you become so religious?"

Jonathan snorted. "Religious? You know better than that. Religion has little to do with it. It's all about Him and what His Spirit does in us. Believe me, when you're faced with death every day, you start to take very seriously what you've been taught from God's Book. And I *know* you, little lady, have been taught God's Word since the day you were born. I was there. In fact, I believe I got most of my Bible learning from your grandma and your pa."

Eliza sat back and actually smiled. She wiped her face again and said, "Thanks, Jon. I…I think I'm going to be all right." She shrugged and looked away. "Maybe, anyway…

The next morning at breakfast, Jonathan noticed Eliza fidgeting with her napkin and avoiding eye contact with the others gathered around the table. He caught the eye of his aunt, who gestured toward Eliza and shook her head in sadness. He and the others tried to keep a cheerful conversation going, but it was strained. Finally, he offered to take a walk with Eliza. Her head snapped up quickly, and she stammered, "Uh, no thank you. I think I'll just go back to my room."

Jonathan wiped his mouth and laid his napkin by his plate. "Let's walk first then you can go back to your room."

She raised her head in protest, but one look into his eyes caused her to clamp her mouth shut.

Jonathan stood, took her hand, gently pulled her to her feet, and walked with her out the door and down the walk.

Eliza kept her eyes to the ground. Her heart was in her throat. The fear of being found out before she could even begin her new mission filled her mind with dread. She couldn't miss her appointment at noon. What if Jon didn't get her back in time? What if they caught her sneaking out? Even worse, what would she do if Jon went with her?

"I should have let you get your wrap. It's chilly out here

this morning."

"Yeah..." Eliza nodded. They walked a block before Jonathan spoke again.

"Last night, you told me you thought you were going to be all right. How are you doing this morning?"

"Hmm? Oh, fine...I'm fine."

"So...what's been on your mind all morning?"

"Nothing. I'm fine."

They walked another block in silence.

"Eliza, I know you're not fine," Jonathan said very gently.

When she didn't respond, he continued. "It's certainly understandable. You've lost your pa. You're staying with people you didn't even know a few months ago. We're at war. I understand. I just wish you'd talk about it. What's going on in that head of yours?"

"Uh...nothing. I'm fine...I...I'm just tired. That's all. I need a nap. Can we go back now?"

Jonathan shook his head and sighed. "If that's what you want."

He escorted her home, where she quietly informed Sally not to expect her for the noon meal since she had a headache and needed to sleep.

Precisely at 11:30, Eliza quietly slipped out of her room, down the hallway to the back staircase, and into the storage room off the kitchen. Knowing Sally was likely in the kitchen preparing the meal, Eliza very slowly and carefully lifted the latch on the door to the shed. She held her skirt tightly against her body as she maneuvered between the crudely built wooden shelves lining the walls of the shed. One set of these shelves cleverly hid the door to a cold, damp, narrow set of stone steps leading down to one of their hidden cellars. It gave her an odd feeling of security, knowing it was there.

She opened the door to the yard no more than an inch

and peeked through the crack before she dared exit. Fearing she might be spotted from one of the windows, she crept along the edge of the property, behind a bank of forsythia bushes until she reached the back gate. Once she made her way down the back alley, she felt safe enough to walk freely without checking over her shoulder every few seconds.

Fifteen minutes later, she entered the square. Her throat clenched as she set eyes on the federal courthouse again, reminding her of that awful day when she was told of her father's death.

Entering Mercer's Mercantile, Eliza shyly scanned the rows of scant supplies. A jolly female voice interrupted her. "Can I be of help, miss?"

"Uh, no thank you. I...um...I..."

Major McDonald's words came back to her. *You must become an actress.*

Standing taller and squaring her shoulders, she confidently stated, "I'd like to look around a bit if you don't mind. I've been cooped up so long at home, it just feels good to get out again."

"Well, I certainly understand that," the portly woman exclaimed. "These are trying times to be sure. If you need me, I'll be in the back sorting what little we have on hand. I'm sure hoping these dear soldiers can keep things safe enough to get a new shipment through."

A man behind the counter watched them with interest. As soon as Mrs. Mercer disappeared through the door, Eliza made her way toward him.

"Have you decided what you want, miss?"

"Uh, do you have any red plaid fabric?" she answered barely above a whisper, her pulse pounding in her head.

Quietly and with a quick glance around the room, he answered, "Down the alley and through the door in the back." His eyes moved quickly to the left then, more loudly, he answered, "No, I'm sorry. We don't have any, but if you come back in a week, perhaps a shipment will have arrived by then."

"Thank you. I'm sure I'll be back," Eliza said as she made her way to the front door. On the porch, she shielded her eyes from the sun and nonchalantly studied the people on the square. She walked down the steps and strolled past the courthouse. Several soldiers lingered on the steps, some in bandages, others propped up on crutches or sitting with bandaged stumps in place of once strong, healthy legs. Eliza shuddered and looked away. In the center of the square stood the charred remains of the old brick courthouse. A few buildings were abandoned and a few held various businesses struggling to cope with war. Several other people were also strolling casually around the square, most likely Union sympathizers enjoying the relative safety of the new military occupation.

Trying not to draw attention to herself, Eliza circled around and walked back to the alley next to the mercantile. Thankfully it was empty. She made her way toward the only door in sight. When she reached it, she peeked back to make sure she wasn't being watched then quickly opened the door and entered.

CHAPTER ELEVEN

Eliza jumped back in fear when she saw an old man in rags slumped against the far wall with several empty bottles scattered around. He didn't move. Was he even alive? Surely he heard her. Holding the doorknob, ready to bolt if necessary, she cleared her throat. Then again, more loudly. Nothing. Thinking she'd made a mistake, she quietly opened the door to leave.

"Wait," came a weak, gravelly voice.

"Who are you?" she asked timidly.

"Who are you looking for?"

"I-I'd rather not say."

"Shut the door, please."

Eliza took a deep breath to steady her nerves then shut the door.

"Good girl," the old man said as he stood.

She kept her hand on the doorknob.

"Eliza?"

"Yes?"

"It's me, Captain Alcorn."

With a giant sigh of relief, she let go of the door and

walked toward him. "I would never have known!"

"Good! This is one of the many things we do. And this is what you'll be doing. How much time do you have before they'll get suspicious?"

"I'm not sure. Things are a little more complicated because Jonathan is here."

"I know."

"How'd you...? Never mind. You somehow manage to see everything... Is that right?"

Captain Alcorn's eyes twinkled. "We better get down to business. We don't have much time. The first thing we need to do is come up with some believable disguises and names for you. Then I'll get you in contact with one or two other spies in the area. That will be it for now."

Eliza's heart beat with excitement. *I'm a spy!*

Captain Alcorn immediately threw water on her enthusiasm. "If you're found out, you will most likely be hanged. If anyone else is found out due to your carelessness, they will be hanged. Understand?"

She swallowed and nodded.

"Are you sure you want to proceed?"

Again, she nodded.

"I would never involve a young female such as yourself in something so dangerous, except I saw in you a determination to do everything in your power to fight this horrendous enemy. Was I correct?"

"Yes, sir. You were. You are!"

"All right, then. Let's talk business. Listen carefully and commit to memory everything I tell you today. Don't write any of this down even after you return to your room. As Eliza Long, you are to remain at home. Conjure up any excuse to do so. Your eyes and hair make you too recognizable. If you must go out, be a shy, mousey little nobody. Wear your hair in a tight bun tucked up under a bonnet. Preferably wear shabby country girl garb, or even black since you're still in mourning. Don't talk to people if it can be helped. Do whatever it takes to not draw attention to yourself, your hair, or your eyes."

He gazed intently at her and shook his head. "I'm afraid those eyes will get you hanged."

She shuddered and involuntarily touched her right eyelid.

"I need you to take this very seriously, Eliza."

"I am, Captain Alcorn. How can I not."

"We have concerns that you are too young for this. But we're at war and desperate for every scrap of information you might be able to dig up."

"I can do this, Captain. I'm sure of it."

"I can't stress enough to you that it's not just your life at stake. It's others as well. Be discreet. Constantly on guard."

Eliza pinched her lips together and nodded.

"Very well. Let's continue. You will be disguised as two different people. One, we'll name Gloria LaRue from Little Rock, Arkansas. Gloria has no family and moved to Little Rock from a farm to the South where you worked as a servant girl. In Little Rock, you made a decent amount of money working as a dance hall girl under an assumed name. Trying to flee the shame of your life, you traveled north to Springfield, hoping to start over. You're ashamed of your past and choose to not speak of it. This way, no one can trace down your history and discover you're a fraud. You must be absolutely believable to everyone who knows you as Gloria LaRue. Understand?"

Eliza nodded.

"Repeat back to me everything I've just told you."

She did. Very successfully, to the captain's obvious surprise, his eyes open wide in amazement. He smiled and nodded.

"Gloria LaRue now works for the owner of a boardinghouse on Elm Street. It's a blue building on Elm Street, just two houses to the east down the alley from Mildred Scott's home. The owner lives there and is working for us. She is expecting you sometime tomorrow afternoon. If for some reason, you can't sneak out, she will understand. She's not going anywhere. Knock three times on her back door and wait. Her name is Elin Johnson. She is in her fifties and has her own story which she will tell you later. You, Gloria, will have your own room there, which, of course, you will not sleep in. But it must at all times appear as if you do stay there. Gloria's clothes will be there, and you will use that room to change in. You will also use a small shed at the back of the property that has a door that opens to the alley. Look for the blue house with an old shed right at the alley. The door is locked. The key is under a rock at the corner of the shed. In the corner of Mildred's property, a small gate has recently been cut in the fence behind the lilac bushes. You will have to find a way to sneak through that gate, down the alley, and into Elin's shed without drawing suspicion. I'm counting on you to be a very smart, very accomplished actress. Understand?"

Eliza nodded.

"Also, and this is crucial to your success, you must become a very good liar. This is war, and it is absolutely necessary that you lie. A lot! Even to those you love. Basically, your whole life will be a lie. Can you do it?"

"Yes. This will be the most difficult part of the job though."

"Remember, you're only acting. And the lives of your loved ones could be in grave danger if they knew the truth. You must lie to protect them."

"I'm certain I can do it, Captain Alcorn. I know I can."

"Good! Now again, repeat to me everything I've said."

She did and he continued. "Gloria is an absolutely beautiful, dark-haired, blue-eyed, talkative flirt. She's the complete opposite of Eliza Long. Eliza's voice will be quiet and low. Gloria's voice is high, very feminine, yet confident, and not at all brash. You mustn't drive off your suitors. And I expect there will be many."

Eliza let out an unladylike snort.

"There will be none of that from the mouth of fair Gloria, please!" the captain said with a sharp glance at her. "Gloria is a Southern belle, a huge supporter of the South. Everything about her is a coquette: the way she dresses, the way she moves. She loves the attention of men, and they will love every bit of attention she will give them, although she does not give the impression that she is a loose woman. She must act in such a way that men will feel very comfortable in her presence, comfortable enough that they might share their life with her, their comings and goings, their frustrations with the war and finally, hopefully, they'll share secrets. That will be your goal. To bring them to a place where they'll share troop movements, troop encampments, any and every detail that has to do with the military. It may seem small to you, but, combined with other reports we get, it may be very significant. I want to know where every officer in Springfield sleeps at night, where he spends his time, how he spends his time, and with whom he spends his time. Understand?"

Again, Eliza nodded.

"Gloria's main job is to collect information. Remember everything you hear then, after you get to your room at Miss Scott's, write it down using the Freemason Cipher, which Elin Johnson will teach you. Hide it in your room where you are certain it won't be found. Your second character will be a twelve-year-old girl named Frances, who actually dresses like a boy. You will also find clothes for Frances in Gloria's room. For your safety, I want anyone who sees you to think you're a boy named Francis, with an i, a misconception that you will not correct. If they manage to remove your hat, they'll see two tightly coiled braids. You can wiggle out of trouble by explaining your name is Frances, a girl's name, and that you never meant to deceive them. Frances' job is to be a courier of the information you've gathered. You will travel with a freed slave who works for us. He will go without you if he feels it's too dangerous, and at times, when speed is important, you will go alone by horseback. Ideally, we want you to go so you can talk directly with the officer in charge, the officer you will be delivering your message to. We'll need you to flesh out the details of your encrypted messages.

"Frances is Elin Johnson's niece, and your story is simply that you're taking food or a message from your mother to Elin or vice versa. They are sisters, and your family lives on a tiny farm in whatever direction you find yourselves traveling. Be shrewd. Pay attention to whoever might stop and question you. Be prepared to change your reason for going in any particular direction. Let George take the lead. He's very good at this."

"George?"

Captain Alcorn smiled. "Yes, George...George Scott. He's the other spy you'll be working with. He has already delivered messages for us."

"I...I had no idea!"

"Of course, not."

"But I've never noticed anything out of the ordinary."

"Well, you haven't been terribly observant lately, have you?"

"Do Mildred and Sally know?"

Captain Alcorn's eyes darkened. "What do you think, Eliza?"

"Uh...I guess not." She took a deep breath. "Does Jonathan know?"

"If Jonathan knows, then we are failing at what we do. He must never find out. Will that be a problem for you, Eliza?" the captain asked quietly but firmly.

"He's very observant."

"Then you will have to be a very, very good actress."

"So, Jonny, how long will you be in Springfield?"

George asked at the evening meal.

Eliza looked up from her plate, keenly interested, not only in Jon's answer but also in George's question. He was an entirely new man to her now that she knew he'd been recruited as a spy. She felt like she'd just met him. He was probably in his sixties or seventies, a little stooped, very thin. It amazed her that Captain Alcorn had even considered him for such a job. He was smart, though, she noted. And very observant, his keen eyes fully fixed on Jon as he talked. Then his brown eyes turned to her and held a slight questioning gaze. She blushed and quickly stared down at her fidgeting hands. Why was he looking at her like that? He was acting much too suspicious. When she raised her head, she saw that everyone at the table was looking at her.

"Whatever is the matter?" she asked, blinking in confusion.

"Jonathan asked you a question, dear," Mildred said.

"What? Oh, I'm sorry." Composing herself, she asked, "What was it, Jon?"

"I just asked if you'd had a good rest. You were still in your room when I got here this afternoon."

"Uh...yes. Thank you. I didn't know you'd returned. I'm sorry."

"Do you think you'd enjoy another stroll after the meal?"

"Yes, very much." As soon as the words left her mouth, she remembered Captain Alcorn's instructions to stay at home. *If you must go out, don't let anyone see your hair or your eyes. Wear a bonnet, be mousey, etc...*

"Uh... I'll need to change first, and, uh...get a bonnet." Although slightly flustered, she managed to flash a dazzling smile Jon's direction. "These beets are exceptionally good, Sally. What did you cook them in? And the pork. Thank God we still have pork to eat. I've heard that food supplies are getting pretty scarce."

The topic of food quickly got their attention. George and Sally, especially, dove into the conversation with glee. Food, after all, consumed most of their day: George finding and storing it and Sally dreaming up a hundred delicious ways to serve it. While they talked, Eliza felt Jon studying her. She squirmed.

"Well, those beets, believe it or not, were cooked in this morning's bacon fat. Sliced thin and slowly fried." Sally shook her curly head and smacked her lips. "Mmm, mmm! There's not much in this world that's not improved by bacon fat."

"And you can thank Jim for that pork," George added. "We went out to Abe Goodman's farm a couple of days ago and slaughtered the two hogs we could find. We smoked most of it out there in the smokehouse and brought a couple of fresh cuts home with us."

"I'm surprised every soldier within smelling distance didn't come swarming down on you. How in the world did you get away with that?" Jon asked with a smile.

Both George and Jim looked sideways at each other and laughed. "We have no idea! Maybe that's it. Just maybe there was no soldiers within smellin' distance," George said, slapping his knee. "We knew we's might be invitin' a heap o' trouble, but it was worth the risk. If we didn't grab those hogs when we could, we knew there'd never be another chance. We couldn't bring 'em into town to butcher. Way too big of a chance of getting 'em stolen! So we figured the only way to do it was butcher and smoke 'em there, hopin' no one would hear or smell what we were up to."

The two men grinned from ear to ear.

"And it worked," Jim added in his slow, deep drawl. "Still don't know how."

"Don't you be forgettin', the two of us was back here holdin' the two of you up before the Lord whiles you was out there gallivantin' around," Sally interjected. "It's not safe out there!"

George leaned over, took his wife's hand in his, and gave it a comforting squeeze.

"I was feeling a little guilty eating like this, when my men would give a month's wages to get fresh pork, but now that I know the risk you two took, I suppose the least I can do is enjoy it," Jon said, pushing back from the table and contentedly stretching his long, muscled legs out in front of his chair.

"Don't you be feeling too awful guilty, nephew," Mildred said in her soft Southern drawl, patting his shoulder affectionately. "I know for a fact some of your men are sitting down to meals very similar to this one. Most of them have family in the area that are doing everything they can to fatten up their boys while they have a chance."

"I'm afraid that chance may slip away soon," Jon said.

"Oh?" Mildred asked with upraised eyebrows.

"You've heard, haven't you, Aunt Mildred, about General Fremont being relieved of his command?"

"I've heard all sorts of rumors, but I'm still not sure what to believe."

"It's true. Fremont received the official letter of dismissal today. The command has been handed over to General Hunter who's on his way to Springfield now. Rumor has it that Hunter doesn't think it's necessary to linger in these parts. Some say there's a pretty sizable group of Confederate forces just outside Springfield. I've heard that's based on faulty reports. Apparently, General Hunter has heard the same. So, in the meantime, we're waiting with bated breath. Do we stay? Or do we go?"

"Well, if it's up to me, I say, stay!" exclaimed Sally, stabbing her fork in the air.

"I wish we could, Sally. I'm still not entirely sure of Lincoln's reason for replacing Fremont," Jon answered, rubbing his whiskered chin. "Some say Lincoln was frustrated with Fremont's reluctance to move his troops to southwest Missouri to help General Lyon back in August."

"We would have won the battle at Wilson's Creek, and my pa would still be alive if Fremont had listened to Lyon!" Eliza declared in a bitter tone. "I say, good riddance to him!"

The others agreed.

"The other rumor is that Lincoln let him go because Fremont declared his own emancipation proclamation for southwest Missouri, which is not his prerogative."

"Well that proclamation has made it easier for me 'n' Jim to go wherever we want. I, for one, thank the good general. That was several weeks ago that he did that, wasn't it?" asked George.

"Back in September, I believe," Jon said.

"Is that why I've seen so many slaves wandering the streets looking for work and food?" Eliza asked.

"Yes, that's the reason," Jon answered. "I'm afraid they're not doing well. Especially the women and children."

"Mildred and I have been getting some rooms ready so's we can take in the little ones without no one to watch after them," Sally said.

Jon nodded appreciatively. Eliza was shocked.

"I-I had no idea! When did you do this?" Eliza asked, feeling betrayed.

"Eliza, dear. It's been no secret. You've just been too occupied with other things to notice," Mildred said with tenderness. "Would you like to help us?"

Flustered, Eliza looked down and stammered, "Uh...n-no thanks. I-I'm gonna b-be busy."

Awkward silence filled the room.

Finally, Jon asked, "Busy? Busy with what?"

"I'm planning to do a lot of reading...and...and writing. I'm not sure. Why?" She looked at them with pleading eyes as she began her new, unwelcome role of actress. "I'm so sorry. Please try to understand. I don't know why. I just feel like this is something I have to do. Maybe it will help me heal from this awful hurt."

"Helping others is often the best way to heal, Eliza," Mildred said softly. "Believe me. I know. It has worked for me," she said with tears in her eyes.

"Maybe I'll help you someday," Eliza said sadly. "But for now, please, just let me do what I feel like I need to. It's how I find peace."

Mildred reached out and took her hand. "Of course, dear. You take all the time you need. We'll use your help when you're ready."

Tears slid down Eliza's cheeks, and she wiped them with the back of her hand. Eliza wept with grief but not for the reason they thought. Hers was the gut-wrenching grief of telling an intentional, bold-faced lie to these precious people who loved her and trusted her.

CHAPTER TWELVE

The next morning, while Eliza was helping Sally clear the breakfast table, Jonathan burst through the door.

"If anyone wants to see General Fremont march out of town, come with me! You'll need to hurry though!"

All three women dropped what they were doing, removed their aprons, and rushed to join Jonathan and the other two men on the big porch. They descended the broad steps and together walked two blocks north to St. Louis Street, where they joined dozens of people waving flags and sending the disgraced general off with good will. Soon they heard and saw the general's entourage, marching east along the street, waving and tipping their hats to their supporters. He and his bodyguard were accompanied by music from a small band. When Major Zagonyi rode by, they cheered and shouted, "Thank you!" to him. It was sad to watch them leave, not knowing what the plans were for the Union occupation of their beloved city.

As soon as they finished the noon meal, Eliza excused herself and went directly to her room. She waited until she saw Jonathan walk out the front gate. Then, very quietly, she snuck down the back stairway, through the storage room, and into the shed. She came up with several excuses for being found going this route, dismissing each one as way too implausible. As she made her way across the back lawn to the lilac bushes along the fence, she suddenly remembered what Captain Alcorn had told her about her appearance. *"If you must go out, be a shy, mousey little nobody."* In the excitement of the morning's events, she had completely forgotten! There she had stood on the sidewalk of St. Louis Street, jumping up and down, waving and cheering, her blue eyes flashing and her dark, curly hair blowing in the breeze. Who had seen her? She shook her head in disgust with herself and squeezed through the cut in the fence, getting her skirt tangled in a blackberry bush.

Cautiously, she made her way down the alley, counting houses, beginning with the one directly behind Mildred's. Sure enough, two down stood a blue two-story house with bushes along the fence, so thick and tall, it was difficult to see the building and impossible to see the backyard. Eliza peeked over her shoulder as she approached the old shed. She bent to feel under the rock for the key and, just as Captain Alcorn had told her, it was there. Quickly she opened the shed door, entered, and locked the door behind her. Her heart was pounding, and beads of sweat trickled down her face.

You've got to calm down, she told herself, hands pressed firmly against her chest. *If you can't do this small thing, how in heaven's name will you be able to do any of what they're expecting of you?*

She wiped the sweat from her face and checked her surroundings. As carefully as Alcorn, or whoever was working for him, had been about every detail, including the gate cut in Mildred's fence and the key carefully hidden under the rock, Eliza thought there might be something of interest in this shed that might easily be missed. So, she snooped around. Everything seemed normal. She did notice, however, a tarp hanging from a workbench. Pulling it aside, she saw a stack of empty buckets tucked next to a pile of old boards. She quietly pulled the buckets out and stooped down to look behind them. Too dark to see and way too many cobwebs. A possible hiding place, only if she was desperate though. She shuddered, pulled back, and replaced the buckets.

The door into the backyard didn't let out even a tiny creak as she pushed it open. *Good job oiling the hinges, whoever you are.* She inspected and found enough of a trace of oil to confirm her guess. The garden behind the house was overgrown and tangled, providing good cover for anyone needing it. Eliza made her way between the bushes to the back porch and very quietly up the steps. *Knock three times on her back door and wait,* she remembered Alcorn saying. So she did. Three firm knocks. Then she waited. And waited. She heard voices inside and thought perhaps she should leave and try to make contact another day. Slowly she backed down the steps and watched the door with expectancy. No one came. Minutes passed before Eliza sighed with disappointment and turned to leave. Then she heard someone clearing their throat. She yanked her head around and saw a tiny woman standing in the doorway, studying her.

"Did you knock, miss?" the woman asked.

"Y-yes," Eliza answered.

"Come up onto the porch so I can get a good look at you, girl."

Eliza obeyed, heart pounding.

"And your name, child?"

Eliza started to stammer an answer but stopped. *What do I say? Eliza? Or Gloria? Is this a test?*

Since she was not yet in her Gloria role, she answered, "Uh...Eliza?"

The woman's eyes twinkled with mischief as she opened the door farther and motioned Eliza inside. "Well come on in, Eliza. I've been expecting you. Follow me."

She turned to the right through a small doorway that led to the back stairway. Halfway up, she very quietly said, "Eliza will only use these stairs. Gloria will only use the stairs in the front." Then she continued up. She led her to a bedroom in the back and closed the door behind them.

Eliza instantly liked this birdlike woman standing in front of her. The mischievous twinkle remained in her sharp yet kind eyes.

"Have a seat, Eliza, and tell me about yourself."

Eliza sat in the chair indicated while the woman poured two cups of tea from a teapot on a small table by the bed.

"I'm Elin Johnson, by the way. Please call me Elin," she said as she handed the cup to Eliza.

"Thank you, Mrs...uh...Elin. Please forgive me. I'm so nervous I can barely hold this cup." Eliza giggled.

"That's understandable. I was, too, when I first started."

"How long have you been doing this?"

"Awhile. So, tell me. What brought you here?"

"S-surely you know, don't you?"

Elin smiled. "Some of it. But I want to hear it from you."

Eliza proceeded to tell Elin of her father's death, her grief, her anger, and her determination to fight the enemy. She told of her embarrassing trip to the Federal encampment and her conversation with both Major McDonald and Captain Alcorn. Finally, she described in great detail the instructions Alcorn had given her when she met him at the square.

"Very good," Elin said. "Now tell me everything that's happened since then, up to this very moment."

Eliza looked at her quizzically.

Elin smiled warmly. "I need details, and I'll explain why after you're finished."

So, Eliza went over every detail she could remember from the time she left Alcorn, including conversations, awkward moments, and who was present. She even shamefully recounted the events of the morning when she forgot to hide herself in the house or under a bonnet.

"Did you talk to anyone besides those from your household?"

"Other than Jonathan, no."

"Did you see anyone paying any particular mind to you?"

"No. As far as I could tell, everyone was paying attention to General Fremont and his men."

Elin stood and paced. "Hmmm... Let's hope that's all." She gently but firmly said, "That was very foolish of you, you know."

Eliza blushed and looked down. "I'm so sorry," she whispered, shaking her head.

"That kind of carelessness could get you killed, you realize?"

Eliza nodded.

"And possibly others..."

"Do you think...?"

"No. Not this time, and not yet since you haven't been active. But...and I'm sure you're going to hate to hear this..."

Eliza stood to her feet. "Please, let me do this, Elin! I won't make the same mistake! If necessary, I'll stay in my room, at least while I'm Eliza."

"Sit down and listen. You were seen. George, of course. But also, another man. He works with us, and he said you stood out. You're too young and too pretty. He feels you're too great a risk, and it would be a big mistake to use you."

Eliza's mouth fell open, and she protested until Elin put up her hand to shush her.

"We still very much need you, Eliza. That's one of the reasons I wanted you to tell me everything. I needed to see for myself what kind of young lady you are. I've seen good things and not so good things. You are extremely observant and have an amazing memory for detail. You're devoted to our cause. You can be very quiet and discreet. I think with time, you can become good at acting and at lying."

Eliza nodded vigorously.

"But you are entirely too impulsive."

Eliza stood again and parted her lips to speak.

"And this just proves it," Elin interrupted. "Sit down, please."

"Oh, my dear, if you only knew how much we want this to work!" Elin shook her head and sat in the other chair.

Eliza choked back unwanted tears of frustration.

"We've been talking to George about this decision, since he's the one you'll be working most closely with. He dropped by this morning. He's afraid for you"—she paused—"but has reminded us that this is war, and we all have to take risks to beat the enemy. He says it would be a shame to not use you. He thinks you can handle it."

Elin took a deep breath. "Therefore, we plan to keep you."

Eliza stood to her feet, hands clasped under her chin. "Thank you. So much. You won't regret this. I promise."

Elin smiled and held out a restraining hand. "Although, you must go through a trial period. Sit, please."

Eliza sat.

"At first, you must practice being the quiet, mousey little Eliza that Captain Alcorn asked you to be. Under the circumstances, I think it would be wise for Eliza to virtually disappear. Not from the Scott household but from everywhere outside of Miss Scott's fence. Use whatever excuse you think will work. Grief, fear, you decide."

"Jonathan often asks me to take a walk with him, and he won't take no for an answer."

"In that case, wear a bonnet, and look down whenever you see anyone. Don't engage in conversation other than with him if it can be avoided. Again, your grief can serve you well as an excuse for your behavior."

Eliza nodded. "I can do that. How long?"

"It all depends on how well you do. Also, never talk to George about any of this unless you are in the back garden. It would be entirely inappropriate for him to go to your room. He came up with the idea of you being interested in plants and gardening. We realize November is not a good month for gardening," she chuckled, "but George is planning to build a greenhouse behind the house so he can try to grow vegetables through the winter."

Eliza was surprised and delighted at this news.

Elin laughed. "It will probably fail, but it's in keeping with his ambitious nature, so no one will question his new project. You are to take a great interest in this greenhouse. That will give you the opportunity to share information in private without drawing suspicion."

Eliza smiled and nodded.

"Also, continue with your story of needing time to read and write. Does Miss Scott have a library?"

"Yes. She has lots of books."

"Very good. To keep up a believable reason to stay in your room, borrow books and actually read them, just in case you're questioned about the contents. The longer we can keep up the deception, the longer we can use you. As soon as we feel that your cover is being compromised in any way, your work for us will have to stop. Understand?"

"Yes," Eliza answered.

"Does anyone else go into your room?"

"Occasionally Sally does, to clean and change the sheets. Usually just once a week."

"Hmmm...that could present a problem. Asking her to stay out would be far too suspicious, therefore you need to keep up appearances even in your room. Have paper and pens and some of your writing scattered across your desk, as if it's an activity you're always in the middle of. Change it every week.

"Also, find a good hiding place for your encrypted

messages that no one, and I mean no one would think to look. This is war. We may soon be under enemy occupation again and at any time your house and room could be occupied by the enemy and searched. If they find anything, you and possibly others will be arrested and maybe executed."

"What would you suggest?"

Elin stood and motioned for Eliza to follow her. She quietly moved one of the bedside tables, squatted down, and pried a section of the mopboard loose. Behind it was a space big enough to hold several folded pieces of paper, which Elin removed.

"This will be Gloria's hiding place, should she need it. Notice that it's on an exterior wall? That's so it will be less likely for anyone else in the house to hear when the board is moved."

Elin quietly replaced the board and the table and continued. "I've noticed that Miss Scott's house has a central chimney. Does your room have a fireplace?"

"Yes."

"Look for a hiding place there. There are probably loose bricks that might have some space behind them. Or check the mopboard and the floor for loose planks. Try to be very, very quiet when you do this. Perhaps wait until the others have gone out."

Eliza nodded, her enthusiasm for her new role growing with Elin's careful instructions.

Elin motioned to sit again. She pulled a chair next to hers, sat, and unfolded the papers she had removed from hiding.

"This," she said quietly, "is the Freemason's cipher. It is what we've chosen to encrypt our messages. It is too time-consuming and cumbersome to write every detail, so we save it for the most important information and remember the rest."

Eliza saw a very confusing mess of lines and letters.

"The biggest risk I'm taking today is to send these papers home with you. Do not let anyone see them. Is that understood?"

Eliza nodded solemnly.

"See these grids with all of the letters of the alphabet? A message can be written using no letters or numbers. The A is in the top left part of the first grid. So an A would be written like this..." Elin demonstrated by drawing what appeared to be half a square. "This represents where the A is on the grid. Do you see it?"

She looked at the grid and back at what Elin had drawn.

"Yes. I understand. But what about the J? It's in the same position as the A."

"Good observation. We make a J the same as the A, but with a dot in the middle to indicate it's from the second square grid."

She then demonstrated how to write an S and a W, both from the same positions on the two X-shaped grids. "Now you try it." She handed a piece of paper to Eliza. "Write your name."

Eliza took the paper and carefully wrote out each letter using lines and dots while constantly checking the page with the cipher. She did it slowly but perfectly.

"Very good!" Elin said with a clap of her hands. "You learn quickly. Now take this with you and practice, practice, until you can write anything quickly without looking at the key. But before you start, be sure to find a hiding place for all papers you'll be working on. In your room and in your clothes. Hide these papers here." She indicated a spot just below her bosom.

Eliza blushed slightly, turned her back, and clumsily stuffed the papers down the front of her dress.

Elin stood to go. "It's time for you to leave. Follow me."

"But isn't there more?"

"Oh, yes. There's much more. But we'll save that for later."

Wanting to ask a million questions, she obediently followed Elin down the stairs and out to the back porch. With lowered voice, Elin bade her goodbye and said, "Remember two things. Practice the code and also being a quiet, mousey Eliza who stays hidden away in her room with her books and her writing. And, do not talk to George about this business. That is all for now. Do not come here again until bidden."

With that, she shut the door. Eliza shook her head in bewilderment.

CHAPTER THIRTEEN

Eliza managed to slip back into the house without being seen, but as soon as she stepped into the upstairs hallway, she was confronted by Sally who stood at her bedroom door, knocking. Both women were startled at the sight of each other.

"Why, Eliza, dear, where have you been? I thought you were sleeping. And why in heaven's name were you using the back stairs?"

Eliza's hand went to her heart. "Oh! Sally! You frightened me!" Composing herself, she laughed. "I'm sorry. I just wanted to stroll around the backyard, see the animals. They calm me. And I used the back way so I wouldn't disturb anyone. I just wanted to be alone. You understand, don't you?"

Sally moved next to Eliza and put a comforting hand on her arm. "Of course, I do, dear. I came up to get you"—her voice lowered to a whisper—"because you have a visitor down in the parlor."

"What? Whoever could it be? I don't know anyone in Springfield, except the people here in this house. And

Jonathan, of course."

"It's a young man. A Captain Henry Goodman, he said his name was. He said you were acquainted."

In spite of her distrust of Henry Goodman, she was relieved it was him instead of someone from a dozen fearful scenarios that had played quickly through her head.

"Yes, we are. Although I really don't want to see him." She gave a resigned sigh. "Tell him I'll be down shortly." She turned to go into her room then stopped abruptly and caught Sally by the arm. "Has Henry seen Jim yet?"

"I don't think so. Why?"

"Henry is the banker's nephew. Abe Goodman's only living relative I know of," Eliza whispered. "Henry Goodman might want to take Jim, and he may have the right. I don't trust him, Sally. I really don't want Jim to end up in Henry's hands. Tell him to stay out of sight."

Sally's eyes were huge. "I will, Miss Eliza!" And with that, she swooped down the stairs in search of Jim.

Eliza checked her face and hair in her mirror, pulled a few stray blackberry twigs out of her skirt then reached down the front of her dress and retrieved the papers that Elin had entrusted to her. She hid them in one of her drawers, under her clothes. Finally, she went down to find out what might be on Henry Goodman's mind. He was pacing back and forth in front of the parlor windows when she entered the room. He saw her and turned, looking her up and down with admiration.

"Well, well! If it isn't the beautiful Eliza Long!"

"Hello, Henry," Eliza said, still standing in the doorway.

Henry's head snapped back. "That's it? An unemotional, 'Hello, Henry'? I was expecting more than that, Eliza We've shared such good times, sweetheart."

"Sweetheart? We've spent time together, Henry, but nothing ever happened that warrants a title of sweetheart," Eliza said, trying to control her annoyance. "And times have changed, Henry."

Henry drew in a deep breath and tried a different tactic. He sat down on the settee and patted the spot next to his. "Come, Eliza. Have a seat. Let's talk. We have a lot of catching up to do."

Eliza walked sedately across the room and sat in a chair facing him. "Yes, we do. You start," she said, trying to take control of the conversation.

Taking a deep breath and clenching his jaw, Henry gave her a short summary of where he'd been and what he'd done in the past two and a half months. "Now, your turn. How did you end up here? I thought you'd gone to Rolla. I've been looking for you."

"Oh?" Eliza was truly surprised at this news. "Whatever for, Henry? And how did you find the time to search for me with all that's been going on?"

Henry's eyes narrowed briefly then he quickly recovered and softened his reaction. "Eliza," he purred, "of course I've been trying to find you. Don't you realize what you mean to me? And after I heard that your father died, I was almost sick with worry."

"Thank you for your concern, Henry. Other than grief, I'm really doing fine."

"I'm so sorry for your loss, dear girl. Your father meant the world to me."

Eliza's hands involuntarily gripped the arms of the chair as she heard his insincere condolences. Her father meant nothing to Henry. In fact, he intensely disliked Henry, a fact that became evident in the days preceding the Battle of Wilson's Creek.

"Our families have been close for generations, Eliza. It's only right that I look out for your welfare now that you're alone."

"My father already made arrangements for my welfare. There's no need for you to be concerned any longer." Eliza stood. "Thank you for coming by."

Henry quickly rose and grabbed her arm. "Don't leave.

Please. There's more we need to talk about."

"Really? All right, go on." Eliza remained standing.

Henry moved a step closer. "Please, let's sit."

She shook herself free from his grip and moved to sit in the same chair as before. He slowly walked behind her and asked very quietly, "What brings you to this particular house, Eliza?"

She turned around and glared at him. "Sit down. I refuse to carry on a conversation with you standing behind me."

He sat on the settee again, irritation snapping in his pale-blue eyes.

"How did you find me?" she asked.

"I saw you this morning on St. Louis Street when Fremont was leaving. Then I followed you here."

"Followed me?" A chill ran down Eliza's spine. "Why didn't you show yourself?"

"I wanted to be sure it was you."

"Why the secrecy?"

He shrugged and grinned. "No reason." He chuckled and leaned in closer. "Actually, there is a reason. I have a very important question to ask you, Eliza. And I'm afraid we might be heard. Would you take a little stroll with me, please?"

Eliza's pulse raced. "No. We can talk in here. No one will hear us."

Henry stood and held out his hand. "I insist. Come. It won't take long."

Eliza remained seated. "You insist? It seems I've heard you say that before Henry. I'm not your slave. We can talk here."

He gaped at her. Anger filled his eyes, but he quickly shook it off and took a deep calming breath. "You are far more stubborn than I remember."

He grabbed another chair and set it next to hers. Leaning in close, he whispered, "I got word that my dear uncle Abe sent a load of valuables out of the city with you and his

100

slave, Jim. I'd like to know what you did with it."

Eliza snapped her head to look at him then stood. "How did you know?"

"It's my business to know! It's my property now that Abe is dead."

"Oh!" Eliza hadn't considered such a possibility. But it made perfect sense.

"Well?"

Something about the expression in his greedy eyes made Eliza pause and hesitate answering him. "Abe told me to hide it and tell no one."

Henry rose quickly to his feet and with one quick stride stood over her. "You can tell me. It's mine," he hissed.

Eliza tried to step back, but his hands shot up and grabbed her arms. He pulled her against his chest and whispered into her hair, "I am Abe's sole heir, and he would want me to have it."

She struggled unsuccessfully to free herself. "Can't it wait? It's in a safe place."

He pushed her back and lowered his eyes to hers. "Eliza..."

"And besides, how do I know it's yours? Do you have proof? Did he leave a will?"

With that, Henry dug his fingers into her arms with a fierce strength.

"Ow! Stop! You're hurting me!" Eliza cried out.

Instantly the door to the parlor slammed open and Jonathan stood there with a thunderous expression. Henry released his grip and stepped back. "Well!" he said. "It looks like we have an eavesdropper, Eliza."

"Get out!" Jonathan demanded.

"Excuse me? Is this your home, Lieutenant?"

"Get out! Now!" Jonathan started toward Henry.

"Yes! Leave and please don't come back," Eliza said. "You're not welcome here."

Henry hesitated then grabbed his hat, gave a slight bow,

and said, "As you wish, my dear."

He walked to the door and turned. "I will be seeing you again, though, Eliza, to discuss this matter further. We are not finished."

Jonathan moved toward him, and Henry quickly walked to the front door and let himself out. When the door shut, she dropped onto the settee and buried her face in her hands, trembling with fear. She felt the pressure of someone sitting down next to her then a hand on her back. Still frightened, she snapped her head up to see, with great relief, it was Jonathan.

"What just happened here?" he asked. "Did the scoundrel hurt you?"

Wiping a few stray tears from her face, she shook her head. "No. Well just a little." She gave a short laugh, rubbing shaky hands up and down her arms. "I might have a bruise or two."

Jonathan swore and stood to chase Henry down but, before he could take more than two steps, Eliza was by his side holding his arm.

"No! Please, Jon. Let him go. He's not worth it."

Jonathan gazed down into Eliza's eyes with such tenderness, her heart almost broke. He took her gently by her shoulders and sighed. "Why was he here, Eliza?"

Eliza couldn't tell him. At least not the whole story. Abe made it very clear that she was to tell no one about the gold. She hated keeping secrets from people she loved. But that was exactly what she would be doing for the next several months, even years if necessary.

"Eliza?"

"Uh...I'm not sure."

Jonathan's eyes narrowed, and he asked, with a tone of sadness, "What did he say to you?"

Turning away from his scrutiny, Eliza walked to the window, trying to collect her wildly racing thoughts. Jonathan remained rooted to the same spot.

Reaching out to finger the delicate lace curtain, Eliza decided to try a tactic that held an element of truth. "H-he, seemed to think I had feelings for him. He even called me sweetheart." She chuckled and turned her head to see Jonathan's face. Her heart melted at the sight of him; so strong, so gentle, so handsome with his piercing brown eyes that could see right through her. "H-he was terribly angry with me when I told him I didn't have feelings for him, that I'd never had feelings for him." She waited for a response. All she saw was sadness. Jonathan said nothing.

Fearing that any minute she would break down under that gaze and tell him everything, Eliza shrugged. "That's all, Jon. Thank you so much for sending him away. Well, I've got work to do, so I better get back to my room," she said lamely and started out of the room. "Goodbye, Jon."

When she walked past him, he reached out and took her hand. Very softly he said, "We're not finished, Eliza."

"I-I really have things to do, Jon," she said, trying to slip her hand free.

He looked down at her and shook his head sadly. "I'm not sure what's going on, Eliza, but I plan to find out. Take a seat."

Trembling, she pulled her hand away and said, "You're beginning to sound like Henry. I don't appreciate being ordered about."

Jonathan took a deep breath. "I made a promise to your father that I'd look out for you, Eliza, and I know without a doubt that he would insist that we have this conversation. Sit or stand, I don't care. But you will stay in this room until you and I have come to an understanding. Is that clear?"

At the mention of her pa and his wishes, she instantly softened. "I'm sorry." She moved to sit on the settee. If Jon sat next to her, it would be easier to keep her eyes down and away from his discerning look. She waited, but he stood over her.

"First of all, you said you had never had any feelings for Henry. When I first saw you with him, everything about your behavior indicated that you were a couple."

Eliza snapped her head up in surprise.

"Weren't you and Henry spending quite a bit of time with each other?"

"No! Well, some time. But that was because Pa introduced us and I didn't know anyone else in Springfield."

"Your behavior, when I saw you walk into the room at your boardinghouse, made it seem you were very fond of him. In his defense, I'm sure he thought the same."

"Well, I wasn't. I've never been fond of him!"

"So, then, that's typical of how you treat a man you're not fond of? That saddens me, Eliza. It's no wonder Henry was a little angry when you'd told him you'd never had feelings for him."

Not sure what to say, she just opened her mouth and stared up at him.

"Is that typical of how you treat men? You play with their affections? Then toss them aside when you're done?"

"What? No! Jonathan! What kind of person do you think I am?"

He sat next to her and gently squeezed the back of her neck. "Oh, Eliza. I couldn't think badly of you if I wanted to. I know you too well." He gave her a quick pat on her back then pulled away. "We do need to get a few things straight though. First of all, and I'm counting on you to be truthful, you've never knowingly entered into a courting relationship with Henry?"

"No, never. If he thought otherwise, I'm sorry. I never meant to mislead him." She turned to look Jonathan squarely in the face. "We'd only taken a couple of walks together. It didn't take long to realize I wasn't comfortable around him, but he was hard to get rid of. What you saw on the day we met with Pa was me trying to cheerfully control the conversation. I hadn't yet gotten to the point of telling him to leave me alone, but I was getting close."

Jonathan was surprised at the intensity of his relief on hearing this information. He chuckled and ran his finger briefly under her chin. Then his eyes darkened and he stared intently at her. "There's more, Eliza, isn't there? What are you holding back from me?"

Eliza's gaze dropped, and she answered, "That's all, Jon. Really."

"I have a hard time believing Goodman's anger was only about you spurning him if, as you say, you'd obviously never been courting."

"You don't believe me?"

"I believe you and Goodman were never courting, but I think there's something you're not telling me. What was the real reason he came to see you?"

Eliza gave an unladylike snort. "I told you that was his reason. What do I have to do to make you believe me?"

"Eliza, tell me there was nothing else that Henry wanted from you."

She repeated verbatim, "There was nothing else that Henry wanted from me. There! Satisfied?" She tried to smile then looked away.

"Are you satisfied?" he asked gently.

Eliza cleared her throat and stood. "Yes, I am. I should go now."

He caught her hand and gently pulled her back down to the settee. "You're hiding something. I need to find out what it is before you leave."

"Really, Jonathan. Don't you have more important things to do?"

"At the moment, no. You're stalling, Eliza. What is it that you're trying to hide? What could it possibly be that you don't feel like you can tell me? Don't you trust me?"

"Of course, I trust you, Jon. It's just..."

He waited patiently.

With a deep, fortifying breath Eliza said, "I'm trying my best to not betray a friend."

"Henry?"

"No, not Henry. His uncle, Abe Goodman. Abe asked me to keep a secret, and Henry wants to know what that secret is."

Jonathan studied Eliza a long time then thoughtfully rubbed his chin. "And, of course you can't tell me what the secret is. I honor that, Eliza. Apparently, Abe knew he could trust you with this secret. And apparently, he had reason to not trust his nephew with it."

"Exactly."

"Did Henry seem pretty desperate to get the truth from you?"

Eliza nodded, with a hint of fear in her eyes.

"Is that why he hurt you?"

She nodded again.

"Was he able to get you to tell him?"

"No! Of course not! Even if he tried to kill me, I wouldn't tell that snake!"

Jonathan chuckled softly. "I'm going to ask a few questions, not to try to find out what this secret is, but to find out, perhaps, the nature of the secret only so I can help you. I'm going to surmise Henry is desperate to finagle this information from you because it has to do with money. I'll bet that ever since the good banker died, Henry's been dying to get his hands on a fortune he's sure is coming to him. Does Abe have any other living relatives?"

"You astound me!"

"It's the only thing that makes any sense to me. And don't tell me any more than that. You need to keep your promise to Abe."

"As far as I know, Henry is Abe's only heir. At least,

that's what Henry said to me."

"I'm also guessing that Abe, like other bankers and businessmen, moved his riches out of Springfield after the battle at Wilson's Creek."

Eliza's jaw dropped.

"It's common sense, Eliza. I'm also guessing Abe told you where he took it so you could find it later. Or possibly he hid some in the wagon you and Jim were driving."

"Jonathan, stop! If I didn't trust you, I'd be really angry right now!"

"Don't worry. You haven't violated your confidence with Abe. I'm only trying to find out just enough so I can be two steps ahead of Henry Goodman. I want you to be safe, girl." He patted her head. "Henry is obviously desperate. He said he wasn't finished with you and that he'd be back. We have to let everyone here know so if he shows up, you can quickly hide. We can't keep him off this property because he's a captain in the occupying army. We'll have to keep you away from him. The only way to do that is for you to stay in your room, which shouldn't be hard since that seems to be what you're bent on doing. I'm afraid I can't be much protection if you go out with me because he outranks me."

Eliza listened and nodded.

"If I have time, I'll check with a lawyer I know to see if Abe left a will. That will settle who actually has the right to know where his money is hidden. Is Abe's wagon here on Aunt Mildred's property?"

"Yes. George and Jim use it all the time to secretly transport food," Eliza said with a twinkle in her eyes. "It has a false bottom." She smiled. "And that's all you're getting from me, Lieutenant!"

They heard a commotion at the front door and went to investigate, Jonathan moving protectively in front of Eliza. "Wait just a moment, Eliza." He opened the parlor door and saw Mildred and her household standing in the entry greeting a skinny, frightened negro woman clutching the hands of two tiny children. Mildred said, "Hello, Jon and Eliza. I'd like you to meet Lucy and her two children. They'll be staying with us for a while."

Eliza moved forward and took Lucy's hands in her own. "Welcome, Lucy. And what are your children's names?" She knelt in front of them as Lucy shyly introduced them.

"This one's Matthias. He's five. And this little one's Abby. She's three." Her voice was so quiet Jonathan could barely hear her.

"Hello, Matthias," Eliza said as she took his hand and shook it then did the same with his sister. Both children hid their faces in their mother's skirt.

"I'm sorry, miss. They be half scairt to death."

"That's all right, Lucy. You'll be safe here."

Lucy dabbed at tears, and the rest of the Scott household looked on with smiling faces. Jonathan was mildly surprised at Eliza's actions. After Sally ushered them upstairs, he leaned in close and whispered to Eliza, "Looks like you might be helping after all."

Eliza shook her head. "No. No, I'll be busy I told you. Nothing has changed."

With that, she went quickly up the stairs and to her room. Jonathan heard her door shut and shook his head. Would he ever understand that girl?

CHAPTER FOURTEEN

Eliza diligently tried to carry out Elin's directions. For the next few days, she stayed in her room, studied the Freemason cipher, and practiced it over and over until she could slowly write it and read it without the key. She snuck quietly around the room looking for a hiding place for her messages, trying to detect loose boards or bricks. She found several loose bricks but, after prying them free of the fireplace, discovered there wasn't enough room behind them to hide anything bigger than a small piece of paper. She found slightly loose boards, but when she tried removing them, the noise was too loud. Finally, while standing on the hearth poking around the fireplace, the heavy mantel moved slightly when she leaned against it. She tried with some difficulty to shove the heavy, thick, wooden board forward a little more and succeeded. Behind it, she found a loose brick which she removed, giving her plenty of space to hide messages. When she replaced the mantel, she was delighted to see that the hole she had created was completely hidden. Quickly she gathered up her cipher work and stuffed it into the hole.

As she stepped down from the hearth, her foot caught on a loose brick. She removed it and the one next to it and discovered another hiding place. Not as big as the one behind the mantel, but this was one that she could use to quickly dispose of incriminating papers if needed. She also asked Mildred's permission to occasionally have a small fire in the fireplace. This she used often to burn the papers with her practice ciphers.

Remembering the instructions to appear mousey, she retired several of her favorite dresses to the back of the closet and pulled out two shabby frocks that she despised, one black to go with her mourning, and one a lifeless gray. She also selected a faded-green calico. Then she dug out her oldest bonnet. As much as she hated to wrestle with her curls, she experimented with plaiting her hair. She was tempted to cut them off then realized she'd need her full head of curls to pull off her Gloria role successfully. Finally, she managed to capture most of her hair in two very tight braids that she wound around her head in such a way that she could easily hide them under a bonnet or under the hat she would use when she was disguised as Frances.

Eliza only left her room to go downstairs for meals. The first time she showed up with her new hairstyle, she was met with curious stares. She quickly explained that she felt that her loose curls were unbecoming for a woman of her age. She found several books in the library which she took to her room to read. She also took notes from those books and left them on her desk for anyone to see, although, as far as she knew, Sally was the only one who ever entered.

Her favorite activity, to her surprise, was her occasional forays into the backyard to watch George build his greenhouse. When she first ventured out, she found George bent over a stack of old windows he and Jim had salvaged from an old, abandoned house. He looked quickly up at her and winked conspiringly, the closest thing they had had yet at communicating their common roles.

"What are you doing, George?"

"I'm going to try to build a greenhouse. If I can get this thing built, I'm gonna move all those plants out of our bedroom into here." George pointed at the back windows of the house where he and Sally had their small quarters next to the kitchen. "We have south-facing windows, and those vegetables are about to take over our bedroom."

"This is an ingenious idea! How big are you going to make it? And how will you heat it? Can I help?"

George stood and chuckled. "Slow down, Liza! One question at a time. Of course, you can help. You might get yer pretty clothes dirty though," he said with a grin. She looked down at her plain gray, very worn dress with patches at her elbows and loose strands of thread hanging from her hem and laughed.

"Now that's the sweetest sound I evah heard from you. It 'bout melts this ol' heart o' mine."

"I think dirt might be an improvement," she said, her eyes dancing.

"That be true, that be true," he said, meeting her eyes with his smiling ones. He turned to look at the pile of windows and boards in front of him. "I have to admit, this ain't an ingenious idea as you said. We had a greenhouse at Miss Scott's farm in Texas. I helped build it. But I'm a thinkin' a greenhouse here at this time will just be an invitation to those scoundrel soldiers to raid."

"That's not stopping you, though, is it?"

He smiled. "No, Liza. We gotta do what we gotta do and pray for the best."

Eliza walked over to a patch of ground cleared of all grass and other vegetation. "Is this where you're going to build it?"

"Yep. Today Jim and I need to dig holes in the four corners for posts. But I have another job for you." He took four small bricks and set them in four corners of an imaginary rectangle on the grass. "This is how big the south-facing wall will be. I need you to carry some of those windows over here and arrange them to fit in this here area. Put the ones with the heaviest frames along the bottom, here." He tapped one side with his foot. "It's fine if they don't fit perfectly. We'll fill in the gaps."

With great delight, she started her job, fitting and refitting windows together in a giant puzzle, while the two men dug deep holes for the corner posts. George then measured out two squares for the east and west walls and asked her to do the same.

The next day, the two men built the frames for the walls using the windows Eliza had laid out as their guide. They also built a solid wall for the north side with a hole for a small brick fireplace in the center. Eliza watched and fetched tools and boards for them as needed.

At first, both men expressed their guilt for asking Eliza to help, but quickly got over it when she expressed her great pleasure in getting to participate. When they started nailing the windows to the frames they had made, she was almost overcome with excitement and asked endless questions.

"Did I do it right?

"What if they break?

"What if they don't fit?

"Where's the door?

"Do you have enough wood?"

The two men laughed and did their best trying to answer all her questions. Several times Sally came out with water. Mildred brought Lucy and her children out to watch, setting the little ones down on the back steps so they wouldn't get in the way. Both children were beginning to act a little less afraid. Eliza sat next to them for a few minutes and tried to describe to them what George and Jim were doing. They didn't say a word, only peered at her with shy, frightened eyes. Lucy managed to say a quiet thank-you to Eliza when she stood to go. Eliza gave her hand a gentle squeeze.

That evening, all nine of them, including Jonathan, gathered around the big dining room table for supper. Jonathan confirmed their worst fears. General Hunter planned to march his army out of Springfield in the morning. And Jonathan would be among those who had to leave.

"General Hunter is not to blame," Jon tried to explain as he ate his last meal with them. "He had orders from the War Department back last week when he first arrived. They ordered him to fall back to Rolla and Sedalia."

"But why? Don't they know the secessionists will come back and take over the city?" George asked, eyes snapping with irritation.

"I'm sure they're aware of that. They just think our troops are needed in other parts of the state more than here." Jonathan shrugged. "I hate to leave all of you."

Eliza listened as if in a trance. She swallowed her food and stared.

Mildred and Sally dabbed at tears. "It's been good having you here, Jonny," Mildred said. "You take care, you hear?"

"I will, Aunt Mildred. I've got good men. We'll do all right." He patted her hand and rose to go.

"Eliza, may I have a word with you?" he asked.

She got up quickly and watched as he gave hugs to Sally and Mildred then shook hands with the men before he took her hand and walked out to the front porch. "I don't have much time. My men are waiting for me. We have a lot to do to get ready to march out in the morning."

"I'm frightened for you, Jon," she blurted out.

He turned gentle eyes on her. "I'll be fine. I'm actually frightened for you, Eliza. I'm not sure what will happen next here in Springfield. A lot of Union families are leaving. Some left yesterday and today. I'd feel better if you could leave, too. I know a family you can travel with.

They're leaving in the morning. There's really no reason for you to stay."

Tears ran down her face. "Oh, but, Jon. This is my home now. Mildred, George, Sally, Jim, they're the only family I have now. Except for you, of course. Especially you, Jon." She sobbed. "Please take care of yourself. I don't think I could go on living if anything happened to you."

"Oh, Eliza, girl. Come here." He opened his arms, and she stepped into his embrace and laid her wet face on his chest. As he held her head close, he gave her final instructions. "If you must stay, then please continue hiding in your room as much as possible, Eliza. You never know who will be out prowling the streets. I've heard some awful stories of pretty ruthless men out there claiming to be soldiers. You're too young and too pretty. I'd rather no one knew you existed. At least during this dratted war. I'm sure soldiers will come here looking for food. Stay out of sight. Let Mildred handle all visitors."

Eliza's head nodded against his chest.

He set her away enough to gaze into her face. "I'll try my best to send letters, but I'm not sure I'll be able to get them to you. You do the same. Not too much information though. Just enough so I'll know you're doing well." He wiped the tears from her face, gave her one last hug, and turned to go. Eliza stood and watched until he was out of sight, thinking her heart would surely break.

Sure enough, the next day, November 9th, General Hunter and his 30,000 men left Springfield, leaving the city open for occupation by the Confederacy. The Scott household grieved, especially for Jonathan. Eliza stayed in her room, not even coming out to help with the greenhouse. She was ashamed of her constant flow of tears. Try as she might, nothing worked to stop them. The pain in her chest only got worse. At the end of the next day, she walked quietly down the back steps to see what progress George and Jim had made on the greenhouse. In the gathering dusk, she could see all four walls standing and the roof in place. She walked over to try the door. It swung noiselessly on its hinges and allowed her to step through. The north wall still had a huge gap in the center. Piled around the hole was a large pile of old bricks ready to be used in building the fireplace and chimney. Eliza admired their work, touching the windows and marveling at her part in this masterpiece. Suddenly, she heard a sound. Turning quickly, she saw George standing in the doorway.

"Sorry if I scared you, Liza." He smiled. "Do you like it?"

"Oh, George! It's beautiful!"

"Well, I don't know 'bout that. But it'll do, it'll do," he said, nodding and grinning. He looked back at the house and lowered his voice. "Elin wants to see you in the morning."

Eliza wanted to jump up and down with excitement, but she had learned her lesson well. She merely nodded and turned away. "When will you start the fireplace?"

"Tomorrow if we're not needed elsewhere," he answered then walked over and showed her how they planned to build it. Jim came out and joined them. Soon, the two men were caught up in a good-natured argument about the best way to build a fireplace.

Eliza went back into the house and left them to their plans. She stood at her window and looked up at the moon, wondering what the next few days would bring. She was more excited than she was frightened. The thoughts that soon the enemy would be close at hand filled her with a renewed desire for revenge. Oh, if she could only be so lucky to come face-to-face with the man who put that bullet in her father's chest! Not likely, but still she almost writhed with agony for her dear, dear pa! If she couldn't pay that scoundrel back for what he'd done to her pa, then at least she could pay a thousand back for what they've done! She clung to the curtains as a terrible unquenchable grief coursed through her body, slowly being replaced with hate. What a welcome replacement it was. Grief controlled a person. Nothing could be done except helplessly wait. Hatred, on the other hand, had an object. Something could be done to attack and destroy that object. Her thoughts were a jumbled mess as she crawled into bed and tried to sleep. She had done her homework, everything Captain Alcorn and Elin had asked of her. She was ready. More than ready. Surely, they could see that. Throughout the night, she kept having dreams with an urgency to pray. But as soon as she woke, she shook off her thoughts and buried her head in her pillow. Finally, morning came, and Eliza obediently dressed in the same drab dress and bonnet as the day before.

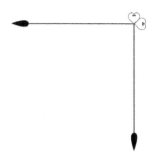

CHAPTER FIFTEEN

Eliza snuck out of the house and through the back gate. George and Jim hadn't started their work on the fireplace yet, which was a great relief. Having Jim working in the backyard would make it impossible for her to leave by that route. George likely had Jim occupied elsewhere. With great care, Eliza let herself through Elin's shed then down the overgrown path and up the back steps. She knocked three firm raps and waited. This time, she didn't have to wait long. Elin opened the door, motioned her to come inside then headed up the back stairs without a word.

When they stepped into Gloria LaRue's bedroom, Eliza commented, "It's so quiet in here."

"That's because everyone has left. All of my boarders were officers in the Federal Army. Yesterday was a sad, sad day for this city."

"Yes, it was," Eliza agreed. "Have you...have you decided you can use me?"

Elin walked over, put her hands on Eliza's shoulders, and looked at her with affection. "Yes. You've done well. And, under the circumstances we find ourselves in, I decided I needed to meet with you earlier than I had expected. Sit down. We have a lot to talk about. It won't be long before this boardinghouse of mine fills up with Confederate officers, and you need to be very comfortable with your role as Gloria LaRue by then."

Eliza sat and listened carefully to every detail.

"You mustn't let them see you come and go as Eliza, so I've decided we need to keep one or two of Gloria's work dresses in the shed." Elin chuckled. "Even her work clothes are fancy, so be prepared.

"I've decided that you will be someone who does some work for me in exchange for room and board. That way, you will have the freedom to sit at a table and socialize if invited, as long as you can also keep up with your work. The work that you will do for me is light housekeeping, taking food to the tables, clearing the tables after the meals, showing guests to their rooms, and, yes, even though this is war and they're not paying for their rooms, we still treat them as guests. As honored guests, actually, since you and I are Southern sympathizers. This is one way I can assure that we'll get officers here. They will always choose the best homes while they're here in Springfield, and mine is one of those," she said with pride. "Because you'll be the only housekeeper, you'll have access to all the rooms. Make sure there is always fresh water in their pitchers. Offer to gather their laundry and see to it that it's bagged, labeled, and returned promptly to the right man. We have a lady drop by once a week to do the laundry.

"You will also be expected to wait personally on our guests, to find things they need, and to run errands for them. Since you won't be able to be here every day, I will also do your duties. If you're not here and someone demands your services, I will tell them you're not available and if I can, I will step in for you. I have a cook, Mrs. Bond, who only comes during the day to help me with the meals. You are not expected to work in the kitchen because

I want you to mingle with the officers as much as possible. Do you play the piano and sing?"

"Yes. Not well though."

"That will do. These men are starved for entertainment of any kind. You are to be very friendly without crossing the bounds of propriety. They must see you as fully devoted to them and the cause of the South. Understand?"

"Yes." She nodded eagerly.

"By your outgoing behavior and attire, it will almost seem to the officers that you are the owner. That is fine, but make it clear that you are not, if asked. Some of the officers staying here may be coming for the second time. They know me, and you will be a newcomer to them. They will probably ask about you. Tell me Gloria's story so I know you're ready and so we can agree, even on the minor things."

Eliza repeated the events of Gloria's life and her time in Little Rock. Elin changed a few details and told her to not be too quick to share her story. "Gloria's not proud of her past and is not anxious for people to know what kind of life she's led. Use your own good judgment on how much to share, but don't change the story we've agreed on. If someone seems determined to hear more of your past, simply act embarrassed and tell him you don't want to talk about it. That's a lady's prerogative."

Eliza's head was spinning with all the information. She cleared her throat and grinned. "It sounds like Gloria will be busy."

"Yes, she will be. I'm afraid there will be days it will be almost impossible to fool the Scott household with your long absences, therefore I've decided it's best for Gloria to work only in the afternoons and evenings, four or five days a week. Have you been able to spend long periods of time in your room without drawing suspicion?"

"Yes, except I almost always appear for the meals."

"Hmmm... You'll have to invent a good reason for

skipping the evening meals."

"I've done it in the past, so it won't seem terribly unusual to them. I'll pretend I'm handling my grief with writing and that I write best in the evening. I'm also rather distraught at Jonathan's leaving. That is the truth, and they're sympathetic."

She chuckled weakly and shrugged. "I'm afraid I might appear to be rather self-absorbed, but they probably already have good reason to think that of me."

"Unfortunately, this is a price you'll have to pay. When the war is over, you may have the opportunity to explain and apologize. But, for now, we need you to be fully engaged in your new role. Come with me."

Elin stood and led Gloria over to the wardrobe where she displayed several beautiful dresses. "Captain Alcorn managed to gather a few dresses that he thinks are your size. I'll leave while you try one on." Before she left, she pulled a crinoline from the closet and laid it across the bed. "Other than this petticoat, wear the same undergarments so you can change clothes in a hurry."

Eliza chose a brilliant blue dress with white lace at the collar and cuffs. She put the petticoat on followed by the dress. It had a tight bodice, full, bell-shaped skirt, and sleeves that flared wide past her elbows. Thankfully she noticed that it buttoned down the front, a new fashion for dresses worn by the rich, unlike the typical dresses of high fashion that had buttons down the back.

Elin entered when she was finished and told her they needed to come up with a hairstyle for Gloria that was fashionable yet easy to do by herself. Elin sat her in front of the dresser mirror and twisted her long curls into a bun that she pinned at the nape of her neck. Loose strands of curls framed her face and clung to her neck.

Elin laughed. "Since I don't think we can control these, let's use them to our advantage. Your hair is too beautiful to hide." She took the strands of curls and quickly fingered them into ringlets, giving a very finished look to the hairstyle. "Now," she said as she unpinned the bun, "let's see how fast you can do it by yourself."

Since this was similar to one Eliza had worn before, she was able to do it quickly. "Very good!" Elin exclaimed. "When you leave here to go back to Miss Scott's, I think the fastest way to handle your hair is to simply remove the bun, twist it tighter, and pin it higher on your head so your bonnet will cover it completely. You'll need to practice so you can do it with lightning speed."

"I'll try," Eliza agreed.

"Also, when you leave to go to Miss Scott's, throw this dress on." She pulled out a simple but beautiful dress of dark-green calico. "I chose this because it's not likely to stand out in the back garden as you come and go. There's an old chest of drawers in the shed full of old tools. The bottom drawer has been cleared out. Put the dress there and quickly change back into your Eliza clothes. There's also another dress out there for you to use. You'll wear these two dresses often as you go about your housekeeping chores during the day. In the evening, dress up in your finest."

Elin went on about precautions that Eliza needed to take as she came and went from both households. They discussed excuses she could make for a variety of scenarios. Finally, Elin told her to put on the green calico and come downstairs to meet Mrs. Bond, the cook, and Charles, Elin's slave. She informed her that Mrs. Bond knew nothing of their deception but out of necessity, Charles did know. He was not privy to secret information, but he knew enough to be of assistance if needed.

After introducing her as their new boarder and part-time housekeeper, "Gloria LaRue, recently arrived from Arkansas," Elin showed her around the downstairs rooms then led her back upstairs to Gloria's room where she told her to demonstrate the correct way to covertly leave. Eliza pretended to change her dress. She took her hair and twisted it quickly into a tight bun, pinned it high on her head, and covered it with her plain gray bonnet. Elin followed as Eliza stepped into the hallway and checked to be sure no one was watching before she opened the door to the back stairs. She went quickly and noiselessly down the steps and out the door. She paused on the porch and checked the garden area before she descended and started down the path. In the shed, she started to change back into her Eliza clothes then realized they were back in Gloria's room. Elin laughed. So did Eliza.

"You knew, didn't you?" she asked Elin.

"There's no better teacher than experience. Let's try that again, starting from the beginning."

They went back to Gloria's room where Eliza grabbed her dress and stuffed it into a simple drawstring bag that she found lying at the bottom of the closet with Gloria's shoes. Then she went through the door out into the hall and repeated her previous steps. In the shed, she changed into Eliza's dress, folded Gloria's dress, and laid it in the bottom drawer of a dresser almost out of sight in a dark corner. She retrieved the key but before she opened the door, Elin stopped her.

"Very good. The only thing I would change is that although you must be sneaky, try not to act sneaky. If anyone should see you, I want them to see Gloria taking a stroll through the garden. Slow down as you walk down the path, trail your fingers along the plants. Not too slowly though. Just try not to give the appearance that Gloria is in a hurry. There's a bench beside the shed. If you notice anyone watching you just meander over to the bench and sit down. I think that covers just about everything. Come over tomorrow evening, let yourself in, go to your room, and come downstairs as Gloria. At that time, I'll show you in more detail what I expect you to do in the dining area and in the bedrooms. The following evening, I'll be having guests, so you can practice. They do not know about our subterfuge." With that, she dismissed her and left.

As ordered, Eliza left Miss Scott's house the next day just before the evening meal. Earlier she had gone to Mildred and Sally and made up a story about starting to write her memoirs. "These are unique and terrible times, and I just feel as if it's necessary for me to capture the events and my feelings on paper while they're fresh."

Sally just stared uncomprehendingly at her while beans dripped off her spoon. Mildred, on the other hand, simply nodded and smiled. But when Eliza said she needed to take food to her room so she could be alone, both women looked sadly at each other.

Mildred finally answered, "If that's what you need to do, Eliza, we won't stand in your way. Please help yourself."

If Eliza hadn't been so determined to fight the hated enemy, she would have quit right then and there. She so hated being deceptive toward people who trusted her. Hoping it would get easier with time and experience, she loaded a plate and sheepishly returned to her room.

When she walked down the dark alley then entered the shed and changed her dress, she felt for the first time she had finally entered the world of espionage. Everything before this had only been training and practice. Today, she truly had to become Gloria LaRue! Yesterday, of course, she had been Gloria for the cook, but Elin had done all the talking. Tonight was her chance to fully transform. She quickly found that the dark shed presented a new challenge. Groping around, she managed to find the drawer with the dress and changed. She entered Elin's house quietly, mounted the stairs, and slipped into her room. This time, she chose an emerald-green dress with a tiered skirt. Quickly she retrieved the petticoat, slipped it over her head then followed with the dress. After buttoning the bodice, she only needed to remove her hair pins and shake her hair loose so the bun she made for Gloria's fair head would be much fuller and softer than the tight bun she'd worn for Eliza. She expertly maneuvered her unruly tresses into submission, forced the free-ranging curls into soft ringlets, and sat back to inspect her work. On the dresser in front of her, she saw a box with a note propped against it. "Try a little rouge and powder... sparingly," the note read. In the box, she found a tiny jar of rouge and a slightly larger one of powder. Since she'd never used either and, in fact, considered them to be borderline scandalous, she was reluctant to try them. But, if this helped distinguish Gloria from plain Eliza, then perhaps she'd try a little. She dabbed a tiny amount of rouge on each cheek and rubbed it in. Then she tried just a pinch on her lips as well. The powder stayed in its jar. Very satisfied with the results, she left the room and walked boldly down the wide front stairs into the entry then right through an arched doorway into the dining room where she found Elin sitting at one of four tables.

"Ah, there you are, Miss LaRue. Are you ready to begin?"

Gloria curtsied and answered, "Yes, I am, Miss Johnson. Where do I start?"

Gloria stayed in character throughout the evening while the cook greeted her and showed her where to go in the kitchen to get the food, while Elin demonstrated the proper way to serve and to address the guests. Elin then showed her where the cleaning supplies were and took her on a tour of the house, instructing her on what to do in each room. "You will only do light work. Dust each room, make the beds, pick up and fold or hang their clothes. Remember, all of our boarders will be men, and most of them are used to being taken care of at home. Most of them miss this level of care and will welcome your attention. Some won't. Please be sensitive to that and leave their rooms alone if that's what they prefer. Never enter a room when a guest is present unless, of course, he's sick. You don't want to give a wrong impression. Some men, though, will already have that impression, no matter what you do, so beware of them and keep your distance. I will give you a ring with a key for each room."

"That will come in handy in case I need to look for important information."

Elin quickly held up a finger to silence her.

"In this closet, you will find bags for laundry. Each bag is labeled with a room number, so we can always return clothes to the right owner. The lady that does our laundry has never failed me yet. She comes every Monday afternoon and returns the clothes on Wednesday."

Elin then walked down the hall to Gloria's bedroom. After they entered, she quietly said, "You mustn't ever talk spy business with me in this house. Don't even hint of it. If you ever see me lift my finger like this again"—she demonstrated—"stop talking or inconspicuously change the subject."

"I'm sorry. I guess I just felt safe."

"Don't ever think that in this house. This room is the only place we can talk. Whenever you need to talk to me, simply invite me here for tea. I'll do the same."

"That sounds simple enough."

"You've done well, Gloria. Forgive me, but I'm afraid it will be necessary for me to always address you as Gloria from now on. If I don't, I'm afraid I'll slip and address you as Eliza and not even notice. Come back tomorrow afternoon, do a little cleaning then dress up for dinner and come down to serve my guests. I'll see you then. Goodbye."

Eliza quickly slipped into Gloria's calico, tightened her bun, put on her bonnet, and left. She remembered to meander down the path and take time to inspect a plant or two before she entered the shed. Once inside, she again quickly and quietly changed her dress, hid Gloria's dress, and snuck down the alley to the hidden gate.

The next day, she snuck over to Elin's in the afternoon and went through the same routine of transforming from Eliza to Gloria as she had the evening before. After doing her hair and applying color to her lips and cheeks, she checked her reflection before leaving the room. Even in the simple calico, she felt almost as if Eliza was a lowly brown caterpillar that had gone through a metamorphosis into a colorful, beautiful butterfly.

When she finished dusting each of the bedrooms as instructed, she changed into yet another beautiful dress and entered the dining room before Elin's guests arrived. Elin took her to the kitchen, handed her a stack of plates, and asked her to help set a table for five.

Soon there was a knock at the door, and Elin asked Gloria to greet their guests. She took a deep breath and thanked God that, in spite of her country background, her father had seen to it she had learned and practiced the social graces. She opened the door and welcomed their guests with warmth and grace. She ushered two elderly couples into the entry hall and offered to take their coats then escorted them into the dining room where Elin was waiting. The meal went without a hitch. The guests talked mostly about the war and their relief that the Federal Army had finally left. They included Gloria in their conversation probably because Elin treated her like an equal. When the meal was done, Elin invited her guests into the parlor. She turned to Gloria and said, "Please come join us, Miss LaRue, when you're finished clearing the table."

When Gloria entered the room, Elin invited her to take a seat and join in the conversation. At first, it was difficult because the guests were staunch supporters of the South and vehemently opposed the North, but she reined in her thoughts and smiled, nodded, and agreed with everything they said. Finally, Elin said to Gloria, "Miss LaRue, I've heard that you can play the piano and sing. Would you be willing to entertain us this evening?"

Gloria blushed and said, "I've told you I'm not very good. Perhaps your entertainment this evening will be comedy, instead of what you might be expecting."

Elin and her guests laughed. "Where did you find this delightful creature?" one woman asked. "I'm already entertained."

Gloria noticed Elin's pleased and somewhat surprised expression as she graciously curtsied to the woman and said, "Why, thank you, ma'am."

Again, the guests laughed when Gloria walked to the piano, sat, and played a simple song with one finger. She turned, smiled at them, and then played a more complicated piece.

The guests clapped. "Bravo, bravo! Can you sing also?"

"Would you like a hymn?" Gloria asked. "Or something fun?"

"Something fun, please. We need it"

"If I play 'Buffalo Gals,' would you sing along?"

And they did, thoroughly enjoying the evening as Gloria played song after song. When they left, they thanked both Elin and Gloria for the beautiful evening and said they would love to visit again soon if circumstances allowed.

When the door closed, Elin quietly asked Gloria to join her upstairs for tea. Once in Gloria's room, Elin clapped her hands with glee. "Gloria! Bravo! You were absolutely perfect! I had no idea you could actually do this so well and so soon! Good work!"

Gloria curtsied again and said, "Thank you, Miss Johnson. I actually enjoyed myself."

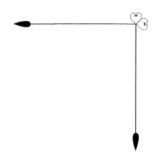

CHAPTER SIXTEEN

For a week, Eliza continued making excuses to stay in her room and then sneaking over to Elin's to practice being Gloria. As long as she was on the property, both women played their roles. The only relief was their time spent in Gloria's room having tea at a small table beside the window overlooking the back garden. Elin made it clear to the cook that Gloria was allowed free access to the kitchen and to any tea, coffee, and food she wanted as long as she made sure Mrs. Bond didn't need it for her meal preparations. Elin also had Mrs. Bond serve them tea occasionally in the dining room, hoping it would establish Gloria's position as being higher than an ordinary servant. It wasn't necessary though, since Mrs. Bond was a simple, uneducated woman who delighted in serving others. She also was in awe of Gloria's beauty and finery. Gloria intentionally allowed the sweet cook to think of her as one of her superiors, although she was very kind to the humble, older woman.

At one of their teas, Elin said, "I think things may dramatically change in the next few days. I just got word that Confederate General McColloch is on his way. He's marching up the Wire Road and should get here in a day or two."

Eliza gasped and covered her mouth. The excitement was almost too much to bear. "How did you...? Never mind." She was learning to stop questioning the flow of information. "How many soldiers?"

"I'm not sure, but one report says that a few Missouri State Guard detachments are following him."

"That means that we could possibly have quite a few guests."

"Yes. I certainly hope we do. We'll have to wait and see. I have something else for you to do before they get here though."

"Oh?"

"I need you and George to carry your first message."

Eliza's jaw dropped. "Are you sure?"

Elin chuckled. "Of course, I'm sure. This is why my niece, Frances, exists. Remember?"

"Yes! Yes, of course! I'm ready. Tell me what to do."

Elin stood and walked quickly to the bureau. She pulled some pants and a shirt from the bottom drawer, along with a long strip of white cloth. "First, we need to create a believable twelve-year-old boy named Francis. Here. Take this cloth and bind up your bosom then put these clothes on." Elin left the room so Eliza could take off Gloria's voluminous dress and petticoat, hang them in the closet, and try to wrap the long strip of cloth around her chest tightly enough that she might be able to pass as a boy or at least like an underdeveloped young girl. Satisfied with the results, she put the gray work shirt on then slipped into the denim overalls. Elin entered the room carrying a ragged brown coat and a soft, wide-brimmed felt hat.

"Let's see what can be done with your hair." She had Eliza sit at the dresser. "Again, it needs to be something you can do for yourself and something you can do quickly.

At first, I was thinking braids would be best, but I'm afraid they would take too long."

"Here, let me try," Eliza said. Although her curly hair appeared to be very thick, it actually wasn't. She divided it quickly into two strands and twisted one until it kinked and coiled into a tight spiral which she pinned onto one side of her center part. Then she repeated it with the other side and followed it up with several more hairpins to ensure they wouldn't loosen. With the hat pushed low on her head, she was passable as a boy.

Elin told her to try rubbing a little bit of dirt on her face and hands when she got outside. "Now, remember, since you're my niece, it won't seem suspicious if you are seen leaving my house. Use the back gate, not the shed, and avoid being seen by anyone. This time, I'll have George pick you up at the end of the alley. People at Miss Scott's are used to George coming and going freely to forage for food or wood. But it's best they never see you. I'm sure they'd recognize you."

"What's the message, specifically? And where do we take it? And who do we give it to? Will I be expected to talk to anyone?"

"George knows where to go. It's a place northeast of here, just off the road to Rolla. There's another courier staying at a tavern there. He knows George. I'm sending you because the two of you traveling together is less suspicious than George traveling alone. Also, I want you to know how to locate this tavern in case I need to send you alone on a horse. I've heard you can handle a musket? George has a rifled musket loaded and ready in his wagon covered by a blanket and some hay. Use it only to save your lives."

Elin then pulled some paper and a pen out of a dresser drawer. "Now's your chance to put all your practice to work. Write out this message in Freemason cipher: *McColloch moving north toward Springfield. State Guards following. Expected to arrive on 18th or 19th. Feel free to abbreviate some of the words, such as Springfield."*

Eliza started to write the message in English first, but Elin stopped her and told her it was important to be able to write what she heard directly to cipher so no messages in English would be found. Painstakingly, Eliza wrote each letter, trying to picture the Freemason cipher grid. It wasn't difficult to remember because it was laid out in an orderly, consistent pattern. It just took time. Finally, she finished it and handed it over for Elin's inspection.

"Very good, Frances." She folded the message and handed it back to Eliza. "Now you need to tuck this into that cloth you bound yourself with and be off. George should be at the end of the alley east of here. If you don't see him, stay hidden and wait. Be ready with a story if questioned. Remember, your ma is my sister, and you're on your way home."

Elin stopped and held up her hand. "Wait here. I almost forgot." She left and came back a few minutes later with a basket. "Take this with you. It's a couple of pies Mrs. Bond baked for your ma." She winked. "Our story might need a little help."

Elin took the younger woman in her arms and hugged her quickly then stepped back. "Drat it. I'm supposed to be tougher than this if I expect to do this kind of work." She dabbed at tears. "I've grown fond of you, Eliza. You've become almost like a daughter. And as counter-productive as it is, I'm truly frightened for you. Please be careful, dear girl."

Eliza put a comforting hand on Elin's shoulder. "I will. I promise."

"Let's pray. You do believe in prayer, don't you?"

Eliza stiffened. "Uh...I used to. But prayers didn't do my pa any good. Either God didn't hear or God didn't care. Either way, I don't have much use for Him anymore."

Elin stood silently, gazing into Eliza's eyes. "Then I'll

pray, since I know without a doubt He hears and He cares."
She took Eliza's hands and prayed a simple but direct
prayer for God's powerful presence and His protection.
"I'll continue to pray until you return safely. We rely
greatly on God's help in this work we're doing, Eliza. It's
much too dangerous to think we can do it on our own. I do
hope your thoughts about God change. I'm sure He's very
saddened by your unbelief." She took Eliza's hand and
squeezed it. "Be off with you now."

Eliza nodded a goodbye and left, her thoughts in a
jumble. Quickly she cast her troubled musings aside and
focused on the task at hand. She walked directly to the gate
and turned right into the alley. Soon she came to an
intersection where George stood next to his mule, stroking
his ears and talking softly. He looked up when Eliza
approached.

"Well, hello there, Frances. Are you ready to head back
to your ma's?"

"Yep, got some pies for her," she said in a scruffy low
voice as she held the basket up.

"Well, if my luck holds out, she might just offer me a
piece when we get there."

"Yep," was all Frances said as she climbed onto the seat
next to George. They drove north to St. Louis Street, then
east, and left the city in silence as dusk quickly settled over
them.

When they reached the outskirts of town, George spoke
in a low tone, "This trip shouldn't have too many risks. I
don't think either army will be on this road. Although
there's always the chance we'll run into a pack of ruffians
up to no good. They're worse than the military. Generally,
they're just mean. Out lookin' for mischief."

After another mile of travel, Eliza heard voices and
laughter up ahead. George quietly pulled his mule over to
the side of the road between some trees and bushes. He
stopped and quietly hummed the first line of "Rock A Bye

Baby" to the mule and murmured quietly to Eliza, "That calms her. She seems to understand that she needs to stand still and be quiet. It's dark enough, I don't think they'll see us."

They waited. The laughter and voices got louder. Soon, about four riders appeared. They acted as if they were drunk. Their conversation was lewd and full of filth, indicating they were on their way to Springfield to visit a Mrs. Thompson and her girls. After they passed and their voices grew distant, George pulled back onto the road.

Eliza whispered furiously, "Poor Mrs. Thompson. Someone should warn her. She and her girls are in danger!"

George chuckled. "Frances, haven't you heard of Mrs. Thompson? I suspect she's up waitin' for those scoundrels."

Eliza's face burned. "You mean...? In Springfield?"

George turned surprised eyes on his charge. "Mrs. Thompson and her girls ain't the only ones."

Eliza stared at him aghast. "That's disgusting! Who would do such a thing?"

George shook his head and chuckled. "Dear Liza, I sure do love that you know nothin' of these goins on." He paused. "I suspect it's something they do just so they don't starve. Or their little ones."

"So, you approve?" she asked in a slightly haughty tone.

He chuckled and shook his curly gray head. "No. Not at all. I just want you to slow down on judging their motives."

"Oh," was all she said for a long time. Then quietly she added, "It's pretty sad when you think about it."

"Yep, Frances. It is, at that."

They continued several more miles in silence. George indicated that the tavern was up ahead on the left. When they got there, she was to go to the door and ask for Thomas Burns. But before they reached the turnoff for the tavern, a loud voice demanded, "Halt! Who goes there?"

George stopped as a man stepped from the bushes with a

rifle pointed at them. George immediately put both arms up in surrender. Frances looked frantically at George then stuck her arms up also.

"Don't shoot! It's just me 'n' Frances, here," George drawled.

"Where are you headed, Frances?" the man asked, lowering his rifle enough to get a good look at the intruders.

"Uh...I'm goin' back home."

"And where might that be, boy?"

"Just this side of Marshfield. My ma's expectin' me."

"Yeah?" He walked over to check the wagon bed. "Whatcha got in here, boy?"

"A couple of pies. My aunt in Springfield baked 'em for my ma."

"Oh, yeah? Pies, huh?" He yanked the towel off the top of the basket, and the delectable aroma of apple pie rose to greet him. "Mmmmm... You don't think she'll mind if a piece is missing, do ya?" he asked as he helped himself by swiping a dirty finger through the center of a pie.

"No, sir. I think she'd be right happy for you to help yourself."

He lowered his rifle and laughed. "Well, in that case, I'll take another. Mmm-mmm. Lordy, that's good," he said, licking his fingers. "You be sure to tell yer ma thanks," he said, waving them on.

After they had ridden several yards, George whispered, "Good job, Frances. I think you'll do just fine."

"Thank you. And thanks to Elin for these pies. We should probably always carry some yummy desserts with us," Eliza whispered. "Good job on that ignorant-sounding voice of yours, by the way."

George chuckled softly. "Been practicin' a while, young'un," he said with the same slow drawl.

Soon he pulled the mule to the left and ambled toward a well-lit building several yards off the road. George stopped at the front door and motioned for Frances to get down and approach the building. "I'll be waitin' right here, Frances," he said slowly.

Frances knocked then opened the door a crack when no one answered. She pushed it open farther and walked in. There were only three men present, one behind the bar and two sitting on stools with drinks in hand.

"Whoa, there, boy! You're too young to be comin' in here. Get lost!" the bartender said gruffly.

"Uh...uh, I'm tryin' to find someone."

"And who might that be?"

"Thomas? Thomas Burns?"

The bartender and one of the men glanced at the third who was slumped over the bar, holding on to an almost empty bottle.

Frances shifted her feet nervously.

Thomas lifted his head and stared at her with bloodshot eyes. "What do ya want," he slurred.

"Uh...Ma wanted me to check on you. She's worried about you."

His head came up, and he squinted in her direction. "Frances? 'Zat you? Why didn't you say so?" He got off his stool and staggered toward her. "How's yer ma? I haven't heard from her in a coon's age," he said as he slung one arm around her and maneuvered her out the door, past the wagon, and down the drive. Eliza was so frightened, she moved toward the wagon, but Thomas' grip tightened. George made no attempt to help her. After walking several feet from the tavern, Thomas forced her to walk uphill into the woods, stopped, and whispered in a kind and sober voice, "Be calm, Frances. I won't hurt you."

She swallowed several times and stared, her mouth hanging open. "You scared the livin' daylights out of me."

"I'm sorry. My actions were necessary. Quickly now. Do you have something for me?"

"Yes." She turned and groped around under her shirt and

bindings for the paper she had hidden there. Blushing slightly, she handed it to Thomas. He muttered a quiet thanks, shoved it down the front of his pants, said, "Goodbye," then walked farther up the hill through the woods.

Eliza stood watching for a moment then went back up the drive to where George was waiting. She climbed into the wagon, and they headed back down the drive. "That's it? That's all I have to do?"

"On this trip, yes. It's different every time. I expect you might be coming here by yourself, in the future, to deliver messages to Thomas, now that you know your way and the people at the tavern won't be suspicious."

"Why wouldn't you come, too?"

"Whenever we need to get a message to Thomas quickly, we'll send Frances by horse. A boy traveling fast on a horse raises less suspicion than an old slave ridin' fast on a horse. And besides, these old bones don't do well at a gallop anymore."

George reined his mule left at the main road instead of toward Springfield. "We need to go home a different way," he explained quietly, "since that same man will likely stop us again. He'll be mighty suspicious if he sees us going back with our two pies still in the basket."

As they made their way on a back road that circled north and rejoined the main farther to the west, Eliza asked about Thomas Burns. "Is he always there at the tavern?"

"Pretty much," George answered. "He's a useless drunk. At least when he's not riding through these hills delivering messages to our troops. He's one of the fastest couriers we have and a sharpshooter to boot."

"So...he's not really a drunk?"

"Naw. He's good at pretending though."

She shook her head. "You should have warned me. He was scary."

George laughed. "He's actually a scout for the same

regiment our Jonathan's in."

"Are you serious, George? Does that mean Jonathan's close by?"

"No. He's probably halfway across the state. And don't let on to Thomas that you know Jonny. As far as Thomas knows, you really are a boy. Let's leave it at that. It's safer for everyone."

Eliza mulled all this information over. "A scout and a sharpshooter and a spy, huh? That's quite a lot of roles for just one man to carry."

They continued on until they reached Springfield where George dropped her off at the same place he'd picked her up earlier. She made her way down the dark alley to Elin's shed where she changed into Eliza's clothes then went down the alley in the opposite direction to the gate in Mildred's fence and quietly to her room. It was late, and she was exhausted. So exhausted, in fact, that the best she could do was crawl into bed with all her clothes on. She pulled the blankets up to her chin and drifted off to sleep with deep contentment in her heart.

CHAPTER SEVENTEEN

Eliza rarely missed breakfast, but she overslept on the morning following her trip to deliver a message to Thomas Burns. A knock at her door was the first thing she remembered. She yawned and stretched and sleepily asked who it was.

"It's me. Sally. Are you feeling well, dear?"

"Come in, Sally."

Eliza threw her blankets back and noticed with alarm she still had her dress on. Sally stepped into the room. "Eliza? You slept in your dress? Whatever for, dear?"

Eliza rubbed her eyes and shook her head. "I...I'm not sure. I barely remember."

"And, Eliza, you have a few sticks tangled in your skirt. What have you been up to, girl?"

Eliza looked down and sure enough. *Drat those blackberry bushes.* "Oh dear, now I remember," she said as she stood and picked the thorny branches out of her hem, trying to collect her thoughts. "I couldn't sleep so I went out to the greenhouse and to just walk around in the back garden."

"Tsk, tsk. You shouldn't be wandering around outside after dark, child. Much too dangerous. From the looks of your face and hands, I'd say you've been digging around in the dirt out there."

Eliza saw her filthy hands and groaned. "Yes, I guess I did, come to think of it. I was too exhausted by the time I got back to my room to care. I barely remember crawling into bed."

"You must be sick, dear girl." Sally put her hand on Eliza's forehead. "Hmmm... No fever. Now, I brought your breakfast to you. Would you like to eat it here? Or come downstairs?"

"Actually, I do think I might be coming down with something. I feel rather faint. I think I'd like to eat up here and stay in bed. Could you also bring something up for the noon meal?"

Sally studied her and shook her head. "What you need, Liza girl, is to stop moping and join the real world."

Eliza schooled her features to appear very sad, even to the brink of tears. "I'll try, Sally. Be patient, please," she said with a pitiful voice.

Sally finally conceded. "I'm sorry. I'm just so worried about you. I know you've been through a lot, sweetheart." She patted Eliza's shoulder. "You just get better, now, you hear?"

At noon, Sally brought a tray with homemade bread and jam and a slice of ham. Eliza still lay in bed, this time with a wet rag draped across her forehead. She told Sally, "Leave the food, please, but don't bother bringing any more. My stomach is upset and I'm terribly tired. I just want to sleep."

Sally muttered under her breath all the way out the door, "There's something strange goin' on with that girl. Somethin's not addin' up."

After Sally left, Eliza again made her way to Elin's.

"Oh, Eliza, thank God you're safe! Tell me all about it, please."

They sat at Gloria's table and went over every detail of the night before. Elin was more than satisfied that Eliza seemed able to successfully carry off being Frances as well as Gloria, two characters as different as night and day.

"Is there any more news, Elin?"

"Nothing has changed. McColloch and his men are still on their way here. I managed to get extra flour and more meat. Mrs. Boyd is making extra bread. The rooms are ready just in case. We'll have to wait and see. It's possible we will have some guests tonight. I think we're ready."

That evening, they found out McColloch was camped just outside of Springfield. Elin sent a disappointed Eliza home. The next afternoon, as soon as she walked into her room, Elin met her and spoke in a softer tone than usual. "Two officers arrived about an hour ago demanding to be fed and housed. When they realized we were Southern sympathizers and that they were more than welcome, they softened their tones. Charles drew baths for them, and they're sleeping now. Mrs. Boyd is doing her best to fix a sumptuous meal for them, poor boys. They stank to high heavens, and they're exhausted."

Eliza wrinkled her nose and said, "Poor boys? They're the enemy!"

"Yes, that is true. But like many of the men from the Ozarks, they may be confused about how they ended up on the side they're on, and they might just rather go home to their families."

"They're officers. I doubt they're confused."

"I just want you to realize they're struggling, too. You can do your job better if you don't hate them."

"I disagree. In fact, it was my hatred of the enemy that caused Major McDonald and Captain Alcorn to recruit me in the first place."

"Just be careful. Don't let them sense your animosity."

"Oh, I won't. If anything, my animosity drives me to fully be the character I have to be. It makes me brave. And I need to be brave."

Eliza dressed in her finest Gloria outfit and went downstairs to dust and set the table for the guests. Before the officers came downstairs, there was a sharp knock at the front door. Eliza could see through the window two bedraggled soldiers. When they saw her, one of them hollered, "Open up, miss! Before we break your door down!"

She immediately swung the door wide and said, "Come in, gentlemen. Please. You are more than welcome. In fact, we've been expecting you."

They looked at each other and raised their eyebrows in surprise. "You have?"

"Yes, of course. Please have a seat in the parlor." Gloria spoke quickly so she could calm their belligerence. "Would you like something to drink?"

The two men took seats, and one leered at Gloria as he answered, "Yes, miss. What kind of alcohol might you have?"

"I'm so sorry. We run a boardinghouse and don't serve any alcohol at all. I'm afraid the only thing I have to offer is coffee, tea, or water." She shrugged and smiled. The men seemed charmed.

"Cool, fresh water sounds wonderful, Miss..."

"Forgive me. I failed to introduce myself. I'm Miss Gloria LaRue." She gave a small curtsy. "And you are?"

The men stood and took off their gloves. One bowed slightly, and the other extended his hand. "I am Captain Frank Jones, and this is Lieutenant Parker. Pleased to make your acquaintance, Miss LaRue. We've come to meet with Major Lee and Captain McKinney. They told us to find them here."

"Would you like to dine with them? We'd be more than

happy to have you."

"Please, miss. Would you please tell them of our arrival?"

"I would be happy to, sir."

Gloria went to the kitchen where she found Elin already filling glasses of water.

"Here, you take these in to them, and I'll introduce myself and go upstairs to tell the major his guests have arrived. And, Gloria...you're doing an excellent job. Thank you."

Gloria entered the parlor and handed them each a glass. Both men stood to receive it then turned as Elin entered.

"Good evening, gentlemen. I hope Miss LaRue has made you feel welcome." She extended her hand. "I am Mrs. Elin Johnson." Each man took her extended hand and gave a slight bow.

"Pleased to meet you, Mrs. Johnson. Is your husband at home?"

"No. I'm sad to say I'm a widow. Mr. Johnson passed on a decade ago. I've been running this establishment almost that long. It keeps me busy and food on my table. Miss LaRue informed me that you're here to see the officers upstairs. I'll go get them now while she prepares your table. But before I go, I'd like to thank you in person for the work you and your men are doing. It is our pleasure to serve you. If there is anything else we can do for you, please don't hesitate to ask."

Both women smiled warmly and left.

Less than ten minutes passed before the officers from upstairs came down to their meal. Elin introduced them to Gloria before she seated them at a table set for four. Elin retired to the kitchen and listened through the cracked door while Gloria carried the first course to the table then hovered close by to see to it that their glasses were constantly refilled, promptly removed dirty dishes, and set the next courses in front of them. In spite of the scarcity of food, Elin and Mrs. Boyd had managed to put together a delicious meal complete with apple pie and thick cream. The men ate voraciously.

And, as hoped, they talked. And talked. Most of the conversation was about the march to Springfield and funny or annoying happenings along the way. Eliza listened carefully to any tidbit of information that might be useful. Her head was swimming, but she managed to be attentive to their needs and did her job flawlessly. Until she spilled water on Lieutenant Parker's hand. She apologized profusely while he reached out and captured her free hand in his.

"That is quite all right, Miss LaRue. My hand has been through worse." He held on longer than what was proper and went as far as to wink at her. She carefully disengaged her hand and went to get a cloth to wipe up the spill.

Captain Jones laughed at his lieutenant. "I must warn you, Miss LaRue, to keep your distance from the lieutenant. He's pretty fast with the ladies, and it's been far too long since he has laid eyes on one as beautiful as you."

She smiled coyly. "I assure you, Captain and Lieutenant, that as much as I appreciate what you do for our cause, you will be very disappointed if you think my appreciation would allow me to be anything other than a lady."

The major smiled and said, "Well stated, Miss LaRue. I assure you that my men"—he stared hard at the lieutenant—"will conduct themselves as gentlemen whenever they are in your presence. You have nothing to fear."

The lieutenant cleared his throat and sat up straighter in his chair. "Yes, sir. I'm sorry, miss."

They went on to talk about news from home and stories of terrible deprivation throughout southwest Missouri and northern Arkansas. At one point, the senior officer, Major Lee told the others that General McColloch planned to stay in Springfield just a few days. "He thinks we're needed more in Arkansas. Although Price, on the other hand, has plans to move north to Osceola. We're in desperate need of more men. His plans are to set up a recruiting camp. Most of the men in the Missouri State Guard are getting close to the end of their enlistment. We can't afford to lose them. He's going to try to talk them into re-enlisting and find more recruits. Hopefully, during the lull of winter, we can grow our forces and set up training camps. Springfield's as good a place as any. As for you and me, boys, looks like we'll be wintering in Arkansas."

The men stood and wandered into the parlor where all but the lieutenant lit their pipes. Captain McKinney stretched and said, "I will be happy to winter in Arkansas. The farther south the better."

"Yes. I'm dreading this winter. I'm afraid it will be unbearable for our men. We're in desperate need of warm clothes and boots but I don't know where we'll get them."

"Unless our boys are fed and warm, I'm afraid morale will drop fast."

They continued discussing the dire straits of their men then talked about their families. Two were married and missed their wives and children desperately. They also expressed their fears for them. "It's very difficult being away and not able to protect them," the major said.

It was late, and Eliza didn't want to interrupt them, so she didn't offer to play the piano or sing. She merely stayed close and filled their glasses with water when asked. Finally, Lieutenant Parker and Captain Jones left, and the two others retired upstairs. Elin met Gloria in her room for tea. They quietly discussed which information might be valuable enough to carry to Thomas then divided the messages between them to write down in code. Eliza wrote, *Price to march to Osceola to set up recruiting camp.* Elin wrote, *McColloch is in Springfield but expected to leave for Arkansas in a few days. Major Lee, Captain McKinney at Elin's.*

"That's enough. If you get a chance, you can fill in more details. It's late, and you're too tired to go anywhere tonight. But as soon as dusk hits tomorrow, I'm sending you on a fast horse. Come here and work in the afternoon then change into Frances and go down the alley to the same place George picked you up before. He'll take you to a place where we have a couple of horses hidden in a cave. From there, you'll go to Thomas. If anyone sees you, they'll probably steal your horse, so stay hidden. Ride through the woods where you can. If you're stopped, same story. I'll send a package of cookies this time. Much easier to carry."

Eliza went home and slept fitfully. Things were happening too fast. She wasn't at all confident she could find her way to the tavern unless she could take the main road. Throughout the night, she had dreams of being chased on horseback then ones of eating cookies and feeding them to her horse. In another dream, Lieutenant Parker's leering face appeared when she opened the door to the tavern then gunshots and a bloody Thomas fell at her feet. She woke covered in sweat and panting for breath.

By the time she arrived at Elin's, both officers had left to spend the day at camp with their men. She quickly made their beds and folded what little clothing they had. She cleaned up their shaving mess, dumped stale dirty water out back, and replaced it with fresh water from the pump. Elin invited her to eat an early supper.

"The sun sets before five. You'll need to eat before you go. Then change clothes. There's not much time left. George said he'll pick you up at five."

She ate and changed quickly, stuffed the messages into her binding cloth, and left by the back gate with a package of cookies in her hand. Sure enough, George was waiting. She paid close attention to the route he took to the cave, thinking she would have to find her own way back to St. Louis Street. When George came out of the cave with the horse, he gave her different directions than she had expected, sending her through the woods and down to a path which would take her directly to the main road a few miles east of the city.

"Yer all wound up, ain't you, Frances? You need to shake this fear off the best you can. Fear will make you do stupid things."

Eliza took a deep breath and rested her head on the horse's neck. "I know. You're right. I couldn't sleep last night. I don't think I'm ready for this, George."

"Now hold on there. Let's walk this through." He told her what she needed to do every step of the way. What to do when she saw someone. What to say if someone saw her. "Be a boy who just wants to get home to his ma," he said gently. "That'll work on most anyone. And I'll be waitin' right here when you get back. This is a good time for your first trip by horseback. The roads are pretty empty."

With that, she mounted and took off downhill until she came to a wide footpath. She followed the path a long way through the woods and across three narrow lanes until she made it to the main road. With great relief, she turned left and took off at a gallop, hoping Elin was praying for her. The miles melted under the flying hooves of her horse. She was shocked to see how quickly she had reached an ancient oak hanging over the road. This was the landmark George told her to watch for. As soon as she passed under it, she was to angle north through the woods, keeping the moon to her right. This way, he'd said, she would avoid the man who had stopped them just two nights before. She remembered his warning to not go too deep into the woods, lest she miss the tavern entirely. She stayed just deep enough she could still see the road. When she came near to where she thought the man might be, she angled even deeper through the trees then circled back, hoping to find the drive to the tavern.

Suddenly her horse neighed. She rubbed his neck. "Shhh, it's all right, boy."

Squinting to see through the dark trees, she spotted another horse up the hill, silhouetted against the sky. She froze and watched. The horse never moved. Eliza waited. The horse remained where it was, and no other sounds could be heard, so she continued on. Finally, she came to the tavern drive. Carefully, she stayed under the cover of trees until she reached the edge of the building, where she tied her horse to a tree out of sight of the front door. She pushed the door open slowly and, sure enough, saw Thomas at his place at the bar. No one else was in sight, so she whispered, "Thomas?"

His head snapped up. "Whatd'ya want," he slurred.

"Uh, Ma wanted me to stop and see you, again. She sent some cookies for ya."

"Cookies? 'Zat you, Frances?" He staggered out the door and down the drive, his arm draped over her shoulder again. Once out of site of the tavern, he walked Eliza into the woods and held out his hand. "You came alone this time?"

Eliza nodded and turned to retrieve the message from the front of her shirt again.

Thomas grabbed her arm and spun her around just as she pulled the papers out. "Why are you digging in there?" He dropped his hand and stepped back when he heard her tiny, embarrassed gasp. "You're a girl? Damn! Why did they send a girl?"

Eliza drew herself up to her full height. "Because I can get information a man can't. That's why," she said indignantly.

Thomas was silent as he studied her face in the moonlight. Finally, he said, "I don't want to know what you feel like you have to do to get this information. It's sad, Frances, or whatever your name is."

"What?" Eliza sputtered.

"Not even this is worth selling yourself for," he said, looking at her sadly.

Again, she sputtered, "What!" This time much louder.

"Give me the message, please, so I can be on my way." He held out his hand.

Eliza stepped back. "I'm not giving it to you until you get this straight, mister! I get my information by waiting on tables at a respectable boardinghouse. And I listen while they talk. That's all!" Her voice rose. "I never do whatever it is that your filthy mind is thinking." Her voice got even louder, and he tried to shush her.

"Never! Do you understand me? Never!"

Before she got the second "never," out, he wrapped one arm around her and covered her mouth with the other. She struggled with all her feeble strength until she realized what she had just done. Then she went limp, and he let her go.

"I'm sorry, miss. Truly sorry for insulting you. I just assumed..." Eliza could detect a smothered snicker.

"Well, your assumption was off, way off!" She stood and tucked her shirt back into her overalls. "I'm sorry, too. I need to control myself better than that if I expect to continue doing this work."

"So, you're Frances, a girl. Now why didn't they tell me? I still think it's a mistake. This is no job for a girl. How old are you, Frances? Twelve? Thirteen?"

"I'm eighteen."

"Well, good job on the disguise. You look like a little girl. It's too dangerous out here. The first chance I get, I'm going to recommend they stop using you."

She stopped adjusting her clothing and stared at him. "Please don't. I'm in a position to get information, and I love doing this. I'd rather die doing this than sit at home doing nothing."

Thomas rubbed his whiskered chin. "You're quite a woman. When this war is done, I think I'd like to meet you."

"Here. Take these before I slap you." She handed the messages to him. "There's more detail than this if you want to hear it." He looked around then led her deeper into the forest where she recounted every detail about troop movements, their lack of food and clothing, possible training camps being established in Springfield, and anything else she thought he might want to hear.

"Thank you, Frances." He walked her down through the trees and up the drive to her horse then took quickly off in the direction of the horse Eliza had seen standing alone in the woods.

Her trip back was fast and uneventful. George was waiting at the cave as promised. She almost collapsed in his arms when she dismounted.

"Let's get you home, Liza girl," were the only words he said the rest of the night.

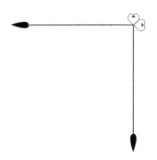

CHAPTER EIGHTEEN

George managed to get word to Eliza the next morning that Elin wanted her to stay home for a few days to rest. The following afternoon, Eliza went out the back door to visit the greenhouse. As she had hoped, George was alone, working on his beloved plants.

"Did you rest, Liza?" he asked quietly when she closed the door behind her.

"Yes, thank you. I'm worried though. I think I should be at Elin's this evening. What if I'm missing valuable information? Those officers are pretty talkative."

"Well, you can put yer mind at ease. I just heard that General McColloch and his men pulled out of Springfield this morning. Have a seat over there and fill me in on yer escapades." Eliza sat and started talking, telling George all about her evening, including the part where Thomas discovered that Francis, the boy was actually Frances, the girl. When she finished, she fidgeted, impatient to get back to work. George watched her and chuckled.

"Look at you. Chompin' at the bit like a filly that needs to be let out to pasture. You need the rest, Liza. And it's best for you to spend a little time around Mildred and Sally, lest they grow suspicious. Continue yer story of grief and needin' time in yer room. But, yer gonna have to be gone a lot if we need to send Frances on a few more trips, so show yer face a little more in the next day or two so they don't think yer dead." George winked at her.

When she finally went back to Elin's to work, she found very little to do. For the last full week of November, they had no guests since there were no Confederate soldiers in Springfield, at least that they were aware of. Elin and her slave, Charles, took several trips throughout the city to presumably locate provisions but primarily to gather information. They would return home with little success. Elin was baffled by the lack of information.

"No one seems to know anything, except that Price is still recruiting in Osceola. We need to be ready, though, Eliza. Don't let your guard down."

Finally, on the last day of November, word reached them that Brigadier General James McBride, commander of the 7th Division of the Missouri State Guard was on his way with 2,000 men. They were expected to arrive on December first.

"I can't spare you to take this information to Thomas yet, Eliza," Elin said as they had tea in Gloria's room. "I'll need the services of Gloria badly. With this many men coming, we may have a full house. And by the time I send you, I'm hoping we will have gathered more information."

As expected, McBride and his troops arrived the next day. Elin had Mrs. Boyd prepare enough food to feed several men. Gloria was dressed and ready when four officers arrived, demanding to be housed and fed. Again, she welcomed them at the door with charm and grace. They softened considerably. But when she announced that their rooms were prepared and their meal would be ready as soon as they settled in, the officers looked like they would bow at her feet. They removed their hats and apologized for their rudeness.

"Please forgive us," said the ranking officer. "We've been marching for days, we're exhausted and hungry, and very few people have been as hospitable as you."

Gloria put her hand over her heart. "I am so sorry. That saddens me greatly. Especially after all you've done for our cause. Please come in and make yourselves at home. My name is Gloria LaRue. I live here and help when needed. I believe Charles is drawing water for your bath, if you'd like one before you eat, that is."

Far beyond what the men had expected, all four of them crowded eagerly through the door and took turns introducing themselves. Yes, they all said, they would love to bathe before they dined. Gloria then showed each to his own private room, where Charles had hastily provided warm, if not hot, water for sponge baths. None of the officers complained since water of any kind for bathing was a luxury. The hungry men bathed hastily and, one by one, descended the stairs to be fed. Gloria was waiting to usher them to the parlor where they would wait until Elin announced the meal was ready. Each man introduced himself as he took a seat. The ranking officer was Major Duncan. The other three were Captains Lewis, Sands, and Forrest, each over a company of approximately 100 men. While they waited for the meal, Eliza played softly on the piano. Two of the tired men put their heads back on their chairs and closed their eyes. Captains Lewis and Sands meandered over to stand at the piano and hum along.

Finally, Elin entered the room and introduced herself. As before, she was profuse in her welcome. The men stood, and Major Duncan introduced himself and his men.

"Please, come into the dining room and make yourselves comfortable. Your meal is ready to be served," Elin said as she gestured the way to the door.

Again, Elin retired to the kitchen to listen at the door while Gloria served the men. Fully at ease, all four men dove into their meals with enthusiasm and compliments to the cook. They seemed to be less talkative than Elin's previous guests, so Gloria decided to prime the pump with seemingly innocent questions.

"You must be exhausted and starving after the long march you just made," she said to no one in particular as she refilled their glasses.

"Yes, ma'am, we are," Captain Lewis said with a smile and a wink. The others nodded and mumbled their agreement around mouthfuls of food.

When nothing else was added, Gloria continued, "I hope you get to stay long enough to regain your strength."

"Me, too," Captain Sands said. "I'm not sure though. The higher-ups will have to make that decision."

Captain Lewis asked, "Do you know anything, Major?"

Gloria was disappointed to observe that the major, although very polite, was not at all talkative. He merely shrugged and continued eating. The others took his cue and ate silently through the remainder of the meal. When it was time for dessert, Elin entered and informed them that they would be served dessert in the parlor. "Miss LaRue will be happy to play for you while you wait if it pleases you."

"Oh, it pleases me greatly," said Lewis as he rose from his chair.

The others laughed at the fact that Lewis was obviously smitten by the fair Gloria LaRue. But before Lewis could make a move, Captain Sands offered his arm to Gloria. She accepted and was escorted to the parlor followed by the good-natured chuckling of the others. Captain Lewis rushed to get to the piano before Sands so he could pull the bench out for Gloria. Major Duncan and Captain Forrest laughed again and sat in the chairs closest to the piano while the other two stood.

"Forgive my men, Miss LaRue. They've been on the field much too long; they've forgotten how to act in the presence of a lady," the major said.

Gloria smiled warmly. "They have been just fine, Major Duncan. I promise you, if they step out of line, you will be the first to hear of it."

He smiled back at her. "Did you hear that, boys? Mind your manners." Then he added, "I don't mean to be forward, but you are *Miss* LaRue, aren't you? You are unattached?"

"Yes, Major Duncan. You are correct." She then started playing lightly on the keys. "Does anyone have a request?"

The two men at the piano were quick with a variety of song requests. Gloria played the songs she knew and encouraged the men to join her in singing. Major Duncan and Captain Forrest simply sat and enjoyed the entertainment silently while Sands and Lewis enthusiastically joined their voices with Gloria's.

Elin soon entered with the pies and more drinks. Gloria excused herself momentarily, hoping her absence would allow the men to talk more freely. Of course, she and Elin found places where they could listen without being seen. But again, the men seemed much more interested in eating than talking. Finally, the major set his plate on the side table, wiped his mouth with his napkin, and leaned back. To Elin's and Gloria's great disappointment he dismissed his men with, "It's been a long, long day, men. I have a lot planned for tomorrow. Why don't you go get some sleep now. You'll need it."

Lewis and Sands both sputtered a protest, but the major quickly silenced them. "That's an order, not a suggestion."

Gloria entered before they could leave, gathering their plates and forks. "Don't go," she said. "The evening is still young."

The men shuffled their feet uncomfortably. Lewis even tried a second time to change the major's mind. "Major?"

"You heard me the first time." He then turned to Gloria. "I'm sorry, Miss LaRue. But my men need their sleep if they are to be ready for tomorrow." He glared at the three captains until they left with quick bows and apologies to Gloria.

When Gloria returned to gather the dirty glasses and tidy the parlor, she was surprised to see the major still there. He was seated comfortably as if he was planning to stay for a while. "May I get you something else, Major?"

"Yes, please. Some more water and one for yourself as well. I'd like to talk to you for a moment, if you don't mind."

A little taken aback, Gloria managed to recover and answer, "Of course, Major. I don't mind at all."

Gloria filled glasses and took them to the parlor. She handed one to the major then sat in a chair facing him. "What did you want to talk about, Major?"

Major Duncan cleared his throat and leaned toward her, resting his arms on his thighs. "Tell me about yourself, Miss LaRue."

Gloria swallowed nervously and took a sip of water, hoping to calm herself enough that she could collect her racing thoughts and answer him in a composed manner. She took a deep breath, set her glass on the end table, and reminded herself what kind of a woman Gloria LaRue was. Now was the time to practice her acting skills more than ever. She settled back comfortably in her chair and sighed contentedly. "What exactly do you want to know, Major?" she asked in a honey-soft voice.

He chuckled softly. "Let's start with, where are you from, and where's your family?"

She gave him a sweet smile as if her memories brought only pleasure. "Ah, Arkansas, beautiful Arkansas. That's where I'm from. And my family. I sure do miss them."

"Where are they now?"

"They died a long time ago. I was told it was cholera." Her mind raced as she constructed a believable story. "First my pa then my two little brothers then Ma. I was only eight, and somehow, I managed to live."

"I'm so sorry, Miss LaRue. That's a horrible thing for a child to have to go through."

"It was pretty awful." Gloria sniffed and dabbed at pretend tears. While doing so, she intentionally rubbed her eyes enough to cause a little redness. "I think God must have spared me from the worst of it though. Neighbors came to help. I was delirious when my ma and my little brothers died." At this, she covered her eyes. Her voice quavered. "I didn't have to watch or hear them suffer at the end. I don't think I could have survived it. Our neighbors, the Smiths, buried them. Mrs. Smith stayed with me until I recovered enough I could be moved to their place."

"Did you stay with them long?" the major gently asked, obviously moved by her story.

Gloria nodded.

"Were they kind?"

She looked at him with red-rimmed eyes. "Oh yes. Very. Although I was never really family to them." She shrugged her shoulders and tried to smile. "They were very poor and needed a lot of help. They only had one son. He was a big help to his pa on the farm, but Mrs. Smith needed someone to help her. So, that's what I did, for the next several years." She shrugged again and flashed a brave yet sad smile at the major.

The warmth in his smile told her that her story had hit its mark.

"It's your turn, Major. Tell me about yourself."

He cleared his throat and said, "There's not much to tell. I grew up in Jefferson City, son of a lawyer, went to good schools, studied law at St. Louis University. I joined the Missouri State Guard at the beginning of the year and, because of my education, was promoted up the ranks very quickly. Although, that promotion was most likely due to a lack of enough experienced men to do the job."

"Are your parents still living?"

"Yes. They're still at their home in Jeff City."

"And your wife?" Gloria asked very innocently.

The major looked at her keenly then chuckled softly. "There is no wife. If there was, I certainly wouldn't be sitting alone in a room with someone as beautiful as you."

Gloria blushed and dropped her head, unable to meet his gaze.

"Miss LaRue, how is it that you have such refined manners and voice if you were raised on a poor farm in Arkansas?"

Without missing a beat, she was ready with an answer. "Both my ma and Mrs. Smith were educated women from the East. I'm still not sure how they ended up married to Arkansas farmers." She shrugged and smiled. "Love, I guess." She smiled sweetly at her pretend memories. "Both of them felt it was important for me to be educated and to learn to act like a lady. So, in addition to the work I did for the Smiths, I was also schooled. Rather relentlessly, I might add. Mrs. Smith was very kind, but at times, I felt like I was more of a project than a daughter." She laughed. "It was good for me though. I actually enjoyed it."

"And after that?" the major prodded gently.

Gloria gave an embarrassed laugh. "I got older, and their son started noticing me."

"I can see why. You have the most stunning blue eyes I've ever seen."

Gloria fidgeted with the folds of her skirt.

"I'm sorry, Miss LaRue. I didn't mean to be forward."

She felt him scrutinizing her.

"If it's difficult for you to tell me about your past, you don't have to say any more."

"It's not difficult. Their son did nothing wrong. He was just very interested in me, and his parents encouraged him. I was very young and very naive. The attention was too overwhelming when I realized that their intentions were for me to marry him. I was only fifteen and scared out of my wits. Besides, as kind as their son was to me, I wasn't at all attracted to him. So, I packed up my few belongings and left."

"And you were only fifteen? Where did you go?"

"I went to Little Rock, hoping to find a job."

"And?"

"I found several. It's not hard when you're young and willing to work hard."

The major studied her intently for a moment then shook his head in frustration. "I'm sorry, Miss LaRue. That is unacceptable."

Gloria sat upright, her heart pounding furiously. "W-what do you mean, 'unacceptable'?"

He stood and walked to the door.

Gloria watched as he stopped, grabbed the doorknob, and shook his head again. She heard an angry sigh just before he turned and studied her again.

"Have I said something to offend you, Major?" she asked as she stood to her feet, hand pressed to her heart.

"Offend me?" He looked almost alarmed that she would think such a thing. "No, dear girl. You have not offended me," He moved toward her and gently took her hand in his. "I am offended, yes. But not by anything you have said or done."

Gloria looked up into his kind, handsome face and reminded herself that he was the enemy. "Then what is it, Major?"

"Miss LaRue, you were only fifteen! Just a child! No fifteen-year-old female should ever be on her own with no one to protect her."

"It happens more than you know. I saw many girls my age and younger in Little Rock with no one to care about them."

"I have a fifteen-year-old sister. I can't imagine her going through what you did. What did you do? Where did you stay?"

She demurely pulled her hand free and returned to her

chair. The major also sat.

"I did what I'm doing now. I went to several boardinghouses and asked for lodging in exchange for work."

"Were you treated well?"

Gloria was very moved by the genuine kindness in the major's tone and expression. She fought feelings of guilt that clouded her judgment. Clearing her throat, she went on. "Yes. I was fortunate enough to stumble across a boardinghouse run by a very nice woman. She seemed to understand that I needed protection as well as work. I slept in the attic and worked hard. She gave me privacy and freedom during my off hours."

The major waited to see if she would add more.

Gloria squirmed inwardly and continued. "After a couple of years, she gave me permission to work part-time for her so I could get another job that actually paid money. I finally got some work as a housekeeper and as a waitress. I saved my money and moved here."

"Why here? Springfield's a long way from Little Rock."

Here it is, she thought. I can't avoid this any longer. She took a moment to appear as if she were wiping her tears away, again rubbing just hard enough to actually bring tears and redness to her eyes.

The major was immediately kneeling at her side, apologizing. "I'm so sorry. I shouldn't have pried. If you don't want to tell me, you don't have to."

She continued to press her fingers into her eyes then took a deep, quivering breath and looked at him with red, watery eyes. "It's not easy, but I want to tell you. I'm not proud of it." She again covered her eyes.

He waited quietly, still crouched by her chair.

With her head still down, she quietly said, "A woman approached me one day and offered me a job at her place. I was shocked at how much she offered to pay me. I went with her, just to see what kind of place it was and, at first, I was certain I didn't want the job. It was a saloon and dance hall. When I refused her, she very quickly explained that she only wanted me to wait tables. They served food there, she told me, and needed someone to work in the kitchen and deliver food to the tables. The pay was very good, and she seemed nice, so I said yes. I continued living at the same boardinghouse though."

Gloria raised her head to gauge his reaction to her story. "I worked there for several months and gradually got used to listening to the music, watching the dancers, and even the attention I got from the men. The people I worked for did a good job protecting me from any kind of lewd talk or aggressive behavior. I realize now, they protected me because they wanted to keep me around and to prepare me for a different kind of work, if you know what I mean."

"I'm so sorry, Miss LaRue."

"Well, I'm happy to say, they didn't succeed." She briefly touched his arm then drew back. "But, they almost did. I was terribly naive. Slowly, very slowly, I became comfortable in that environment. Once I was asked to deliver alcoholic drinks to a table because the women at the bar were busy. Soon it became a regular part of my job. The other girls who worked there were friends to me, the only real friends I had. Most of them lived there and, at first, I just assumed it was the same arrangement I had at my boardinghouse. Lands, was I ever foolish!" She covered her face in embarrassment before continuing. "The woman I worked for told me if I would work exclusively at the bar and be willing to dress as her saloon girls dressed, she would increase my pay significantly. I refused. As much as I liked my new friends, I detested the way they dressed. She asked if I might be interested in dancing instead, since the pay for that was almost twice what I was making. The dancers seemed to be the nicest, and the clothes most of them wore were a little more modest than the saloon girls. When I hesitated, she called one of the dance hall girls over to talk to me about it. I'm so ashamed to tell you this, but she managed to make the job seem almost honorable. She explained that there were different levels of performances and that mine could be the most modest, and I could leave if I felt uncomfortable and go back to helping serve tables."

Again, Gloria looked at the major to gauge his reaction and to determine how far to go with her story. His eyes held nothing but compassion.

"I accepted the position. I danced for them for about two months before my eyes were opened to what the other girls were doing. And...what was eventually expected of me." She shook her head in frustration. "In hindsight, I can't believe I was so blind. By the time I realized what kind of establishment it was and what was expected of me, it was too late. I was branded as one of them. The only thing I could do to save my reputation was to leave." Looking him squarely in the face, she said, "I knew a family that was coming here, and they let me travel with them. So, in answer to your question, that is why I'm in Springfield, Missouri, so far from Little Rock."

Major Duncan covered her hand with his. She stared at his large, strong hand completely covering hers and, against her wishes, felt pleasure. "Please don't tell anyone else," she said in a small, weak voice. "Mrs. Johnson is the only other person that knows."

"I won't. I promise. But, Miss LaRue, you have nothing to be ashamed of." With that, he stood to his feet and drew her up with him, never letting go of her hand. "I must retire now. Thank you for your company. I know we've just met, but war sometimes necessitates the, shall we say, the setting aside of the slowness of society's rules of getting acquainted with someone of the fairer sex." He stumbled over his words. "What I mean to say is, forgive me for seeming to be forward, but might I address you as Gloria in private? And could we meet again sometime soon?"

Gloria was stunned. And flattered. It took strength to

continue her role. "Of course, Major. It would be my pleasure. And what should I call you in private?"

He raised her hand to his lips for a brief kiss. "Call me Joel," he replied in a husky voice.

CHAPTER NINETEEN

Eliza rode furiously through the cold December night. She was totally transformed into Frances again, so much so, she felt an almost giddy sense of freedom. Keeping her eyes peeled for any signs of riders up ahead, she could feel the crinkle of paper under her bindings and the bulk of a small Colt revolver under her belt. The paper was the message she carried to Thomas Burns. The revolver was a gift, delivered unexpectedly to Elin the day before by an unknown man.

Three days had passed since Major Duncan had made his intentions known of a casual courtship with Gloria. Elin told Eliza to encourage that relationship. "The potential for valuable information is huge." She also asked her to continue working as Gloria for the next two evenings, hoping to dig up more information. On both evenings, after hearty meals and a relaxing time in the parlor, Major Duncan again sent his three captains away so he could spend time alone with Gloria.

As Eliza rode, she shook her head in frustration with herself. In spite of her declared hatred of the "enemy," she was struggling to stay emotionally detached from Major Joel Duncan. He was a kind, compassionate gentleman to the core. Guilt had been nagging at her each day that she had sweet-talked him and pried for information. He was as closemouthed with her as he was the first day they met. Finally, Elin decided it was time to send Frances to Thomas with what information they had managed to gather. They had met and talked in hushed tones in Gloria's room late after Major Duncan had retired for the night. Together they had written the message, *Gen. James McBride arr. in Spr. with 2,000 men on the first. More troops have come in since then. Possibly 4000 here now. Major Duncan of the 2nd Regiment, 7th Division Missouri State Guard, and his Captains Forrest, Sands, and Lewis staying at Elin's.*

Eliza's roles as both Gloria and Frances filled her with excitement and purpose. It was becoming more and more difficult to mope around the Scott household as sad, pitiful Eliza, she thought as she rode, leaning forward over the saddle, pressing her legs into the horse's heaving sides. The cold wind stung her cheeks and caused her eyes to tear up. She chuckled to herself as she realized she was growing to dislike the Eliza Miss Scott knew. Some days, she dreaded walking back into the house and back up to her room. It was interesting how her spy job had evolved. Not once had it been necessary to use any of the carefully sought-out hiding places in her room. Maybe that time would come. For now, the transition back and forth from Eliza to Gloria to Frances was going without a hitch.

Up ahead, Eliza saw the branch from the old oak tree hanging over the road. She slowed to a walk then angled north through the trees and around to the drive to the tavern. As she dismounted and approached the door on foot, she heard a "Psst," coming from the trees to her left. Cautiously she made her way toward the sound, hand on her revolver.

"'Zat you, Frances?" came a familiar drawl from the

woods.

"Yeah," she answered with a low, scruffy voice.

"Got some cookies from yer ma?"

"A few," she answered as she worked her way deeper into the woods.

Through the darkness, she could barely make out Thomas' outline. He put a hand out in greeting. She relished the feeling of his strong warm hand around hers.

"Your hands are like ice," he said as he reached out to take her other one. He held both between his and blew warm air on them.

She closed her eyes and enjoyed the comfort. *Ahh. This feels so good,* she thought before she snapped back to reality and pulled her hands away. Impatiently she turned to dig her message out of the binding around her chest. Thomas chuckled behind her.

"Here," she said a little more brusquely than she'd intended. Thomas took the papers but his eyes never left hers.

"So, what's got you all in a dither, little missy?"

"Nothing. I'm fine."

"Was it having a handsome man holding your pretty little hands in the middle of a dark forest?"

"Leave out the word handsome, and maybe you're on to something."

Thomas laughed. "Ah, Frances, you and I definitely need to meet after the war."

"If you can find 'Frances' after the war, you're welcome to meet her," she answered with a smile.

"Don't forget who I am and what I do. I have my resources. I know how to get information."

"And don't forget what I do. I'm very good at disguising myself and hiding."

"I'd recognize those blue eyes anywhere. I don't think you could effectively hide those."

She looked down and shuffled her feet.

"Do you have anything to tell me besides what's written in here?" he asked as he lifted the paper she'd given him.

"No, that's about it. Sorry, there's not more." She went on to fill him in on a few details.

"I see you're carrying a pistol this time."

"What?" Frances saw where the pistol was completely covered by her coat.

"I'm trained to see these things. Especially trained to quickly observe what weapons are accessible to people around me. I'm glad you have it. Do you know how to use it?"

"Aim and shoot. It's not difficult."

He stared at her soberly for a long moment, causing her to squirm under his scrutiny. "Maybe someday I'll give you a quick lesson. In the meantime, don't be hasty to use it." His tone left no invitation for further banter. "Goodbye, Frances. Take care of yourself."

He turned to leave then stopped and came back to her. "I almost forgot. It's possible I won't be at the tavern if you come in the next week or two. My company will be operating in the area and I'll be farther on up the road with some of my platoon. Take the second road to the right and start whistling 'Silent Night' after you've gone about a mile. We'll find you, I promise."

For the next few weeks, Eliza busied herself making Christmas preparations at both the Scott household and Elin's boardinghouse. She helped Mildred and Sally work with Lucy and her two children to string popcorn and cut star shapes from colored paper. George and Jim had stumbled across some toys in a burned, abandoned building on the outskirts of town: a wooden horse and wagon with no wheels for five-year-old Matthias and a small dollhouse for three-year-old Abby. After much scrubbing, a coat of paint, and the addition of four wooden wheels, the two men were like two kids in their anticipation of presenting their gifts on Christmas Eve. Sally made a doll and a ball from rags for the children, and Eliza bound paper together to make a drawing book for each child. She found two pencils and some charcoal to include with her gift.

Elin and Gloria also worked to bring a measure of Christmas joy to the boardinghouse. They kept reminding themselves that everything they did was to make their boarders as happy and as comfortable as possible so in the end, they would let down their guard and share information. But, as they hummed Christmas carols and helped Mrs. Bond with the baking, Eliza couldn't refrain from a desire to genuinely bless their Confederate officers.

Major Joel Duncan continued his courtship of Gloria. She demurely allowed it to continue, visiting into the night, taking short strolls down Elm Street, holding hands as they sat on the porch swing, bundled in separate blankets. Once, when he leaned in for a kiss, she turned her face away and whispered an apology, "I'm sorry. I'm not ready for that yet, Joel. It's not you. I...I just don't feel like it's proper...not yet anyway."

"No need to apologize, Gloria," he said as he let his arm linger around her shoulders. "It just confirms to me that you are the proper young lady I know you to be. I'm sorry if I've been too forward."

"Oh, not at all. You've been nothing but a gentleman. I think you've actually helped bring a measure of healing to me, Major." Gloria looked away as soon as she uttered those words.

"Please don't be embarrassed. You have nothing to be ashamed of," the major said as he pulled her closer and gently kissed the top of her head.

In reality, Gloria's heart was stabbed by the deception. His kindness only made it worse.

On Christmas Day, none other than General Sterling

Price rode into Springfield to establish his headquarters for the winter. Finally, the four officers boarding at Elin's started talking about military matters. Over the next couple of days, Elin and Gloria heard much enthusiastic talk about General Price's plans. Apparently, Price had been offered a promotion as a major general in the Confederate Army instead of his present role as general over all of the Missouri State Guard. This promotion was conditional, though, on Price recruiting more men and bringing them, and all of the Missouri State Guard, officially into the Confederate Army with him. Elin and Gloria also heard that Price had established his headquarters on Boonville Avenue just north of the square.

Five more officers showed up at Elin's door, which made it necessary to put two men in each room. Even the fair Gloria LaRue moved in with Elin on the first floor so her room could be used. It tickled the women to watch their first boarders bully the newcomers into proper, gentlemanly behavior while they were in the presence of the two ladies.

By December 28th, Elin felt it was time for Frances to ride again. So, in spite of the freezing conditions and a thick covering of snow, Frances took off with her carefully worded cipher and a sack with several gingerbread squares for her "ma," each wrapped in red paper and tied with white ribbon. As Frances and her horse made their way into the woods, they entered a quiet wonderland, branches thick with sticky snow. Fat snowflakes drifted slowly down. When they broke through onto the road the horse's hoofbeats were muffled as they trotted down the snow-packed route.

After a slower than usual ride, Frances discovered that Thomas was indeed missing from the tavern. She quietly made her way down the tavern drive then left onto the main road. As she guided her horse northeast, she kept to the right side, peering ahead lest she miss a break in the trees indicating a side road. Almost a half hour passed before she found the first road. Another fifteen minutes passed before she made out another narrow break through tall oaks and thick bushes buried in sticky snow. It seemed more of a wide path than a road, but she followed it. After what she guessed was a mile, she whistled "Silent Night" in a weak, barely audible wheeze. Fear gripped her heart, and she shivered from the cold. She was sure she had taken the wrong turn but she kept on, not knowing any other alternative than going back. Every time snow fell from the trees in soft plops, she jerked around in fear. She was sure she saw dark figures hiding among the trees. Numbly following Thomas' directions, she continued riding and continued whistling.

Finally, she heard the click of a rifle and a voice commanding her, "Hands up!"

Her horse bolted in fear, but she managed to rein him in and put her hands in the air. "Don't shoot!" she squawked.

Two men approached from behind with rifles aimed at her. "What's your business here?"

"Uh...nothin'. Just trying to get home to Ma before I freeze."

The men made their way to the front of her horse, one lowering his rifle and taking the reins from her hands. The other kept his rifle pointed at her head. "What's your name, young'un?"

"Frances."

"Well, Frances, you're under arrest," the man with the reins said as he slipped her revolver from under her coat. "Any more weapons we should know about?"

"No, sir."

"Dismount, please. And if you make one false move, my buddy will put a bullet through your head."

Frances slid to the ground and kept her hands raised as the soldier checked her saddle for weapons then ran his hands over her, beginning with her boots. "Well, well. What do we have here?" He pulled a small knife from her left boot.

"Looks like we've got a liar, that's what," said the soldier with the gun. "Tie him up."

"What tune were you whistling, Frances? We could barely hear you."

"S-silent Night."

"Hmm... Your name is Frances and you're whistling 'Silent Night'?" He glanced over at his companion. "That's good enough for me. I don't think we need to tie him up."

His companion protested, "I don't like being lied to."

"All right, then. Turn around, boy."

Frances obeyed, and the soldier bound her wrists then helped her mount her horse. He took the reins and led her deep into the woods until they reached a few scattered tents. Men, wrapped in blankets, sat in tight circles around campfires. Both soldiers dismounted in front of the largest tent. They helped Frances down and led her inside where four men sat huddled together around a map lit by two lanterns placed at each end. Immediately and with a huge sigh of relief, Frances laid eyes on Thomas Burns. As soon as he saw her, he jumped to his feet.

"You actually made it! I was hoping you wouldn't have to come this far, especially in this weather. Have a seat, Frances. Men, get her a hot drink, pronto! She's got to be half frozen." He reached to help her sit down then noticed her wrists were bound. Glaring angrily at the two that brought her in, he demanded an answer. "What's the meaning of this?"

"Sorry, sir," one of the men stammered as he cut the rope away with the knife they'd confiscated. "He...she lied to us and, and, gosh darn it, sir! We didn't know he was a she!"

"That doesn't matter. Was she whistling the tune I said to listen for? And did she tell you her name was Frances?"

Both men nodded sheepishly.

Thomas then looked at Frances. "Don't tell me you drew

your gun on them!"

"No. I didn't have a chance. They took it away from me."

"As I ordered. I wanted them to get it before you had a chance to shoot them. But this?" He held up the rope they used. "This was uncalled for. Get a blanket, a hot drink, some grub, and see if you can dry her coat before we send her back."

The men scrambled to obey, and Thomas turned to introduce Frances to the other three men in the shadows of the tent. But before he could utter a word, the commanding officer stood abruptly, took two long strides toward Frances, and grabbed her by both shoulders. Thomas stepped back in alarm.

Eliza instantly recognized the eyes that bored into hers. Her beloved Jonathan, eyes full of shock, unbelief, and wrath. Instinctively, she tried to shake free and run, but he had her locked in a painful grip. Jonathan's jaw was clamped shut, his breath deep and loud as he tried to maintain control.

"Everyone, out!" he barked. His men scrambled to obey. "Burns! You stay!"

He kept his grip on Eliza and glared at Thomas. "I know this girl," he hissed.

"Jon, I..." she said.

His grip tightened. "Not a word from you, missy!" he said between clenched teeth as he stared down at her frightened face.

Just then, the two arresting soldiers entered the tent with a hot drink and food for Frances. They stopped at the door.

"Set it down and go saddle my horse," Jonathan ordered sharply. "I want both mine and Frances' horse ready to go in five minutes."

"Yes, sir!" both men answered as they backed out through the tent flap.

"Captain?" Thomas quietly asked. "What do you plan to

do?"

"Take her out in the woods and thrash her within an inch of her life, that's what I plan to do, Lieutenant."

"Sir?"

"Show me the message she brought," he ordered.

Thomas handed the folded paper to Jonathan. He released Eliza and reached out to receive the ciphered message. After reading it, he returned it to Thomas. "Is this the first message you've received from this Frances," he asked, breathing deeply.

"No, sir."

Jonathan ran his hand over his eyes then looked at Eliza with eyes blazing.

"Jon..." she said again.

"Hush!"

"How long has she been carrying messages?"

"To me? Over a month, sir."

"Is she only a courier?"

"No, sir."

Jonathan walked away from them both and stood with his back to them. Without turning, he asked, "As far as you know, Lieutenant, to what extents has she gone to get this information?"

"As far as I know, she has not in any way compromised her good morals, sir."

At this, Captain Jonathan Monroe turned.

"Jon?" Eliza said in a weak, frightened voice.

He glared at her. "You certainly don't know how to follow orders, do you, Frances? I want nothing but silence from you! You'll get your chance to explain later. But not here. Do you understand?"

"Y-yes, sir."

Turning to Thomas, he said, "You should have informed me that you were using a woman courier."

"It was never my plan, sir. I thought she was a boy at first. That's what she led me to believe. I tried to stop her, but she talked me out of it."

"I'm afraid she's good at talking people into ridiculous notions," Jon said as he stared at her. Eliza heard the men arrive with the horses. Jonathan grabbed her arm and moved her toward the exit.

"I'm leaving with Frances now. At risk of jeopardizing this spy ring, I won't reveal to you or anyone else who Frances actually is, but, as of now, this little lady's role has ended. You will have to find someone else to do her job."

"But, sir! She's extremely valuable. At every level. I don't think it's possible to find anyone else to do what she does," Thomas protested.

"I don't care, Lieutenant," he spit out. "She's valuable to many people on a much deeper level than this." He indicated the encampment with a nod of his head. "You won't be seeing Frances again." With that, he shoved Eliza toward her horse, helped her back into her wet coat, and stood next to her until she mounted. He then mounted his own horse, reached over to grab her reins, and took off.

Eliza gripped the saddle as they crashed through the snowy woods. She dreaded the moment Jonathan would finally bring their horses to a stop. Never in her wildest imagination had she anticipated this meeting. No amount of acting would rescue her now, she thought. They rode hard for what seemed like miles until Eliza realized she was completely lost. Her hands were numb from the cold and she thought she'd lose her grip. Finally, she cried out in desperation, "Jon! Stop!"

He stopped and turned just as she slumped to the side. Instantly he was next to her, gently easing her to an upright position. He reached out to pry her frozen fingers from the saddle and warmed them between his own. "We have about a mile to go. Here. Wear my gloves. Can you make it?"

She nodded. "Where are you taking me?"

He didn't answer. After she put the gloves on and grabbed the saddle, he took off again, this time slower. He looked back repeatedly to see if she was okay. Finally, he slowed to a walk and squeezed the horses between thick evergreen branches to a small clearing. Eliza could barely make out the dark shape of a tiny log shack in the center. Jonathan dismounted and walked to Eliza. Grabbing her arm, he pulled her gently but firmly from her horse. He stood next to her until she was steady on her feet then led her to the door of the cabin. They had to duck their heads to pass through into the cramped space beyond.

"Stay here while I build a fire and take care of the horses," he ordered and guided her to a bed in the corner. He helped her out of her damp coat and threw a blanket around her shoulders.

Shaking from fear and from cold, she did as he said. Soon, he appeared at the door with an armload of wood. He went to a stone fireplace, gathered dried grass and kindling from a basket by the hearth, and set about starting a fire with flint and his knife. After several tries, a spark and a small plume of smoke rose near his determined face. He bent over and coaxed the fire with his breath and additions of grass then kindling. He added small sticks until there was a strong blaze then carefully arranged bigger fuel in a teepee around it.

With a quick glance her direction, he patted a spot on the hearth. "Sit over here and get warm." He rose and crouched to exit through the door.

She had noticed a lean-to on the side of the cabin and assumed he'd take the horses there for shelter and possibly food, something her horse needed since, by now, she would have returned him to the cave and George's care. How worried George must be. Would he be waiting for her when she got there? Outside, Jon spoke gently to the horses, followed by a soft whinny in reply. She sat in dread of the moment he'd finish his work and walk through the door. The fire blazed hotter and ignited the small logs. Eliza stretched out her frozen fingers closer to the warmth as the one-room cabin took on an eerie glow from the flames. On the bed in the corner was a pile of blankets. In the other corner stood a small table with three tree stumps for stools. A coffee pot, tin plates, and mugs indicated this was not an abandoned place. She assumed it wasn't Jon's first time here.

The sound of the heavy door scraping open sent alarm through her, and she yanked her head around to see Jonathan enter with two sacks: hers and the one he had stuffed with the food his soldiers had provided. He set the sacks on the table, grabbed the coffeepot, and stepped outside to fill it with snow. When he returned, he hung the pot from a hook on a rudely constructed crane and maneuvered it over the flames. He then opened the sacks at the table, rolled two stumps close to the fire, and brought a plate of food to Eliza.

He sat down next to her with a plate for himself and simply said, "Eat," in a tired, gruff voice. On each plate sat a neatly wrapped square of Elin's gingerbread. "What's this?" he grunted, pointing at his small, red package.

"Gingerbread," she answered meekly. They each ate the food from Jonathan's camp then opened and quietly ate the gingerbread.

When they were finished, Jon returned their plates to the table, poured hot water into two tin mugs, and added coffee. He handed one to her with an order, "Drink."

She drank the bitter brew and waited for the storm. When she was finished, he took it from her then pulled her hat off her head. "Let your hair down so it can dry," he said in a voice tinged with fatigue. She loosened her hair and let the long, dark curls fall over her shoulders so they could take full advantage of the heat. He sat next to her and stared at the fire, his features hard, his jaw clenched. Finally, he dropped his face into his hands then turned to look at her.

"I am tired, terribly sad, and so angry I'm afraid to speak," he said as his eyes bore into hers. "Explain yourself, Eliza."

"I-I'm not sure where to begin."

"How about you begin by telling me why you ever dreamed up this insane notion," he said through clenched teeth.

"I'm sorry..."

"Don't tell me you're sorry!" he barked. "Your apologies won't do any good. Just tell me why."

"I wanted to avenge Pa's death, that's why, Jon," she answered with a defiant lift to her chin.

Jonathan shook his head and said, "Ah, Eliza. And you think this is what your pa would want?"

"Maybe..."

"Maybe? Have you completely lost your senses, girl?" The anger was back in force. He stood and paced back and forth in the small room. Finally, he stopped next to her and said, "Your pa made me promise I would watch over you if anything happened to him. It's a vow I mean to keep, even if it costs me my life, Eliza."

"You haven't broken your vow to Pa," she said softly.

"I will certainly break it if I let you continue in this foolishness."

"I'll be fine."

"That is nonsense!" he barked and started pacing again. "I order you to immediately stop doing anything connected to this spy ring you've entangled yourself in."

Eliza was silent.

"Eliza! Did you hear me?"

She nodded.

"And you'll do as I say?"

Eliza stared at the flames and didn't move.

"Eliza?"

Eliza trembled. "No, Jon. I can't do as you say. This is too important."

He stared at her. She stared back.

"Is someone forcing you?"

"No."

"Then you are free to choose whether you continue or not?"

"Yes. And I'm choosing to continue. You can't ask me to sit and rot in that house while a war is going on around me."

Jonathan moved to sit beside her. "Eliza," he said with desperation. "If you're caught, they will hang you! Don't you realize the danger you've put yourself in?"

"I fully realize the danger. But I don't care. This is war. People die. My pa died." Her voice choked. "I hate this horrible, cruel enemy. I want to make them pay. I can't sit at home and do nothing, Jon."

Jonathan put his face in his hands. Eliza was shocked when she realized he was hiding tears. He wiped his face, stood, and walked away. "Do you know what drives me? What keeps me going day by day, Eliza?" he said very quietly.

Eliza stood and moved across the room to stand next to him. She placed a comforting hand on his back.

"It's the people in that house in Springfield that you seem to despise. You and Aunt Mildred. George and Sally. The thought of protecting you and fighting so I can walk through those doors and see all of you again. The hope that soon, all of this will be over and life can go back to normal. A life that all of you will be a part of." He ran his hand over his face and struggled to compose himself.

Eliza was silent for a long time. Then she said very quietly, "I'm sorry, Jon. So sorry. But I can't make myself look forward to that time. Nothing will ever be the same now that Pa's..." She pulled her hand away from Jon's back and covered her face as she broke down and sobbed.

Jonathan took her in his arms. "Oh, Eliza, lass," he cooed into her hair. "Shh shh. I'm so sorry, girl."

They stood wrapped in each other's arms until Eliza's sobs were under control. She pushed away, wiped her face, and said, "I need to go, Jon. George is waiting for me. He's probably out of his mind with worry."

"George? So, he's a part of this?"

Eliza stood rooted to the spot, realizing her blunder.

"Who else in that house knows what's going on?" The anger was back in his voice.

"No one else. Just George. Please, Jon. Don't mention his name to anyone. He could be in danger."

"Danger? Imagine that. Are you the one that dragged him into this?"

"No. He was involved before I was. I was as shocked as you when I found out."

"Is George the one responsible for getting you involved?" Jonathan asked with steel in his tone.

"No."

"Then who's responsible for dragging a female into this? A mere child at that! I have a score to settle with him!"

Eliza drew herself up to her full height and raised a defiant chin. "I won't tell you! And in case you haven't noticed, I am not a child!" With that, she spun away from him and twisted her hair into a knot.

Jonathan put out a hand to stop her. "Eliza, please. Just listen to reason."

She shrugged him off and walked away while continuing to fix her hair.

"I could arrest you, you realize? And have you locked up just to protect you. To keep you from this foolishness."

She glared at him as she grabbed her hat and shoved it on her head.

Jonathan took two long steps and grabbed her shoulders, "Eliza, please listen." He paused and took a deep breath. "You don't understand, do you?"

Eliza cocked an eyebrow, waiting for him to explain himself.

"It's you, Eliza. I care about every person at Aunt

Mildred's, but it's you who keeps me going in this war. If anything happened to you," his voice cracked. "If anything happened to you, Eliza, I think I'd die!" He gave her a gentle shake and walked away. After standing with his back to her for several long minutes, he quietly said, "I'll get the horses ready." Then he threw his coat on and walked out.

Stunned by his words, she still managed to get dressed to leave. She pulled at the heavy door and walked out into the snowy night where she found Jonathan standing by the horses. He silently helped her into her saddle and handed her a pair of gloves. Mounting his horse, he announced, "I'll ride back with you. Once we get close to Springfield, you can lead the way to George."

Eliza started to protest but stopped as soon as Jonathan held up a hand for silence. He grabbed her reins and took off through the dark woods.

CHAPTER TWENTY

Eliza stretched and rolled over in her warm comfortable bed. She had slept through the entire morning and part of the afternoon. Sunlight was shining through her west-facing windows. The house was silent. Memories of last night and early morning reconstructed in her tired brain. True to his word, Jonathan had made her lead him to George who was faithfully waiting at the cave. After Jonathan pulled George aside for a very heated, private talk, he returned to Eliza and gravely ordered her again to stay home. "I want you to be there, Eliza, when I come back."

She rubbed her eyes and yawned. Jonathan's words at the cabin drifted back into her thoughts. What he had said could easily be taken wrong. Was she more to him than a beloved little sister? She pushed the thought aside and sat up. There was no one she cared about more than Jon. He said he'd die if anything happened to her. The emptiness would be unbearable if he was gone. But she had always thought it was a deep brotherly bond he had for her. Was there more? Is that what he'd tried to tell her? She shook her head and stood to dress so she could go downstairs and face Mildred, Sally, and possibly Jim. It was again time to construct a believable story for this household that must be getting very suspicious.

That evening, she snuck over to Elin's and took up the role of Gloria just in time to help serve at the evening meal. After sitting at the piano and playing several songs for the officers in the parlor, she again stepped out for a walk with Major Duncan in the cold evening air. When he put his arm around her, her thoughts immediately flew to Jonathan. Guilt gnawed at her conscience as she exchanged insincere words of endearment with this kind, gentle man she could no longer see as the enemy. If he knew what she was doing, he could have her arrested and possibly hanged. On the other hand, if Jonathan knew what she was doing at this moment, he, too, might want to string her up. The duplicity of it all caused almost unbearable guilt.

For the next few weeks, life continued on this same path. George told her in no uncertain words that because of Jonathan's discovery of them, they were to postpone as long as possible any more trips as couriers. "Jonathan ordered me to stop using you as a spy. He'd have my hide if he knew you were still in this thing." He shrugged and went on. "We can't stop, Liza. This is war. We have to do our part. For now, though, just listen for every scrap of information you can get. Commit to memory everything that could possibly be important. Write it down and hide it in your room at Mildred's. Don't leave anything behind at Elin's. We can't risk having one of those officers search your room if they become suspicious. It's too dangerous."

So, Eliza did as George instructed. She did all the work required of Gloria and listened carefully whenever she was near the officers. When she returned to Mildred's, she carefully translated the most important pieces of information into the Freemason cipher, wrote them on small scraps of paper, and hid them in her room. Nothing was ever written in English. Occasionally she'd sit at her desk and hastily work on her journal, copying sections from the books at her desk, writing about her pretend depression and small tidbits about the people in the Scott household, all a pretense just in case Sally or Mildred entered her room to clean or to change the bedding.

As the days passed and the officers staying at Elin's boardinghouse relaxed, Gloria found to her delight that the tongues of the men were finally loosened. And also, finally, there were many military activities for the men to talk about. It seemed as if Springfield had become one giant military camp. General Sterling Price was operating from his headquarters on Boonville Avenue and was furiously recruiting and training new soldiers. At one evening meal, Captain Lewis announced that Price had managed to recruit 3000 men and more were coming in every day.

Late one afternoon, Major Duncan showed up at Elin's with a horse and buggy and asked Gloria if she'd like to take a ride with him. As he drove through the streets she was amazed at the beehive of activity. Tents and crude huts were scattered throughout the vacant lots. Some of the regiments were marching on an area of open land they had converted into their parade grounds and, much as she hated to see their progress, she was very impressed with the unison of movement and the obvious discipline of the men. When she commented on the good behavior of the soldiers, Major Duncan told her there were strict rules for the troops encamped in Springfield.

"No swearing or drinking allowed. Even loud noise will not be tolerated. All lights have to be out by ten o'clock. There are two drills a day, morning and afternoon, which no one is allowed to miss." Major Duncan expressed great pride in the army he served.

He went on to tell her that General Price had gone as far as issuing a command that no officers or soldiers were allowed to harm the property of the citizens of Springfield. No fences or shrubbery or fruit trees or even ornamental trees were to be damaged. All foraging in and around the city was strictly outlawed by Price unless authorized by him.

Only the week before, a group of soldiers had showed up at Mildred's home and rudely demanded all the food in their larder. Mildred and Sally gathered a good amount of food and handed it over. The sergeant in charge then handed them a small handful of "Missouri scrip," worthless bills printed by the Missouri Confederate government based in Neosho under Governor Jackson. Thankfully, both of Mildred's hidden cellars were undiscovered.

As they were making their way back to Elin's, they heard sounds of cheering on the square. Major Duncan turned their buggy around and trotted to South Street then drove to the square. When they asked what the commotion was about, they were told a supply train from Arkansas had just arrived with a huge amount of provisions for the soldiers. The major quickly drove Gloria home so he could ride down to headquarters to help supervise the distribution of supplies.

When Eliza got back to her room at Mildred's house, she was chomping at the bit to get vital information to Thomas. She hastily wrote just what she'd learned that afternoon: the conditions of the Confederate soldiers in Springfield, where they were staying, and where most of their training was taking place. She also wrote about the rules concerning their daily behavior and the rules forbidding unauthorized foraging and pillaging in the county. Finally, she wrote about the supply train. Determined Frances would ride that very night, instead of hiding theses new messages, she tucked them into her bodice, along with the others she had written that month. She went to the greenhouse to find George. He wasn't there, so she started pacing in the backyard, hoping he'd see her. Finally, after twenty minutes or more, he came whistling around the corner of the house with a sack thrown over his shoulder.

"Well, hi there, Miz Liza. Are you wantin' to git yer hands dirty again? I got me some new plants."

"I'd love to! What do you have?"

They both entered through the greenhouse door and started digging in the far corner where he had room for more plants. He held his hand up for silence as soon as she started talking. With his head, he indicated the direction of the house. "Both Sally and Jim have been acting mighty suspicious. It's best we work for a while and actually get our hands dirty. Sally was watching you from the back window."

He pulled a few plants from his bag and raised his voice. "I dug these up from Abe's garden. Some roots that might still have some life in them. These here are beets and these are potatoes. We'll have to put a good amount of straw on top to keep 'em from freezing since they're way back here in this cold corner." He looked in all four directions and whispered, "What's up?"

Eliza spoke in very low tones as she continued to dig. "It's time. I have a lot. We can't wait."

"Tonight?"

"Yes."

"Let them see you wash up. Eat with us tonight. Then let them hear you go to your room. Leave from here while they're making noise cleaning up in the kitchen. I'll get word to Elin that Gloria needs an evening off."

Eliza did as told. She had a relaxing meal with the entire household, including Lucy and her children. After the meal, she acted exhausted and yawned several times while helping to clear the table. Mildred noticed and told her she wasn't needed.

"Dear girl, you're tired. We have more than enough hands to do this work. You go on up and get some sleep," she said kindly as she put an arm around her and escorted her toward the stairs.

Eliza entered her room, checked to make sure all the messages were still tucked safely in her bodice, opened the door, and made her way down the stairs and out the back door. She meandered through the backyard and checked to make sure Jim wasn't watching. She entered the greenhouse and walked between the rows of plants, thankful for General Price's orders for his soldiers to not bother the citizens' yards and gardens. Soon, she opened the rickety door and carefully walked through the yard toward the back corner. Certain no one was watching, she squeezed behind the bushes and through the gate. As always, Frances' clothes were waiting in Elin's shed and, as always, she could rely on George to be waiting at the end of the alley.

For the first time, they were stopped by soldiers before they left the city. Three men rode up and asked where they were going in such a hurry. Eliza remembered at that moment she had forgotten to pack some goodies for Frances' ma. Her heart started pounding as she tried to come up with a believable story.

They both started talking at once. Eliza backed off and let George take the lead. "I'm jes' driving Frances here back home to his ma. He's been visitin' his aunt Elin. She's sendin' some goodies back to her sister," he drawled as he held up a sack he'd placed at his feet.

"Let's see what kind of goodies you have there. Hand it over," one soldier barked.

George did as instructed. Eliza prayed that George had actually filled it with food. To her delight, the soldiers pulled out several small loaves of bread and about a dozen cookies.

"There's a lot in here," one soldier said as he looked squarely at Eliza. "You have a big family, boy?"

"Uh...yes, sir. But you can help yourself if you want. My ma wouldn't mind at all."

"Don't mind if I do. Here, boys. Have a cookie. And I

think we'll take one of these loaves," he said as he handed treats to the others. After tossing the sack to George, he asked, "Where's yer ma live, boy?"

"Just outside of Fair Grove," Frances answered, realizing that was the direction they needed to go to reach the cave.

"Be off with you, then. And watch out for them freebooters. They're everywhere, and I'll guarantee they'll take more than a few goodies. They're likely to take your life."

Thankfully, the December snow had melted enough that the roads were clear. George's mule trotted along the frozen ruts with little difficulty. After George saddled her horse, Eliza packed one loaf and a few cookies in the saddle bag and mounted.

"I'll be here when you get back, Liza. Be careful, girl," George said as he reached out and squeezed her hand.

Snow still covered large shaded areas in the woods. Once she got to the road, she was able to ease into a smooth canter. Knowing that Union forces were possibly still in the area gave her some comfort. But the thought of possibly seeing Jonathan again filled her with a confusing mix of emotions. Fear and dread dominated her thoughts. She was determined she'd avoid any such meeting, so she watched for any sign of movement around her.

Soon, the lights of the tavern appeared through the trees. Eliza eased quietly off her horse and tied him to a tree. She listened for Thomas, hoping he'd be hiding among the trees again. Nothing but an eerie silence. She cautiously pushed the door open, desperately hoping he'd be inside. Several men lined the crude bar, some with heads down. Soft snores rumbled. Apparently, no one had heard her, so she cleared her throat and asked in a low, husky voice, "Uh, is Thomas here?"

"Close the door, you eejit!" one man growled. "Yer lettin' the cold in!"

At that, one of the sleeping men raised his head and glared at Eliza. "'Zat you, Frances?" he slurred.

He slid off his stool and staggered toward her.

"I haven't seen you in a coon's age, boy. Thought you and yer ma had forgot about me."

"Well, I might forget about you, but Ma never would," Eliza replied as Thomas threw a heavy arm around her and guided her toward the door.

He continued to stagger, leaning heavily on her as he steered her toward their usual meeting spot in the woods. She was beginning to think that this time, he was actually drunk. But as soon as he stopped, he immediately dropped his arm and stood tall.

"Captain Monroe was right. You don't know how to follow orders, do you?"

Eliza glared at him.

"I heard him as plain as day order you to stop this spy business."

"I don't take orders from him!"

Taking her chin firmly in his hand, he said, "Well I do. And he told me I was to stop using you."

"I don't think that's your decision to make, Thomas. I've got valuable information, and I'm the only one in a position to carry it. In fact, I'm the only one in a position to gather it."

Thomas ran his fingers through his hair in frustration. "All right. Hand it over."

She turned around, dug several pieces of paper out of her bindings, and placed them in his outstretched hand. "The most important piece of information is that Price is recruiting and training thousands of new men. They have to be stopped!"

Thomas pocketed the scraps of paper. In a low voice, he said. "Take this information back with you, Frances. Listen carefully. The Union just created the Army of the Southwest, headed by General Curtis. His orders are to push Price out of Missouri. He has already gathered several thousand men at Rolla, and thousands more are on the way. Some have already advanced to Lebanon. In a matter of weeks, they'll march on Springfield."

Eliza almost squealed with excitement but quickly covered her mouth.

"Quit acting like such a girl, Frances," Thomas said with a small chuckle. "Now that you have this good news, do you think you can listen to your Captain Monroe and lay off the spying?"

"I'll do it as long as it's necessary."

He shook his head. "You're a fool, Frances." He patted his pocket. "The captain will probably have me court-martialed if he finds out I got this information from you."

"Don't tell him."

"If he asks, and he will, I have to tell the truth."

"Huh," she snorted. "This whole spy business is made up of lies. What's one more?"

He narrowed his eyes. "I only lie to the enemy. Not to my friends."

Eliza lowered her head in shame. "To do my job, I have to lie to my friends, too. My whole life has become a lie. I hate that part of it," she whispered.

To her great surprise, Thomas pulled her against him and held her in a gentle hug. "Hopefully, it will soon be over. Take care, girl. I'll see you back in Springfield at the end of next month, if not sooner. That's a promise." With that, he turned and disappeared into the dark woods.

Eliza stood there a while and tried to watch for him. Finally, she sighed and walked down through the trees to her horse. When she reached to untie the reins, she heard movement to her left. A branch snapped under the weight of someone's step, quickly followed by someone clearing his throat.

"Uh, Frances? Could I have a word with you?"

That voice! She knew that voice! With horror, she

swung up into the saddle and tried to turn the horse around. Hands grabbed the reins, and that familiar voice demanded she dismount immediately. Before she could obey, a man pulled her roughly to the ground and yanked her hat from her head.

"Frances, Frances, Frances... What a naughty boy you are. Or should I say girl?"

With a sickening feeling deep in her being, she looked up into the face of Henry Goodman!

Henry started pulling pins from her hair, releasing it into cascades of tangled curls.

"Stop, please!" she begged.

"Dear Eliza! What have you gotten yourself into?" He dragged her down the drive. She held on to the reins hoping to escape. "As soon as I heard your voice back there in the tavern, I thought it might be you. I knew you were up to some sneaky shenanigans when I heard you were gallivanting around Springfield today with a Confederate major."

When they stopped, she released her anger. "Henry Goodman! I demand that you release me! What has gotten into you? I'm surprised at you! And besides, who told you about me and the major?"

"A friend."

"You have Confederate friends?"

"This is Missouri, Eliza. We all have friends on both sides. You certainly do."

"What I do is none of your business!"

"Oh, be quiet, woman! We need to make this quick and get out of here. You and I never finished the conversation we started back in November. Remember? You were about to tell me where you hid Uncle Abe's gold."

"He made me promise to tell no one."

"He's dead, Eliza. I'm his heir. The gold is now mine, and I demand to know where you've hidden it."

"How do I know you're telling the truth?"

Henry dug his fingers deeply into the flesh of her arms. "If you refuse to tell me, dear girl, I will expose you for what you are. Those Confederate friends of mine will consider you quite a prize."

Eliza shuddered and stared into his leering face, unable to believe even Henry would stoop so low. She took a deep, calming breath and realized now was as necessary as any time to use her acting skills.

"I will tell you on two conditions. One, you take your filthy hands off me."

Henry smiled and let his hands drop to his side. "And two?" he asked.

"As soon as I tell you, you will allow me to mount my horse and ride back to Springfield. If you don't, I promise I will give you no end of trouble."

Henry nodded. "It's a deal."

"East of here on this road, there's a small cabin deep in the woods, surrounded by cedars. I was scared to death the day I found it. Everyone was running away from Springfield, and the road was crowded. I don't remember the exact location, but I'm sure I could find it again, and I'm sure the gold is safe. I turned right on a small road, probably the second or third from here. Then I rode about a mile and then went left into the woods quite a ways."

Henry growled his dissatisfaction. "Describe the cabin."

"It's small with a low roof and a lean-to shed on one side. There's a stone fireplace inside. It didn't look like anyone had been living there for a while."

"If it's the one I'm thinking of, some Union soldiers have been making good use of it lately. How do I know the gold's still there?"

"It's not there. It's in a hollow tree about a hundred feet straight back from the lean-to."

"All of it?"

"All seven bags."

Henry's eyes gleamed as he gave a low whistle. "Seven

bags, eh? That's a lot."

Eliza mounted. Henry reached out and grabbed the reins. "If you're lying to me, Liza, there will be hell to pay."

"I know. I'm not lying. See for yourself." She regained possession of the reins and galloped down the drive.

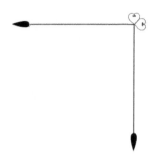

CHAPTER TWENTY-ONE

Eliza rode harder than she had ever ridden in her life. Henry Goodman frightened her. It went beyond the fear and distrust she had of the enemy. This was a fear of someone that was truly mad. The look in his eyes as he squeezed her arms was fueled by something deeply evil. She shuddered and dug her heels into the horse's side. When she pulled up to the cave, George rushed to her side, helped her down, and led both her and the horse into the cave.

"Shhh. Settle down. Both of you," he cooed to them. "What happened, Frances? I've never seen you like this."

Eliza backed up to the cave wall and slid down to a crouching position. She buried her face in her hands and cried.

George tore the saddle and blanket off the horse and started wiping the sweat off its heaving sides, all the time humming softly. He worked and waited.

Finally, Eliza vigorously rubbed her face and looked up at him. "I had an encounter with Henry Goodman."

George let out a low whistle. "And?"

"Well, apparently he also knows who I am and what I'm doing."

George's head snapped up. "Well, that sounds pretty serious. It's probably best we listen to Jon and not send you out there again."

"For the first time, I'm actually afraid to go out again. I think Henry might kill me next time."

George stopped wiping the horse's side and faced her. "Kill you? It's that bad?"

"He's trying to force me to reveal where I hid Abe's gold."

"Whoa! Slow down there, girl. What's this gold you're talking about?"

Eliza looked down and shook her head in frustration. After taking a deep breath, she went on. "I'm sorry. I forgot that you didn't know. I'm surprised you don't. You know everything, George."

George chuckled. "I try, but I've obviously missed something really big. Tell me about it."

"I'm sworn to secrecy, so you have to keep this to yourself. I trust you with my life, George. Way back in August, on the day we fled Springfield, Abe asked Jim and me to hide some gold. Now that Abe's dead, Henry insists the gold is his, and he's been after me to tell him where we hid it. He's so desperate, I'm beginning to suspect he's not in Abe's will and knows it. Why else would he be so sneaky and mean?"

"Makes sense. If he was the legal heir, he would just go through Abe's lawyer." George led the horse deeper into the cave to some hay and water. When he came back, he asked, "So, did you tell him where the gold is?"

"I gave him a false location. He believed me enough to let me go. Although he warned me, if I had lied to him, things would get bad for me." She groaned. "That's where I messed up, George. Messed up real bad. The place I named is not that far from the tavern. That's where he caught me.

By now, he's probably already found out there's no gold there. I should have made up some place way out in Rolla. It would be days, maybe weeks before he found out I lied to him."

"Well, in the meantime, you should be safe back in Springfield."

"No!" Her head shot up. "He has people in Springfield. Confederate friends. He said he'd expose me if I didn't cooperate. They know where I live, and they even know about me working at Elin's! Apparently, they've been watching me and Major Duncan."

"Shhh... It's all right, Liza. We'll work on a plan. I'll see to it that you're safe."

They got into the buggy and started for Springfield. "First of all, I want you to keep the Colt on you, loaded and ready. Then we'll discuss some good hiding places for you at Miz Scott's and at Miz Johnson's. We'll use the hidden cellars. We just need to pick the easiest and fastest ones for you to get to."

"Oh, George! I almost forgot. I have a report that's so good, you're going to cry!"

"Cry? You underestimate me, Liza."

In spite of her fear, she chuckled.

"Well? Out with it, girl."

"Thousands of Union forces are gathering in Rolla with orders to drive Gen. Price and all the Confederates out of Springfield within the next few weeks!"

George stopped his mule and stared, open-mouthed, at her. She just smiled and nodded. George grinned from ear to ear and took his hankie out to wipe his eyes.

Eliza slapped her leg and chortled "I knew it! I knew this would make you cry!"

"I ain't crying! I'm laughing inside! And that always brings tears of joy to my face!"

"Call it whatever you want, George. In my book, that's crying."

He laughed and slapped the reins over the mule's back. "Giddyap, there, girl! Let's get on home."

Realizing they might have very little time to prepare for Henry's revenge, George and Eliza started work immediately the following morning. George decided to have a meeting with the others in the Scott household and let them know part of the truth about Henry since they were all aware of his unwelcome visit to their house months before. George told them he had heard Henry was in the area and was making threats toward Eliza. "I'm not sure what he plans to do, but he can't be trusted. We need to come up with a plan to warn Eliza and get her hidden if he happens to show up," he explained.

Jim stood, wringing his hat in his hands. "He's a mean one, that young Goodman is! Nothing like his uncle Abe! We can't let him get his hands on our girl!"

"Why in heaven's name does he want to harm Eliza?" Mildred asked.

"I know!" Jim declared. "It has to do with a secret that Abe had. I'm not free to say more than that." He hung his head and continued to wring his poor hat.

"But why is Eliza involved?" Sally asked.

"She just is, Sally," George said as he rested a comforting hand on his wife's back. "Not by her choice though. It happened before she came to us. Abe involved her because Eliza's pa and Abe were very close, even had business dealings between them."

Understanding passed from his eyes to Jim's. Jim nodded.

"Have you told Eliza yet?" Sally asked.

"Yes. I thought it best to tell her first. As you can imagine, she's terrified, poor girl."

Mildred lifted concerned eyes toward the stairs. "That's

all that poor, grief-stricken girl needs. One more thing to drag her down."

"I told her last night. She cried and went back to her room. We may not see her for a while."

They went on to make plans to put strong locks on her door and to make an escape route to the cellar with the hidden entrance in the back shed. They devised signals to use as soon as Henry or any unidentified man approached the house. "Visitor at the gate," meant there was time to escort Eliza to the hidden cellar. "Visitor at the door," meant Eliza was to stay in her locked room, the whole house was to lock every door, and the men were to stand on either side of the house with shovels or hoes to use as weapons if necessary. Mildred planned to point a loaded shotgun at them through the window as she asked them to state their business.

As they made these plans to protect their helpless, grief-stricken Eliza, she was busy working as the fair Gloria LaRue, less than two blocks away. She and Elin sat in their room having tea together. Elin sipped hers slowly as she contemplated the story Eliza had just shared.

Eliza tapped her foot impatiently and said, "I'm afraid we don't have much time."

"Act in haste, repent at leisure, Eliza. Let's pray first," Elin said calmly as she set her teacup aside and bowed her head.

Eliza gaped in disbelief then reluctantly bowed her head.

"Heavenly Father, we need your wisdom. Please protect us all as we do Your work. Amen." She raised her head and smiled confidently at her charge. "First of all, am I to understand that this Mr. Goodman now knows you as Eliza, Gloria, and Frances? All three?"

"Yes," Eliza answered.

"Hmmm. That is surely cause for concern. And he's threatened to expose you?"

Eliza nodded.

"That means Gloria and everything we've constructed around Gloria must come to an end. In doing this, I will try to salvage what I can of this boardinghouse. As far as we know, he suspects only you. I'll do whatever I can to maintain my innocence so I can continue this work."

"I'm so sorry," Eliza said, "especially if this in any way endangers your life."

Elin shrugged nonchalantly. "It's one of the expected consequences of the kind of work we're doing. But it doesn't give us an excuse to be sloppy. Right now, we need to be more diligent than ever. We need to come up with a believable story for your absence, and we need to destroy anything on this property that might link your spy work to me. All of our Freemason notes, for example, and your clothes in the shed."

"Major Duncan knows I have no family. Maybe we should just say I disappeared without a trace and you are absolutely befuddled by it."

Elin stared out the window and thought for a moment. "Hmm... That might work, especially since we'll only have to pretend for a few weeks, if, in fact, our soldiers arrive, as you've heard, soon, and drive out these Confederates."

"You could even elicit the major's help in finding me. That should throw him and the others off."

So, that was the story they decided to go with. Eliza went back to Miss Scott's to hide in her room, and Elin effectively grieved the loss of Gloria, who had grown very precious to her as well as being indispensable in helping with the boardinghouse. She wrung her hands as she told the officers that night, "I'm afraid she's met with a terrible misfortune because she left her belongings here. I know Gloria. She wouldn't just leave. Can you help me find her,

Major?"

The officers were visibly shaken, but none more than Major Duncan. His military training enabled him to stand before them in a composed manner, but his eyes told another story. He stood rooted to the parlor floor, eyes wide. He swallowed several times before he spoke. "Men, spread out and start searching. Lewis, I'm putting you in charge of making sure every square inch of this city is covered. Go!"

After his men left, he turned to Elin. "Miss Johnson, may I have your permission to search your property for clues?"

Without hesitation, she answered, "Please! Do whatever you need to do," as she prayed that they hadn't left any incriminating evidence behind.

He searched and found nothing except one thing that caused Elin's heart to pound as she listened to his report. "You're right, Miss Johnson. It's obvious her departure wasn't planned, based on what she left behind. But I did discover one very disturbing piece of evidence that really frightens me."

Elin's hand went to her throat. "What is it, Major?"

"Your shed has been used quite a bit recently. Someone has been coming and going frequently from the alley behind your property, through the shed and into your backyard. Do you have an explanation for that?"

Elin let her fear drive her response. "No! You mean to say someone's been coming into my yard, unbeknownst to me?"

"It certainly appears that way. If it were only a path to the shed from your yard, I wouldn't be concerned. I'd assume it was just you or your help. But it's obvious someone's also been coming and going from the alley. The grass is trampled right to the back door of your shed. That makes me wonder what's been going on. You know of no one who would be using that route?"

"No one. This is frightening, Major. Do you suppose it could be soldiers sneaking around looking for food?"

"Possibly. I hope that's all it is. I'm afraid it might be more sinister than that, though, now that Gloria has disappeared."

Elin stared and waited for his explanation.

"You and I both know that Gloria is beautiful. She draws attention wherever she goes, especially from these men of ours who are starving for female company." At this, he ran his fingers through his hair and groaned. "I'm so sorry, Miss Johnson. I blame myself for this."

She reached out and laid her hand on his shoulder. "What do you, mean, Major?"

"I'm responsible for many, many soldiers in Springfield getting a glimpse of her beauty. All the walks and buggy rides we went on together got her out there in the public eye. I'm very aware of how a man's mind works, Miss Johnson. Especially during these terrible times when our men are deprived of the company of females. They're starving for a female presence. When they see a young woman like Miss LaRue, some of them go almost mad. You've seen the other officers under your very roof. Even those good men have difficulty conducting themselves like gentlemen." At this, he looked at her with desperation. "I don't mean to shock you, but this war has put me in contact with more than a few men that are far, far from being gentlemen in their conduct and certainly in their minds. They are lower than even I could ever have imagined. They would stop at nothing to get their hands on a woman like Gloria."

Elin's hand covered her mouth in horror. "You mean...?"

"I believe Gloria's been abducted. Taken by someone who has been spying on this house and waiting for the best opportunity to act. I know she liked to wander around in the backyard. They probably knew that and watched her, waiting for just the right moment to act."

Relieved and slightly amused, Elin stood behind the parlor drapes and watched Major Duncan leave on horseback to start his own search for the girl who had captured his heart. She prayed that the search wouldn't lead to Mildred Scott's house and, if it did, they would be adequately prepared.

In the meantime, Eliza stayed in her room, leaving only for meals. Even then, her presence in the dining room caused the others to be on edge. They were terrified they couldn't get her hidden fast enough if someone happened to show up for an unannounced visit.

January melted into February with no sight of Henry or his accomplices. The weather was unseasonably warm at first, but, as Missouri winters go, it soon turned brutal with noisy sleet beating down on buildings and trees and soldiers on both sides huddled in tents and around fires. George worked tirelessly to save the greenhouse plants. One evening he appeared at Eliza's door and knocked. Sally approached from the top of the stairs just as Eliza opened the door.

"What is it, George?" Sally asked, eyes as big as saucers.

George put his arm out and pulled her close. "Shh... Everything's gonna be fine, woman. I just need to move Eliza to a safer place for a while."

"Wh-what do you mean?" Eliza asked.

"Get your things. I'm taking you over to Frances' house." At this, George winked and nodded toward the sack with Frances' disguise. "Someone told me he saw Henry. We don't have time. I can sneak you out the back and down the alley."

Eliza quickly grabbed the sack filled with Frances'

clothes while Sally wrung her hands and fretted. "Where are you taking her? Wouldn't it be safer here? Who in the world is Frances?"

"Shhh... Quit worrying, Sally." George drew her into his arms and hugged her. "Frances lives close by, just down the alley. Henry wouldn't think of looking there for her. She'll be much safer. Tell the others after we leave. And be prepared for Henry to show up. If he breaks into the house, don't fight him. I don't want anyone getting hurt. I'll come back as soon as I can."

As soon as they reached the backyard, George whispered, "I'm so sorry to involve you again, but it's an emergency. Our men could be killed if someone doesn't warn them. You're the best and fastest choice we have right now." He ushered her into the greenhouse. "You've got to change into Frances fast, and I can't think of a safer place to do it. Thanks to your Major Duncan, soldiers everywhere know to report a female with blue eyes and curly dark hair, so we can't risk you being seen in the alley."

"But what if they're watching?" Eliza asked, nodding her head in the direction of the house.

"I can make up a story if I have to. At this point, they're the least of our worries. Hurry, Eliza! Lives are at stake."

Eliza quickly changed, pinned her hair up, pulled her hat tightly over her head, and rubbed dirt over her face. When she emerged, George led her to the makeshift gate that led to the alley and hastily filled her in on details. "Elin contacted me. She said the officers are packing up to leave. Apparently, they know Union forces are coming. General Price found out a week ago and couldn't get the reinforcements he asked for, so they're leaving Springfield as we speak."

Eliza's heart pounded with joy at this amazing news. "But, why do you need Frances?" she asked as they hurried down the alley to the waiting buggy.

George whispered, "Trust me. I'll fill you in on details

on the way to the cave."

As they drove through Springfield, she was amazed at the activity. It was as if someone had stirred up a hornet's nest. Everyone was much too occupied to even notice a boy and a slave making their way through the dark streets to the edge of town. When the houses thinned, George quietly explained to her why Frances was so desperately needed. "It goes against my better judgment to send you, but I don't know what else to do, Liza. I'm so sorry."

He paused when two soldiers rode toward them. She tensed in fear, but the soldiers apparently had more important things to tend to than two seemingly harmless travelers. They merely nodded a greeting and rode on past.

George exhaled, before he continued. "Most of the Confederate troops are making a mass exit from Springfield soon, but a detachment of soldiers is being sent either tonight or early morning to engage our forces east of here. Our men need to be warned, Eliza. Do you think Thomas will be at the tavern?"

"I never know. He usually is, but under these circumstances, I'm not sure."

"Give him the message if he's there. If he's not, keep riding toward Lebanon until you're stopped by our men. Give them the message and ask for their protection. Don't try to come back tonight. Find a secure place and stay hidden until it's safe to return."

Heart pounding with excitement and intense commitment to get the message out as soon as possible, the two arrived at the cave, readied the horse, and parted ways. "I'll wait here until midnight. If you're not here by then, I'll assume you're under the protection of our men. May God go with you, Liza."

Eliza took the familiar route, through the woods, down to the Wire Road, and left toward St. Louis. She rode hard, knowing how crucial this information was to the Union troops. If Henry appeared before she delivered her message, she was prepared to shoot him. Or so she tried to convince herself. Just before she came to the drive to the tavern, she decided to cut through the woods to see if she could find Thomas' horse where he always tied it. If his horse was there, it would be certain he was at the tavern and she could safely approach. Fear threatened to choke her as she got closer. Anybody could be out here, including Henry and his cronies. She dismounted and stealthily crept between the trees, ice-covered branches brushing noisily across her arms and legs. She heard a familiar soft whinny and slowly made out the shape of a horse tied to a tree about twenty feet ahead. With a huge sigh of relief, she realized it did, indeed, belong to Thomas. She tied her horse to the same tree and quietly made her way down the wooded slope to the tavern. Before she reached the door, a man exited the building and staggered down the drive past her. His gait was familiar, so she dared clear her throat and whisper, "Thomas? Is that you?"

The man yanked his whole body around and staggered back to her. Eliza pulled the Colt out of her pocket and took aim. "Stop or I'll shoot!"

He stopped instantly, but instead of raising his hands as she expected, he laughed. A wonderfully familiar laugh. "Put that thing away, Frances. I'm not gonna hurt you."

"Thomas?" she squeaked. "Oh, thank God it's you! I've got some..."

Thomas quickly wrapped his arm around her and interrupted her flow of excited words. "You've got some goodies from yer ma? Good! I've had a hankerin' for somethin' sweet." As he jabbered on, he guided her back into the woods toward the horses.

To her surprise, after they had walked several yards up through the trees, Thomas abruptly yanked her around to face him. He was livid. "What are you doing out here at a time like this? Don't you know what's about to happen? Couldn't it wait? And what's going on that caused you to blow your cover down there and blather like a scared little girl?"

Eliza straightened and shook free from his grasp. "I did not blather like a girl!"

"Yes, you did! And you still are, for that matter. What's got you all worked up, girl?"

"They're on the move! The Confederates are! They know you're coming. Price didn't get the reinforcements he asked for, so the whole lot of them are packing up to leave Springfield as we speak. But a detachment is on its way here to attack our forces. They should be here tonight or early tomorrow morning."

"What? How many?"

"I don't know. But I had to come! You had to be warned!"

"Tonight, you say?"

"Or early in the morning."

Thomas let out a low whistle then jumped into action. Eliza followed him to the horses. "Please, Thomas. Can you take me somewhere safe? For now? I don't want to ride back tonight and..."

"Meet the enemy on your way?" he finished for her. "Yes. By all means. Follow me." And off they went crashing through the trees farther up the hill then down into a ravine where they rode for about two miles. Thomas stopped then hooted like an owl. Soon, two men on horseback approached from the hill to the north.

"Frances, meet Frank and Larry. I believe you've all met before," Thomas said quickly. "Frank, come with me. Larry, escort Frances to the Rogers' farm this side of Lebanon. She is to hide in their cellar until one of us comes to get her." Turning to Eliza, he said, "Did you hear that? Stay there until we come for you. There's enough food and water for several days."

Eliza nodded. Thomas reached out and laid his hand on her shoulder. "You've been a great help to us, Frances.

Thank you."

"You're welcome. I'm so glad I can help."

He leaned down and got his face close to hers. "With that said, can I expect you to obey orders for a change? When I say stay in that cellar, I mean it. It's an order."

"I will. I promise."

"Let's ride!" Thomas motioned to Frank. "We don't have much time!" And with that, they disappeared down the ravine, into the dark woods.

Larry tipped his hat toward Eliza and said, "I'm really sorry about the last time we met, ma'am."

"Were you one of the two that tied my hands before you took me to Thomas?"

"Yes, ma'am." His head hung sheepishly. "I'm sorry. We didn't know."

"That's all right. You were just doing your job."

He turned his horse and led her back up the hill in the direction he'd just come from. They made a wide arc and headed back toward the Wire Road, a few miles northeast of the tavern.

"Are you from this area?" Eliza asked after they'd traveled down the road a mile.

"Yes, ma'am. I hail from Ozark," he answered in a soft drawl.

"Isn't that where Jonathan Monroe's from?"

"Captain Monroe? Yes. I used to help him on his farm."

"Oh really?" Eliza was surprised. "So, he's a captain now? That happened fast. He was a lieutenant back in August."

"The good men get promoted fast because we need them. And the captain's the best you'll find anywhere. I'd gladly take a bullet for him."

At that exact moment, Larry's body stiffened, a shot pierced the stillness of the night, and he slumped to the side. His horse bolted and ran. Before Eliza could react, she was surrounded by men on horseback, yanked from her saddle, and thrown roughly up against a tree. Momentarily she lost consciousness. She woke to the hard, frozen ground under her head and a heavy boot pressing down on her chest. She gasped for air and heard gruff voices in the dark.

"Did you get him?"

"Yeah, he's dead all right?"

"Well, she's gonna die, too, if you don't get yer dirty foot off her. She's awake. Get her up."

Several men grabbed her and pulled her to a standing position. She reeled and almost slipped from their grasp. One man wrapped his giant, beefy arms around her and threw her up against the tree again.

"Careful, Tex! Yer gonna kill her!"

"So? Isn't that what the boss wants?"

"Not yet, you idiot! He wants answers first. Then he said we can have a little fun with her before we string her up."

Eliza stared into the face of evil and, from deep within her bitterness and rage, she made a bold pitiful yet stupid move. She spat in his leering face. Not once but over and over again as long as she could work up enough saliva. The men froze. Then they laughed. Hilariously laughed. Eliza's fury grew. She yanked free from Tex's grasp and swung her arm at him. He grabbed it and shoved her against the tree with his body.

"She's gonna be fun! Let's get going before those troops get here." The apparent leader tossed a rope to Tex and he threw her to the ground, yanked her hands behind her, and tied her wrists tightly together. Piercing hot pain shot through her shoulder as he pulled her to her feet and tried to put her on his horse.

"She's riding with me. Your saddle can barely hold you, you big lummox."

"Aww, Pete. Come on. I want her."

"She's not yours, idiot! Help her up in front of me. There's room."

"She'll fight you," Tex said. "You can't handle her."

"Oh, you think so?"

Pete jumped down, pulled Eliza toward him, and slapped her face. "Do you like that?" He hit her again. "I've heard all about you, woman. Your lying, deceptive ways. Your sneaking around, getting information any way you can. You're nothing but a whoring spy destined for the gallows. I would never hit a woman. But in your case, I take great pleasure in it. If you so much as twitch a muscle when you're in the saddle with me, you'll get more of this." He struck her face with the backside of his hand. The force of the blow sent her head sharply back. She saw stars and felt blood pour out of her mouth.

"Well, who's killing her now?" Tex laughed.

"Shut up, Tex! Get on the horse, whore." He shoved her forward and roughly grabbed her foot and placed it in the stirrup. Several hands grabbed her and lifted her beaten body to the saddle. Pete immediately swung up behind her and wrapped one arm tightly around her waist. He then leaned over and whispered in her ear, "Let's see how much whoring you're willing to do to save your pretty little neck." Then he straightened with a husky laugh and hollered, "Let's ride, men!"

CHAPTER TWENTY-TWO

On February 12, 1862, about ten miles east of Springfield, a small detachment of Confederate forces attacked the approaching Union troops. After a brief skirmish, the Southern soldiers quickly retreated back to Springfield to join the mass Confederate exodus down the Cassville Road to Arkansas.

The next morning, Jon and his men watched as Union Brigadier General Samuel R. Curtis rode into Springfield with over 10,000 troops. They found the city vacated by the enemy. The streets were lined with citizens cheering the return of their army. To Jon's great delight, many Springfield families accompanied the soldiers as they finally dared to return to their beloved home after being gone since the Battle of Wilson's Creek in August. The army marched straight to the square and raised the Union flag over the courthouse.

Jonathan looked up in time to see the Scott household join the celebration. With loud cheers, they followed the crowd to the square where they tearfully witnessed the flag raising. He maneuvered his horse their direction, dismounted, and swept his aunt Mildred and Sally into a joyful embrace. When he stood his eyes darted around.

"Where's Eliza?"

George hung back as Sally tried to explain. "George had to take her to a safe location because that scoundrel Henry Goodman is after her."

Instantly Jonathan stood and pinned George with a piercing stare. "Take me to her!" he commanded.

The two dismissed themselves from the others and walked purposefully down South Street. When they reached Walnut, George turned and looked at Jon with grief etched in his old eyes. "You will probably want to kill me after you hear what I've got to tell you, Jon. And I don't blame you. I did what I did because this is war and I was desperate to save lives."

"Where is she?" His voice was edged with steel.

"I don't know, but I think she's safe."

"You think?" Jonathan's voice rose as he glared at George.

"She took another message to Thomas two nights ago. The message that Confederate troops were planning to attack you on the Wire Road as you approached the city. Did you get the message? If you did, that means she's safe."

"Yes, we got it. As usual, it came through Thomas, but I thought you'd be decent enough not to send her again, George. You've got a lot of explaining to do. But, for now, we've got to find her."

"I told her as soon as she delivered the message, she was to ask for protection. Is Thomas around? He should know where she is."

"I'll find him. He rode into town with my men and me."

As Jonathan turned to mount his horse, George reached a hand out and grabbed his arm. "If anything happens to her, Jon, I'll never forgive myself." He choked back a sob. "I'm so sorry. I blame no one but myself."

Jonathan mounted and looked down on the old man. "I blame us both, George. Pray hard."

The square was still filled with soldiers and celebrating citizens when Jonathan rode back. He quickly scanned the crowd for his men. Most of the local soldiers had been given permission to locate their families for long-awaited reunions, but, as far as Jonathan knew, Thomas Burns had no family in Springfield. After walking his horse around the perimeter of the square, he spotted Thomas talking and laughing with a group of women.

"Burns!" he barked.

Thomas mounted his horse and made his way through the crowd to follow Captain Jonathan Monroe a short distance down St. Louis Street. When they broke free from the mass of people, Jonathan turned his horse and pulled up next to Thomas. He didn't try to hide his anger.

"Why didn't you tell me it was Frances that delivered that message?"

"I'm sorry, but there was no time. I knew we had to act. She's in good hands, Captain. I sent her with Larry."

Jonathan scowled. "And where, exactly, did Larry take her?"

"To the Rogers' farm in Lebanon. I told her to stay in the cellar until we came to get her."

"And just when did you plan to get her?"

"Uh...now, sir. Right after we marched on Springfield."

"When were you going to give me this information?"

Thomas stared at his hands.

"Burns?" Jonathan growled.

Making eye contact, Thomas answered, "To be honest, sir, I was hoping I wouldn't ever have to tell you. My plan was to get her safely home before you found out."

Jonathan's eyes narrowed. "Are you keeping any other secrets from me?"

"No, sir. This is the first and last."

"Get Frank and a couple of others. Meet me here in five

minutes. We're all riding out to get her. And hurry!"

Two hours later, all five soldiers rode up to Rogers' farm. Thomas and Jonathan quickly dismounted and approached the entrance to the cellar.

"Shouldn't their horses be here?" Jonathan asked nervously.

"They're probably in the barn."

Jonathan pulled the heavy door open and descended the stone stairway. "Eliza? Are you here?"

The silence was deafening. Thomas lit a lamp and held it high. "Frances? Larry? It's safe. You can come out."

Both men called again and searched the small space frantically, hoping to see any sign of them. With a voice filled with dread, Thomas said, "Captain? None of the food's been touched."

The two men stared at each other in the lantern light, both momentarily paralyzed.

"Quickly! Let's spread out and search the grounds," Jonathan ordered.

After searching the house, the barn, two sheds, and the surrounding fields, the men gathered together again to strategize. Filled with a combination of anger and fear, Jonathan had a difficult time thinking clearly. Thomas suggested that they ride back to the place he last saw them, carefully checking every tree, bush, and rock on their way. So they wouldn't miss any clues, they fanned out but stayed within sight of the person on either side. They rode through thick brush and over rough ground for an hour before they saw anything. Frank was the first to see Larry's horse.

"Over here!" he hollered to the others. As they approached, Larry's horse gave a welcoming ninny and then dropped her head to a huddled figure on the ground. Frank dismounted and threw himself onto his friend with a wail. "Larry?"

Jonathan and Thomas joined him and gently rolled Larry over. Dried blood covered his face and chest. Thomas checked for a pulse. After a moment, he looked up with hope in his eyes. "He's alive!" he announced to Jon's amazement. "At least for now."

Jonathan leaned over and peered into Larry's unconscious face. "Larry? Can you hear me?" He shook him gently and Larry moaned. "Where's Eliza?"

"He doesn't know Eliza, sir. Only Frances," Thomas gently reminded him.

"Where's Frances, Larry?" Jonathan tried again. "Did someone take her?"

Larry's head lolled to the side.

"Is he gonna die?" Frank asked.

Jonathan sighed and stood to his feet. He rubbed his hands over his face and replied, "I hope not, Frank. We need to get him to a doctor as soon as possible. Frank, you and Joe, take him to my aunt's house at 420 East Walnut. Have my aunt Mildred get a doctor. The rest of us will continue to search these woods for clues. Then we'll go back to Springfield, get a good night's rest, and continue the search first thing tomorrow morning."

Eliza woke to darkness, pain, and bone-chilling cold. She lay still with her head on the frozen dirt floor for a long time, just listening and trying to make sense of her situation. Dim morning light filtered through cracks in the walls of a shack of some sort. Her head and shoulder throbbed. Blood trickled from her nose and filled her mouth. When she tried to sit, she realized her hands were still tied behind her back. With great effort, she managed to scoot herself a few feet until she bumped against something solid. Using her head and bound hands, she braced herself and pushed up into a sitting position and stared into the dimness.

Confusion and fear filled her. Scenes from the days before came to her in snatches: memories of slipping in and out of consciousness while being held in Pete's vise-like grip, being jerked from Pete's horse for a quick meal and a cold night under the stars, Tex and Pete fighting, both of them shoving and hitting her. It had seemed to take forever to reach the place she now found herself. She shivered violently, whether from cold or fear she wasn't certain. Today was likely her last. She remembered hearing repeatedly the plans to hang her once they arrived at their camp. After they'd had their fun with her, of course.

Were they done?

Was beating and terrorizing a young woman enough fun for those monsters? She desperately hoped it was. Was today the day they'd obey their boss and finish her off?

As much as she longed for her misery to be over, she was gripped with an undefinable fear. Not fear of dying but fear of what came next. She had denied God over and over again. Yet she couldn't deny His existence. Unexplainably, as she sat in the cold darkness, she knew beyond any shadow of doubt that He simply...was.

He seemed to have made that clear to her on her tortuous journey south. The words, "I AM," had flitted through her mind over and over again. She realized now that she'd never really doubted that He existed, that He filled everything, everywhere. She'd just allowed her anger at Him to grow into something that bordered on hatred. How could she face Him now?

She longed to die and slip into oblivion. To be completely gone forever. She heard a low sobbing groan and realized it had come from her. Hopeless tears streamed down her face.

Voices and movement interrupted her thoughts. Laughing men approached. She wanted to sink down and disappear into the dirt she sat on. The door creaked open. Pete and another man entered. The morning light had increased enough that she could see their leering faces. Pete carried a bundle of clothes.

"Good morning, princess," he said, followed by laughter from both men. He threw the bundle at her feet and leaned down to untie her hands. His breath reeked of alcohol. "We've talked and decided that maybe, just maybe, your life is worth sparing." He stood and kicked the clothes toward her. "Put these on and don't try anything funny, whore."

Eliza glanced down at what appeared to be a dress. She picked it up and spread it out enough that she could see it was very low cut. The other man shoved a wet rag in front of her face and gruffly ordered, "Clean up. You're a disgusting mess."

Eliza lifted one hand to her face and felt dried blood on her forehead and fresh blood oozing from a wound as well as blood still dripping from her nose. She could feel the grit of dirt everywhere. The men stood over her and watched hungrily. A new fear gripped her. She handed the dress and rag back. "I would never wear a dress like this."

Pete snorted. "I was wondering how far you'd be willing to go to save yer scrawny neck. Perhaps you're not understanding us, whore. It's this or the noose."

Eliza stared back at him and said defiantly, "The noose, please."

Pete swore loudly and kicked her in the ribs. Eliza tried to suppress a scream as she slumped to her side. Pete grabbed her hair and pulled her back to a sitting position. "Hand me that dang rag, Ben." He roughly scrubbed her bruised face with the cold rag.

Eliza squeezed her eyes shut and silently prayed the only prayer she could manage. "God, help!" It came from deep within her spirit, and she meant it with every fiber of her being "Forgive me! Oh God! Forgive me. Please, please forgive me!" Tears streamed down her face.

Pete slapped her. "Quit yer blubbering." Glancing up at Ben, he ordered, "Get that lantern over here. Let's see what we've got." Ben held the lantern close to her face. Pete let out a low, lusty whistle. "Whoa baby. She's a beauty." He grabbed her chin and forced her to look at him. "Listen to me, doll. You can save your life. It's your choice. You put that dress on and fix yourself up for us, then you live. If you don't do it on yer own, we'll strip you down and do it for you. And then, when we're done with you, we hang you." He pressed his lips to her ear and hissed, "If you cooperate, we might even make it pleasant for you. If you don't cooperate, I promise, it will be"—he paused for a moment and grinned—"torturous. And you don't want that, do you, hussy?" Standing, he glared down at her. "I'll give you the rest of the day to think it over. It ought to be an easy decision. Life or an agonizing death. Either way, you'll be in that dress by the end of tomorrow. You got that, whore?"

Eliza wiped her eyes and stared at him.

"She's not answering you, Pete," Ben chuckled.

"Shut up, Ben!" Pete roared as he bent and lifted Eliza by the hair to stand in front of him. "Maybe what you need is a sampling of what's to come." He pulled her into an embrace and forced a hard, unyielding kiss on her. "See? That's not so bad, is it? It's more of this, sweetheart. Willingly from you. Or it's a noose thrown over a branch of that tree out there. Of course, that'll be after we're done with you. Understand?"

Terrified and repulsed, Eliza nodded.

"Good. Ben's gonna bring you some food, and I'll see you after we get back. In that dress, I hope. This shouldn't be that hard for you. You've had a lot of experience in this occupation, I've heard."

"You're wrong," she managed to whisper.

He laughed and ran his fingers roughly through her

tangled hair. "I'll be thinking about you all day, doll. Don't disappoint me." He shoved the rag into her hand. "And get that bleeding to stop. It's disgusting."

CHAPTER TWENTY-THREE

Early on the morning of February 14, Captain Jonathan Monroe put together a search party made up of the best men he had: sharpshooters, scouts who knew every ridge and ravine of the rugged Ozark countryside, and men who could track a deer for miles. Twenty determined men rode down the Wire Road toward Lebanon before the sun glowed in the east. Thomas led them to the exact spot he had met Frank and Larry and transferred Eliza into Larry's care. From there, they rode toward the place they had found Larry the night before, combing the woods for every possible clue as they rode.

After half of a mile of slow riding, Matthias Jones, one of Jonathan's best scouts, held his hand up to stop the men closest to him. He pointed to the ground ahead. "Big disturbance in the leaves up there. We'd better dismount."

Thomas, riding next to him, made a circle motion with his hand and ordered the others, "Do a perimeter search." He and Matthias carefully and slowly entered the area straight ahead, taking one step at a time as they studied the ground and every rock, bush, and tree.

Jonathan stood on the outside, intently watching their every move. His head snapped to the right as someone shouted, "Found a bullet!" Quickly securing his horse to the closest branch, he made his way down the hill toward the commotion. Jeremiah Fox studied the angle of the bullet's entry before he pried it loose with his knife. He handed it over to Jonathan. "I suppose it's possible this is the one that wounded Larry, but there's no way to know for certain."

Jonathan studied it for a moment. "It's from a Colt revolver," he said. "So, I'd say it's safe to assume it's not from a hunter." He pointed in the direction the bullet had come from. "Look for blood," he ordered. Jeremiah and another tracker obeyed.

"Frank, where are you?" Jonathan hollered.

"Here, Captain!" came Frank's voice from up the hill near the central search area. The two men made their way through the trees toward each other.

"Yes, sir. What do you need?" Frank asked.

"I want you to get two of the best trackers and continue out to where we found Larry. He was bleeding pretty heavily. Try to track it to the source then get back to me."

"Yes, sir!" He saluted and left to gather up his horse and two men to go with him.

When Jonathan returned to Thomas and Matthias, he saw Thomas holding a slip of paper. "What do you have there, Lieutenant?"

Thomas motioned for Jonathan to enter the center of the search area. "I figured Frances, er, Eliza, would be smart enough to leave a clue if she was able to." He held up the paper. "She was here, Captain. She was most definitely here."

Jonathan took the paper and unfolded it, revealing a code that was pure gibberish to him. His eyes locked with Thomas'. "Do you think she intentionally dropped this? Or was she searched, and this is what they found on her?"

"I'm certain she dropped it. If they found this, they would have kept it, as evidence against her or possibly even to decipher the message if possible."

Jonathan nodded and looked at the paper again. "And you're sure this was hers?"

"One hundred percent positive. It's the message she delivered to me."

"What else can you tell me?"

"Well, as you can see, the ground is covered with tracks: horses and people. We're guessing anywhere from ten to twenty people. Apparently, they were here for a while. Not for the night though. Just long enough to take care of whatever ugly business they were up to."

"Any blood?"

"We couldn't find any on the ground, but we did find some on that tree over there."

"On a tree?" Jonathan asked as he walked over to investigate. Matthias was standing next to it and pointed to the blood spot about five feet from the ground. "What do you think happened?"

"Captain," Thomas spoke from behind him. "We also found this tangled in the bark next to the blood." He held out several strands of dark wavy hair.

Jonathan reached out and took the hair in his hand. "It's hers. No doubt in my mind." He lifted his eyes to Thomas. "Not only does this mean they have her, but they slammed her up against that tree. They mean her harm, Burns. And they've had her for days! Who knows what else they've done? We've got to get to them as fast as possible. Which direction did they ride out?"

Thomas motioned for a soldier to come in close. "What did you find, Sergeant?"

"They rode out on the same path they rode in on. But we'll be able to track them with no problem. It goes southwest of here then veers more to the south. Another lone rider took off at a gallop to the northeast. We think that was probably Larry."

"I sent Frank and a couple of others that direction. Ride out to get them and return here as quickly as possible. We'll mount up and leave as soon as they arrive."

Eliza lay face down in the dirt, fist pressed against her mouth and tears streaming from her eyes. Every sound caused her to jump with terror. Her simple, heartfelt prayer continued between sobs, "God, forgive me. What a fool I've been. Forgive me and deliver me from this evil."

Her weeping gradually shifted from hurt and fear to a deep, deep sorrow of her heart. "Forgive me and take me home. Please, please, Jesus," she begged, "take me home." After what seemed like hours, she drifted into a fitful sleep then woke suddenly with a gasp.

Someone had entered the room. She was certain of it. Heart pounding, she painfully pushed her bruised body into a sitting position and turned her head, frantically searching the room for whoever had come in. Blackness filled every corner. She heard thunder and saw an occasional flash of lightning through the slats. "Jesus?" she uttered, barely above a whisper. Nothing.

Eliza sighed and dropped her head into her hands. Her fatigue was bone-deep. Pressing the heels of her hands into her eyes, she slumped forward and longed to sleep for eternity. Her head nodded forward as her broken body surrendered to sleep. She was vaguely aware of the wind whistling through the cracks. Thunder rumbled in the distance.

Suddenly, Eliza felt light and warmth enter the room. She lifted her head and opened her eyes. Nothing but the same darkness and bone-chilling cold surrounded her. Yet something was, without a doubt, different. The light and warmth continued. She couldn't see it, but somehow knew it was there. All around her. And in her. The very air seemed to sparkle with it. Then, unexplainably, deep within her spirit, something stirred. In awe, she slowly sat up straight and simply basked in the stirring. The knowing. Supernaturally knowing, beyond reason, that Jesus Christ was *present*!

None of her five senses were engaged, yet what she sensed inside was stronger than anything she had ever experienced in her life. He was in her and all around her. His love filled her very soul. His joy overcame her despondency. His power conquered her fears.

And His thoughts filled her thoughts. "You are forgiven. You are Mine, now and for eternity. I have called you by name. My daughter. Don't be afraid. I will not leave you."

Pete and his men rode north, intending to bushwhack any unsuspecting Union soldiers or sympathizers in retribution for taking control of Springfield. Their blood lust was powerful. Being the undisciplined gang that they were, though, the liquor flowed freely, the talk got louder, and the men became careless. As they approached a farmhouse in Christian County, the men started firing through the windows before they saw anyone. Before they knew it, rifles were firing at them from both the house and the barn. Two of their men went down. Pete was enraged. He ordered them to take up positions behind fences, rocks, or anything big enough to provide cover. Then he goaded them on, foot by foot, to advance on the poor farming family, never easing up on the gunfire.

Half a mile north of there, Jonathan heard the shots and held up his hand to halt his men. Thomas rode up next to him and asked, "Should we engage? It could mean hours more before we get back on this trail again."

"Let's at least investigate. It's our duty. And who knows? This might lead us to Eliza."

They rode off the trail and up a hill between them and the battle. Just before cresting the peak, they stopped. Jonathan, Thomas, and Matthias left their horses and crept forward. It didn't take long to assess the situation. Thomas held binoculars to his eyes.

"Well, I recognize at least two of those scoundrels. Pete Crawford and his sidekick. They spend considerable time gettin' soused at the tavern. I've heard enough talk from them to know he leads a group of Confederate bushwhackers. Up to mischief all the time."

"Could they be the ones who took Eliza?" Jonathan asked.

"Very possibly. They operate out of Taney County, but those two have been seen in Greene and Webster Counties a lot."

"Do you think we have enough long-range rifles to do the job from here?" Matthias asked.

"We have enough to at least start the job from here. I'd guess there's about twenty firing on those buildings. I want you two to get Fox, York, and Dawes to join you up here. You're our best marksmen. I'll divide the rest and go there and there." Jonathan indicated areas thick with rocks and brush on either side. "When I signal, start picking them off. Shoot to kill. They're our enemy. If they leave cover and run at you, we'll start firing. If they run away, we follow. I want prisoners who will talk. Got it?"

"Yes, sir! Pete's mine!" Thomas said over his shoulder as he and Jonathan made their way down to their men. In very little time, all of Jonathan's men were in place and he gave the signal. Immediately shots were fired and five men went down, including Pete. Pete's men fired back. Several ran for their horses, mounted, and galloped off. About seven were trying to find cover from bullets that were coming from every direction. Four of them stood to surrender with rifles held high above their heads, begging for the gunfire to cease. One man hidden behind a rock was shot before the other two also surrendered.

"Throw your rifles down, put your hands high, and walk out to the well," Jonathan hollered. "Cease fire!" he bellowed when a gunshot came from the house. "We mean you no harm!"

Jonathan and several of his men cautiously approached their prisoners. He had them searched for hidden weapons then lined them up and studied their faces. "Were you in the party that abducted a young woman about three days ago just north of here?" he asked. He had his answer as soon as he saw their downturned eyes and shifting feet. He continued to study them before he decided how to divide them.

Looking up, he saw an elderly man and young boy approaching from the house, rifles aimed loosely in his direction. In turn, his men had their guns trained on the man and boy. Jonathan held up a hand in greeting. "Hello. Captain Monroe of Company B of the Missouri Volunteer Cavalry, and my men. Are any of you hurt?"

Both man and boy lowered their rifles and approached with big smiles. "No! Thanks to you getting' here in the nick of time! There's three scared females in the house, and they're fine, too. What can we do to help?"

"Could you house some prisoners for a day or two? If they give you any trouble, you have my permission to execute on the spot!" He made sure all six prisoners heard him.

"Well, sure! We'd be happy to. You can put 'em in the barn. Hopefully in chains. I don't want the likes of these varmints getting' loose and goin' after my family."

"If you find chains for me, I'll gladly use them," Jonathan answered. He then selected two of the captives and told his men to bind their hands behind them and find their horses. He directed the others to a room in the barn where they were bound hand and foot. The horses were rounded up and put in the corral. "I'd let you keep these horses, except our army needs them. After this fool war is done, I'll see what I can do to send a couple back to you in gratitude for your help."

Jonathan and Thomas then took the two carefully selected prisoners aside and began interrogating them. Both of them looked at each other and refused to talk. Jonathan pulled his revolver out and held it to the head of the closest man. "I'm sick of talking! I've killed one man already today, and I'd be more than happy to get that number up to three! You give us the information we want, right now, or you die!"

"I'll talk. Don't shoot!"

"Jake," his companion growled in warning.

Immediately Jonathan's gun shifted to point at the speaker. "Take him behind the barn and shoot him!" he barked at Thomas.

"Yes, sir!" Thomas quickly obeyed, knowing it was a ruse.

Jonathan pointed his gun at the remaining man. "You talking?"

"Uh...y-yes, sir! W-we did capture a female spy up north of here," he stammered.

"Where is she now?"

"At our camp, just outside of Forsyth."

"Is she all right?"

Jonathan's heart sank when he saw the shame on the man's face.

"What did you do to her?" he asked through clenched teeth.

"N-nothin' We didn't do nothin'. It was Pete and the others."

Jonathan grabbed him and slammed him against a tree.

"What? What did they do?"

"Shoved her around and roughed her up a bit. That's all. She's alive though. Honest!"

"How many men are at your camp now?"

"Just two or three," he stuttered, "plus those that rode off just now."

"You're going to get on your horse and lead us straight to your camp, you understand?"

"Y-yes, sir."

"Any funny business, and you'll get a bullet through your head. If we get Miss Long out of there safely, you get to go home."

"Mount up, men!" Jonathan hollered. "If we ride fast, we can catch up to the ones that ran. I'm guessing they're heading straight back to their camp. I want to engage them in battle before they get there. Otherwise, we'll risk shooting Eliza."

His well-trained men were on their horses and riding hard in less than five minutes. After an hour of relentless pursuit, they spotted their prey, drew their rifles, and started shooting. About half of the surprised bushwhackers went down and the others scattered into the woods and took up firing position behind rocks. Captain Monroe's men had time to do the same. But there were twenty disciplined marksmen versus four frightened backwoodsmen. After the first one was picked off, the other three surrendered. They were quickly bound hand and foot and tied to trees, with the threatening promise they'd be taken care of later.

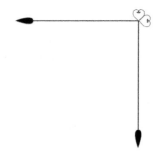

CHAPTER TWENTY-FOUR

Eliza woke with a jolt to the sounds of gunfire and screams of pain. She sat up and wrapped her arms protectively around herself, waiting for the worst, shaking with fear. Her time had come. She heard men hollering from every direction, angry and demanding. She strained to listen but couldn't make out the words. Hope stirred when she realized these were different voices. She dreaded the sound of Pete, and he was usually the loudest when there was any hollering going on. But his voice was strangely absent.

The gunfire ceased.

She crawled over to the door and weakly and painfully managed to stand. It was evening and too dark for her to see anything.

Then, like a shout from heaven, she heard a very familiar, very welcome sound. Jonathan! "Where is she?" he growled loudly from a campfire about fifty feet away.

"Here I am!" Eliza croaked barely above a whisper. She tried again. "Here, Jonathan!" but sobs broke up her cry. Slumping to the floor in weakness and desperation, she stuttered through tears, "I'm here, please come!" With that, she blacked out.

Jonathan held a revolver to the head of a scrawny, filthy teenage boy as the lad pointed then led him to what appeared to be a run-down chicken coop. "Sh..she's in there," he said and pointed. The door had an old rusty padlock on the outside.

Jonathan quickly handed the boy off to Thomas and cried out, "Eliza? Eliza, are you in there?" Silence. He pressed his eye to a crack and tried to see but couldn't. Turning to the boy, he asked, "Do you have the key?"

"N...no, sir. Pete always kept the key with him, and he's not back yet."

A menacing growl formed deep within Jonathan's gut. "Eliza!" he hollered loudly. He pressed his ear to the crack. Total silence. He picked up a rock and smashed it against the lock several times before it broke then tore it from its place and almost ripped the door from its hinges in his haste. What he saw lying in a heap just inside the door broke his heart. Quickly, he dropped to his knees and gently wrapped his arms around his broken girl.

Thomas, in the meantime, checked for a pulse. "Captain, she's alive!"

Jonathan's tear-streaked face lifted to Thomas. Then he gazed at Eliza and very tenderly took her face in his hands. "Eliza? Eliza! Are you there? It's me, Jonathan. I'm here."

Eliza stirred, and a weak moan escaped her swollen lips.

"Wake up, girl. We're here to take you home. Would you like that?"

In the light of a lantern that Thomas now held over her, Jonathan could barely make out a tiny smile and a nod. He also saw, to his great horror, the rest of her beaten, bloodied face. Both eyes were black, one swollen shut. Her grotesquely swollen lips had numerous cuts. Dried blood covered most of her face, and fresh blood oozed from a gash on her forehead. He cradled her; her hair was matted with blood, and the wetness of fresh blood still dripped from a wound on the back of her head. He briefly rested his forehead against hers. "Oh, Eliza," he groaned in agony.

Looking up, he composed himself and returned to command mode. "She's lost a lot of blood. We need to assess her wounds and get her to Springfield as quickly as possible! She needs a doctor!" He motioned for Thomas to come closer with the lantern and told the others to leave. Gently he rolled her onto her back. She groaned. He ran his fingers over her arms and legs, checking for open wounds and broken bones. When he squeezed her left arm, she gasped in pain and opened her eyes.

"Jonathan, you came," she said, barely above a whisper.

He reached down and cupped her cheek in his calloused hand. "I'm here to take you home. You're safe now, Eliza." His voice choked as she turned her face into his hand, weeping with relief.

"I'm sorry, Eliza, but we're going to have to move you. Can you tell me where you hurt?"

She nodded and answered, "Everywhere. It doesn't matter. Just get me out of here."

"We don't want to do any more damage. Your arm might be broken. Possibly other broken bones we need to splint before we move you. Where do you feel the most pain?"

"My arm, my shoulder, my head, and...and my side." She pointed as she spoke, using her right hand. Her left arm seemed to be useless Jonathan noticed.

Thomas went to the door and told his men to cut branches for splints. He said to Jonathan, "We may have to put together a travois to move her. I don't think she'll be strong enough to stay in a saddle. And I'm afraid riding with one of us will be too painful."

"I'm afraid you're right. Check around for wagons,

first."

Thomas left Jonathan alone with Eliza so he and his men could search the enemy camp for a wagon. They found an old one that had several rotting boards but decided with a few quick repairs, it would be better than dragging Eliza on a travois. Either way, it would be a rough trip for her, possibly excruciating. But it had to be done. All of the men had months of experience watching their comrades suffer, but none of them felt prepared to watch a female suffer.

Jonathan and Thomas gently wrapped Eliza's head to slow the bleeding then went about the uncertain job of splinting possible broken bones. It was obvious Eliza was in pain, but her relief at being in the hands of friends instead of the enemy caused her to endure the pain in happy silence. Soon, they had her loaded in the wagon with as many filthy blankets as the men could gather, wrapped around her to protect her from the cold and the jostling of the wagon as it made its way over the rocky terrain back to Springfield.

As much as he dreaded having his aunt Mildred and her household go through the shock of seeing Eliza in her battered, bloody condition, Jonathan couldn't think of a better place to take her. When they arrived, he ran up the porch steps and into the house, calling for them. Mildred, Sally, and George rushed from the kitchen, all asking questions at once. Jonathan silenced them with his hand.

"We found her, but she'll need a doctor. George? Can you run and get Dr. Jameson? Tell him it's an emergency. Mildred and Sally, Eliza needs a female to wash her. She's..." He choked. "She's covered in blood. And I'm pretty sure she has several broken bones. You'll have to be gentle."

Sally's hands flew to her mouth. "Lands, Jonathan!

What's our girl been through?"

Mildred dropped heavily into the nearest chair to compose herself. Jonathan excused himself to go help transport Eliza into the house and up the stairs to her room. He, with the help of Thomas and the two women, carefully removed the blankets. Eliza woke enough to notice her surroundings and smile. Then she drifted back into oblivion.

The two men excused themselves so the women could undress and bathe Eliza's filthy, bloody body. While they worked, Jonathan boiled water in the kitchen then hauled it up to the hallway and knocked. Sally appeared at the door with tears streaming down her face.

"Is she awake?" Jon asked.

"She woke once. Jonathan? What's the meaning of all this? Who would do such a thing?"

"We can talk about it later. For now, we just need to help her pull through. Do you need more rags to wash her?"

"Yes, please. Lots more."

Mildred covered Eliza and motioned for Jonathan to carry the bucket in. He set it down and leaned over the bed. "Eliza? Can you hear me?"

Her blue eyes opened just inches from his face. She smiled and answered with a weak, "Uh-huh." Alarm replaced her smile when she saw Mildred and Sally. "I'm so sorry. This is all my fault. I...I didn't mean to ever bring this to your house."

"Hush, dear girl!" Aunt Mildred said as she gently wiped dried blood from Eliza's face. "How could this possibly be your fault?"

"Oh, but it is!" By now Eliza was sobbing. "You weren't ever supposed to find out."

Jonathan leaned over her, his nose inches from hers. "Hush. Don't talk about it anymore, Eliza."

"They don't need to know?"

"Don't need to know? Just what are you talking about,

nephew?" Mildred asked pointedly as she stroked Eliza's hair.

Jonathan rose to his full height and looked down at the three women, his eyes narrowing. "This is war. Eliza's been attacked by the enemy. At this point in time, that's all you need to know." His stern countenance kept them both from further protest. "Just help Eliza heal then protect her. That's what I'm asking of you for now." He turned abruptly to leave, trying to hide his unwelcome tears.

Over the next several weeks, Eliza slowly healed. Doctor Jamison made daily visits at first then weekly. His diagnosis on his first visit was shocking to her and to the two women who stood sentry next to her bed. "Several ribs and her left arm are broken. Her left shoulder has been dislocated. Numerous cuts and bruises over her entire body, loss of blood, and possible internal injuries."

Mildred dropped abruptly into the nearest chair at hearing the news, fanning herself in an attempt to regain her composure. Eliza reached over to touch her arm while she whispered, "I'm so sorry, Aunt Mildred."

Mildred patted her hand. "I don't want to hear another apology from you, dear girl. When you pull through this, then you can explain everything if you feel the need to. I love you and trust you, and there's nothing you can say to me that will change that."

Eliza smiled and nodded. For the next few days and weeks, Mildred put action to her words, to the point Eliza finally relaxed and allowed this dear lady to truly mother her. Two weeks after her rescue, she opened up and gave Mildred a brief account of her spy work without naming names. She told about her spiritual condition since her father's death and how she had finally surrendered to Christ while in captivity. Mildred was fascinated and overjoyed.

The two of them spent long hours talking about what it meant to be a redeemed child of God, poring over scripture together with Eliza discovering that she had stepped through a door into a bigger more exciting adventure than anything she had ever experienced.

Ephesians 2:4-10 thrilled her to the core of her being.

"But God, who is rich in mercy, for his great love wherewith he loved us, even when we were dead in sins, hath quickened us together with Christ, (by grace ye are saved;) and hath raised us up together and made us sit together in heavenly places in Christ Jesus: that in the ages to come he might shew the exceeding riches of his grace in his kindness toward us through Christ Jesus. For by grace are ye saved through faith; and this not of yourselves: it is the gift of God: not of works, lest any man should boast. For we are his workmanship, created in Christ Jesus unto good works, which God hath before ordained that we should walk in them."

Eliza truly felt as if God had reached down and grabbed a corpse when He delivered her. Then He raised her up and pulled her close so she could, from that moment on, literally sit with Him in a heavenly place. The sense of His presence and love had not left her. She basked in it every day. Reading the words that God planned to continue to show her "the exceeding riches of his grace in his kindness toward" her, filled her with an indescribable joy. The realization that she was God's "workmanship, created in Christ" to do good works, that God had already ordained for her, caused her to start each day with excited anticipation.

Elin Johnson dropped in for a visit one day, introducing herself to Mildred as a neighbor who had heard of Eliza's kidnapping. "I met Eliza once when she was out taking a walk," she lied. "I took an instant liking to her and thought maybe I should do the neighborly thing and drop in for a visit." Her genuine kindness was evident in her voice, so she was welcomed in and ushered to Eliza's room where the two of them had a wonderful reunion. They decided Elin would come back often, but Eliza should avoid going to Elin's house since Mrs. Boyd, the cook, and Charles, Elin's slave, still knew nothing of the spy ring.

"If the Federal troops stay here, we may never need to resume our activities," Elin said. "But it's war, and we should be prepared for anything." Elin continued to visit and soon, she, Mildred, and Eliza were having regular Bible studies together.

At first, Jonathan stopped by daily to check on her, usually with Thomas in tow. He told her that their duties would most likely take them away from Springfield for days and sometimes weeks at a time. He explained that his entire company of 105 men had joined the newly formed Missouri State Militia. They and two other companies, composed of mostly Greene County men, had formed a new regiment under Colonel John Richardson. The primary purpose of the Missouri State Militia was to maintain order in the state and to protect its borders from further Rebel invasion.

Thomas filled her in on the activities of the Federal forces stationed in Springfield. Eliza delighted in every scrap of news she could get. Apparently, the soldiers spent the first few weeks cleaning the city up. Streets were littered with fallen tree limbs, trash, and animal droppings. Abandoned houses and businesses were cleared of debris, raccoons, possums, and all manner of vermin that had taken up residence.

Elin was also full of news about the rapid changes taking place. Soon, businesses that had shut down reopened, and new businesses moved into vacated buildings. The post office reopened, and mail started running again. By the beginning of March, the Presbyterian Church opened its doors for services, a telegraph line was completed connecting Springfield to Saint Louis, a new newspaper began publication, and a steam mill opened, providing the farmers in the surrounding areas with US currency for their wheat and corn.

On March 10, Elin rushed in full of excitement. "Have you heard?" she asked the group of people gathered at the table. "We've won the battle at Pea Ridge, Arkansas."

George and Jim whooped, jumped to their feet, and a did jig. The women watched and cheered. "The whole city of Springfield is celebrating!" Elin continued. "People are ecstatic. I predict by tomorrow there will be a huge celebration."

She was right. People from all over gathered on the square. Bands played. Speeches were delivered.

Soon, Eliza heard word that the wounded were arriving. "Where will they put everyone?" she asked, remembering the nightmare of too many wounded crammed together in one place.

"I'm not sure," Elin answered. "I've heard they're opening a new military hospital for Union soldiers in northeast Springfield. The courthouse, a church, and a few homes are already full with the wounded that General Price left behind. There are several hundred of them."

George and Jim walked in one morning shaking their heads. "It's a sad sight, watchin' all them wounded men bein' carted down the streets," George said, wiping his hand across his sweaty brow. Sally moved to his side and put an arm around him. "Let's just pray this will end soon."

"In spite of what we're seein' out there, it sure does seem that most folks truly believe our city won't be abandoned again," George reassured his wife.

Soon, Mildred's household watched with great pleasure as the city established itself as a major storehouse and supplier of goods for the Army of the Southwest.

Businesses, farms, and families thrived again with the confidence they would be under the continued protection of Union forces.

In May, Jonathan dropped by to announce that General Egbert Brown was appointed commander of the Southwest Division of the Missouri State Militia. Jonathan set his hat on the hall table, ran his fingers through his hair, and winked at Eliza. "He's setting up his headquarters in Springfield. My Company will be under Brown's control." His eyes twinkled. "And guess what? We'll also be stationed in Springfield."

Eliza jumped out of her chair at that news. "For how long?"

Jon's smile warmed her. "Not sure, but I'm thinking it will be for quite a while. We've set up our encampment on the south side of the city. That's only a ten-minute ride from here."

Eliza instinctively grabbed his hand and held it to her cheek. "I'm so happy to hear this. Now maybe you can drop by here a little more often than once a month."

By then, Eliza was almost restored to full health and able to help Mildred and Sally with their growing household, which she did with joy, seeing it as work that God had ordained for her, as she had read numerous times in the book of Ephesians, *"For we are His workmanship, created in Christ Jesus unto good works, which God hath before ordained that we should walk in them."*

In addition to Lucy and her two children, two more former slave women, Jessica and Sarah, and their eight children had recently moved into one of the spare bedrooms upstairs. One day in mid-May, Eliza walked into their room with tea and crackers. She had met them downstairs the previous Sunday when Aunt Mildred held an impromptu Sunday service with her new charges. The children immediately retreated to a far corner, and both women stood ashamedly to their feet, taking the tray from Eliza's hands and bowing their heads. Eliza gently asked a few questions, trying to engage them in conversation, but the fear and distrust were such a barrier, she got nothing more than names and a few shy nods. Eliza was deeply moved by their shyness and fear. It was difficult for any of the newcomers to make eye contact, particularly with her and Mildred. When Jonathan or Thomas visited, the women cowered in their rooms until the men left.

After her first attempt to visit their room, Eliza was aware of their crowded conditions: two women and eight children in one bedroom. She returned to the kitchen, praying all the way. Later when Mildred walked in, Eliza asked if they could have a little meeting to discuss the needs of their houseguests. They compared notes and suspected that these precious ladies and their children had suffered unspeakable abuse and that they needed to be very gently dealt with. Eliza suggested she move into Mildred's room so one of the families could have her room. Mildred's eyes crinkled with pleasure. "Only if you're sure, dear."

"Aunt Mildred, I can honestly say, it would delight me," Eliza answered as she reached out to take the older lady's hand. So, they did just that. As they helped Jessica, the younger of the two former slave women, move her meager belongings and her three small children into her new room, neither Mildred nor Eliza let her know it had recently been vacated by Eliza. Sally soon put the two women to work, knowing it was the only way to help them regain a sense of belonging. While they worked, Eliza and Mildred took turns visiting the children: reading to them, encouraging them to play in the yard. It wasn't long before the youngest would eagerly crawl into their laps as they sat to read. Soon, the older children trusted them as well.

In the afternoons, Mildred and Eliza started visiting the makeshift hospitals, taking food and ministering to the sick and wounded, both Confederate and Union soldiers. When a wounded Confederate officer thought he recognized Eliza, she smiled, told him he was mistaken, excused herself, and never went back. After a while, she realized she needed to limit her visits to only the Union hospital.

By early summer, reports were reaching Springfield of the dangers of traveling outside the city. Large numbers of angry, former Confederate soldiers of the Missouri State Guard had not re-enlisted with General Price because he had moved on to fight east of the Mississippi. They chose instead to stay behind so they could fight to regain control of Missouri. Marauding bands took to the bush, resorting to plundering, robbing, even murdering, all supposedly under the authority of the Confederate States. It got so bad that General Egbert Brown of Springfield ordered that any member of a band of guerrillas caught committing a crime against the laws and authority of the United States was to be shot on the spot and anyone harboring them was to be arrested.

Jonathan and Thomas Burns were the bearers of this alarming news as they both leaned back and stretched out their long legs under Mildred's table after a satisfying meal of Hopping John stew and cornbread. Thomas reached out and grabbed Sally's hand as she passed. "Thank you, dear lady, for the scrumptious food. Will you marry me?" She whacked him gently on the head with her free hand and pulled away.

"You ain't nothin' but a troublemaker, Thomas. I need to have a word with your mama," she said, chuckling gently.

Eliza laughed and glanced at Jonathan. Immediately she turned away and blushed when she realized he had been watching her. She stood to help Sally and Lucy clear the table, wondering what was wrong. Why would it rattle her so much to find him watching her? It certainly wasn't the first time. Where was this unexplainable shyness coming from?

Both men retired to the porch with Mildred, George, and Jim. Sally took a towel out of Eliza's hand and whispered, "Get on out there, where you belong, girl. There's two lovestruck soldiers just dying to spend time with you. Are you blind?"

Eliza's hand flew to her mouth. "Sally! Hush! Don't say such things!"

Sally faced her, hands on her hips and a huge smile stretched across her face. "And why not? Someone's gotta wake you up! Those two have been like puppy dogs hanging around here for the past few months, and you've got your head in the clouds. It's about time you wake up and at least give 'em a morsel now and then."

Again, Eliza covered her mouth in shock.

Sally swatted at her and said, "Don't you be misunderstandin' me, now. I mean, give them some attention. You been too busy with all your do-goodin', you don't have nothin' left for poor Jon. If you could've seen that poor boy when you was all broken and bleedin, back when he brought you to us, you'd know..."

"Know what?"

"He's smitten with you, girl."

Eliza blushed again and shook her head. "You've got it all wrong, Sally. Yes, he loves me. Always has. I love him, too. Like a brother. And that's all!" Eliza sliced her hand through the air to make her point clear. "I'll go out there, but I don't want to hear any more about this!" She yanked her apron off, threw it at Sally, and stormed out, leaving Sally chuckling behind her.

CHAPTER TWENTY-FIVE

Through the long hot summer of 1862, southwest Missouri continued to see the guerrilla bands spread fear and chaos throughout the rural areas. Jonathan's company was often sent out to hunt them down and take as many captives as possible or, as ordered by General Brown, shoot on sight if they were seen violating the law and not surrendering. General Brown at one point thought he may have to abandon Springfield because Southern forces were building up in the southwest. Brigadier General Schofield ordered him to stay because of the valuable military depot located in Springfield. He also advised Brown to build several fortifications on high ground throughout the city.

So, in late August, work began on the forts. All five were to be simple earthworks called redoubts, constructed mostly of dirt taken from a ditch that was dug around the fort site. Bastions were built at the corners to hold artillery. The largest fort, covering ten acres, was called Fort No. 1 and was built on a site about a mile northwest of the square. Fort No. 2 was built on West Walnut Street just south of Fort No. 1. Plans were made for Fort No. 3 to be built on the north side, Fort No. 4 south of the square within easy walking distance of the Scott household, and Fort No. 5 east of the square. At the end of August, Brigadier General James Totten marched into Springfield with 1200 men and took charge of the building of the forts. He ordered all able-bodied men not in the army to work to that end, including prisoners of war and slaves. Businesses were allowed to operate only two hours a day so that they wouldn't interfere with the construction of forts.

Both George and Jim spent long, backbreaking hours digging the trench around Fort No. 1. Surprisingly, though, both men were sent home to rest after working twelve straight days. They walked into the house when the others were sitting down for breakfast. George dropped a small, heavy sack on the table. "We even got paid. That beats all, don't it? The officer in charge handed this to me after he told us to go home and get some rest. Told us to not come back for a week. If this is a picture of things to come, I think I'm gonna like it."

Sally scooped up the bag of coins and handed it to Mildred, who in turn pressed it into George's hand. "It's yours and Jim's. You've earned it." Jim stared at the floor. George looked into the eyes of the lady who had given him his freedom several years ago. Tears formed as their eyes met, and he simply nodded.

Lucy and Jessica stopped in their tracks and silently watched the exchange. Eliza saw them exchange smiles as they continued setting the table. What a strange and wonderful household, she thought as she looked around the table. George, Jim, Mildred, and Eliza sat, receiving food from Sally, Lucy, and Jessica. When all was ready, Sally took her place at the table in time to pray with the others. Jessica and Lucy put food on a tray to take upstairs for the three families living up there. Sarah, the other former slave woman, was upstairs making beds and emptying chamber pots. Sarah's two oldest daughters had the job of waking, bathing, and dressing the other eight children.

Autumn faded into winter, and the Scott household continued to thrive. The number of soldiers in Springfield during September reached 20,000. Many were used as prison guards and others sent out to patrol the rural areas. Guerrillas were being arrested on a daily basis and taken either to the prison on State Street or to the jail at the courthouse. Jonathan and Thomas were often gone for days at a time but still managed to find time most weeks to drop in for one of Sally's meals and to linger on the porch or in the parlor with Mildred and Eliza.

One unseasonably warm Sunday in December, just before Christmas, Jonathan asked Eliza to take a walk. Thomas stayed on the porch with Mildred, George, and Sally. Eliza noticed a quick flash of irritation in his eyes as she rose to join Jonathan. An uncomfortable feeling stirred deep within her as she walked down the steps and out the gate. She shook it off and chattered randomly, glancing up now and then to see Jon nod, a smile on his strong, handsome face. When he looked down at her, she instantly turned away, overcome by unexplainable shyness. They walked in silence for a while. Then Jonathan asked, "Have you heard anything from Henry?"

Eliza shuddered. "No, thank God. Not since almost a year ago. Why?"

"He's been missing since about that time. Either he's dead or he deserted."

"Deserted? Isn't that a hangable offense?"

"Yep, sure is. I've heard rumors he's been seen riding with a renegade group up near Osceola."

"A Confederate group?"

"Yep."

"Nothing about him surprises me."

"Do you think he was involved in your kidnapping?"

"I've wondered about that. He threatened to turn me over to Confederates if I lied to him about, about

241

something..."

"About Abe's valuables that you hid?"

Startled, Eliza looked up at him then remembered he had partially guessed at the truth a year ago when Henry showed up at Mildred's house demanding answers from her.

"Uh...yes. And, of course, I lied. So, no telling what he did. I still can't believe he'd go to that length."

Jonathan stopped and turned her to face him. "I'm not surprised. I can't think of a better explanation for your capture. And, Eliza, I'm not sure he's done. The reason I know he's missing is because we've been searching for him. I'm quite certain his absence points to his guilt. And I don't think he's done with you. He wants what he thinks is his."

"Is it his? As far as I know, he's Abe's only heir."

"If he's truly his heir and knows it, then why is he so sneaky and mean trying to get the truth out of you? If Abe's gold is his, he can go through legal means to get it. Something's fishy."

Eliza's eyes got big. "Who told you it was gold?"

Jonathan grinned from ear to ear. "You did. Just now, Eliza."

She smacked his arm. "You tricked me, you scoundrel!"

Jonathan laughed, grabbed her arm, tucked it into his, and continued their walk down Walnut Street. "You've never been good at hiding things from me, you know, Eliza. I can read you like a book."

"Huh! There's a lot you don't know, mister! So much you don't even have a clue about," she smirked.

"In due time, I'll have it all figured out. For now, though, be on the alert. I don't think Henry would dare show his face in Springfield, but he's unpredictable."

Eliza shuddered. "He still occasionally haunts my dreams."

Jon watched her with concern. "I'm sure he's not the

only one haunting your dreams after what you've been through."

She nodded. "It's not as bad as it was at first. But even then, every time my dreams woke me, God was waiting. He was always right there as soon as my eyes popped open." Eliza looked up into Jon's face. "It was so amazing, Jon. God knew exactly what I needed. His Presence in my room was so real, I almost felt I could reach out and physically touch him."

Jonathan smiled and kept walking. "You've truly changed, Eliza. You've lost that bitter anger that seemed to drive you. It's good to see. Really, really good." He patted her arm, and Eliza smiled, filled with warmth at his praise.

Christmas came and went, with all eight adults living at the Scott house doing everything they could to make the day special for the ten children in their care. With the fireplace lit, all eighteen, plus Jonathan and Thomas, gathered in the parlor and exchanged gifts. Rag dolls for the girls and carved animals for the boys. Jonathan surprised them all with a piece of peppermint. The children received their gifts with wide-eyed wonder, asking their mothers for permission to take the wrapping off. After watching the young ones play for a few minutes, they all made their way to the large dining room table to partake in a meal that Sally, Lucy, and Jessica had prepared.

The children listened in wide-eyed wonder as Jonathan told the Christmas story. Eliza was struck by his knowledge of the details and by the respectful way he held the Bible. His deep, gentle voice kept the children captivated as he smiled at each child, making eye contact with those who were confident enough to look at him.

Soon after the dawning of the year 1863, word reached

Springfield that President Lincoln had issued a proclamation that all slaves were now free. George had heard the news on the square and rushed home to announce it to the others. Eliza noticed that Jim dropped into a chair and covered his eyes. She walked over to stand next to him, briefly patting him on the shoulder. He looked up and, with tears in his eyes whispered, "That means I don't belong to Henry no more, Liza!" With that, he bent over as if in pain, stood, and quickly walked out of the house. Eliza's eyes darted to George and Mildred. Neither appeared to have noticed. Sally took off at a run up the stairs to relay this incredible news to Lucy, Jessica, and Sarah. Suddenly, everything about their future and the future of their children had changed dramatically.

Eliza slipped out the back door and wandered through the yard, hoping to find Jim. She heard muffled moans intermingled with gagging sounds from behind the greenhouse. Torn between a desire to comfort him and a realization he needed privacy, she stood still as a statue and prayed. When his crying changed to soft sniffling, she approached. "Jim?"

He yanked his head around and when his eyes met hers, he sank to his knees and wept some more. "I'm so sorry, Miz Liza! I'm just so relieved, I don't know how to handle myself."

She walked close enough to rest her hand on his head. "Oh, Jim! Please don't apologize! I...I didn't know this was weighing so heavy on you. I didn't even know you'd belong to him."

"Oh yes! Miz Liza! I think about it almost every day! Henry is Maatah Abe's only heir. As soon as Abe died, I belonged to Henry. War is awful, but if it's keepin' me out of the clutches of that evil man, then I want it to never stop!" He dropped his head in shame. "I'm so sorry! That's mighty selfish of me. But I've seen him with slaves, and it's a living hell!" Again, he covered his face with his hands and wept.

"Jim, I'm so sorry. I didn't know you were burdened with this. I wouldn't have let him have you, you know."

"Thank you, dear girl. But there's nothin' you could've done to stop him. I know. I've seen this before."

"So, what are your plans now, Jim? When the war's over, I mean. Where are you going to go?"

Jim stood and looked at her. Then he bowed his head and said in a voice so quiet, she could barely make out his words, "A few months ago, Miz Mildred read to us from the book of Ruth in the Bible. She read some words that stuck in my heart, cuz I was desperate to belong, truly belong to someone. You see, when Mastah Abe died, I wanted to die with him. He was the closest thing to a pa I ever had, Miz Liza."

Shame filled Eliza's heart. "I'm so sorry, Jim. I was so consumed by my own grief, I never noticed."

"No offense, Miz Liza, but I never expected no white person to notice. 'Specially not you after what you was going through. Mastah Abe was the only one that ever cared about me. But then I met you and Mildred and Jonathan and...well...you're all different, somehow." He wiped his eyes and dug a piece of paper from his pocket. "When I heard that maybe Henry had deserted and gone over to the Confederates, I thought there might be hope that he'd go to prison and couldn't ever claim me..." Jim studied the paper in his hands. "So, when I heard those words in the book of Ruth, I asked Mildred to copy them down for me. They're for you, Miz Liza." Tears streamed down his face as he handed the paper to her. "Don't read it yet. Wait until I walk away. Then you can read it and have time to think of your answer." He started to walk away then turned and said, "If your answer is no, it's all right. I'll be fine."

Eliza watched him go then unfolded the page with Mildred's handwriting. Through her tears, she read:

"Entreat me not to leave thee, or to return from following after thee: for whither thou goest, I will go; and where thou lodgest, I will lodge: thy people shall be my people, and thy God my God: Where thou diest, will I die and there will I be buried: the Lord do so to me, and more also, if ought but death part thee and me."

Slowly, Eliza folded the paper and clutched it to her heart. She knew her answer before she was done reading. But she was uncertain of her own future. She was quite certain her father had sold their farm north of Springfield just before moving here at the onset of the war. But she knew nothing of the whereabouts of that money or any of her father's money, for that matter. Even if he had money in Abe's bank, was it still there? As far as she knew, she was destitute and had nothing to offer Jim: no home, no work, no food. Nothing! She was completely dependent on Mildred's kindness. Shamefully so. As soon as this war was over, if not sooner she vowed to herself, she was going to find a way to support herself. Her answer to Jim would be an unequivocal yes, but she had to make it clear to him what her situation was. She might not be able to feed and house herself, much less him. Wiping her nose and drying her eyes, she walked across the yard to deliver her answer.

At that same moment, Captain Jonathan Monroe and Lieutenant Thomas Burns were riding side by side on a patrol with Jon's company south of Springfield. Thomas seemed to be in a particularly sour mood that day. Jonathan knew Thomas well enough to know it would just be a matter of time before he heard the cause of his discontent. There was a thin coating of snow on the ground, the sky was a deep blue, and the air still. Only twenty of Jonathan's men rode that day, planning to join the Fourteenth Missouri

State Militia Cavalry on a scouting expedition to Beaver Station close to the Arkansas border.

Finally, Thomas let out a snort of disgust. Jon continued riding in silence, waiting patiently for his friend to vent. "I don't understand you at all, Monroe," Thomas growled.

"What are you talking about, Burns?"

"You! I'm talking about you!"

"What about me?"

Thomas reined his horse in and stared at Jonathan who eased his horse to the side of the road and stopped. He waited for Thomas to join him, motioning his other men to ride on.

"What in the world is eatin' at you, Lieutenant? Out with it," he demanded.

Thomas just stared at his friend for a minute before he asked, "Do you love Eliza?"

"Of course I do. I've loved her since the day she was born."

"That's not what I'm talking about and you know it! Do you love her now, the way a man loves a woman?"

"That's none of your business, Lieutenant!" Jonathan snapped.

Thomas brought his horse up beside Jonathan and looked him squarely in the eyes. "Oh, yes, it is my business. I'm in love with that woman and, if you're in love with her, too, I'll back off. But if you're not, then I'm declaring my intentions right here, right now!"

"What? You can't be in love with her! What are you talking about?" Jonathan's voice rose.

"And why not? She's certainly desirable. And as far as I can see, no one has laid claim to her." They glared at each other. "Well?" Thomas persisted.

Jonathan ran his fingers through his hair and stared at the horizon. With a frustrated sigh, he answered his friend, "Yes, I love her, confound it! And if you must know, I plan to marry her someday!" He started to ride away, but

Thomas reached out and grabbed his reins, pulling his horse to an abrupt stop.

"Actually, this is not a surprise to me! But it's not enough!"

"What? What do you mean, 'it's not enough'?"

"I've been fairly certain of this for months! But Eliza doesn't have a clue. Don't you think she deserves to know?"

"We're in the middle of a war, here, in case you hadn't noticed. I'll tell her when the time is right."

Thomas glared at Jon. "War or no war, she's a woman who needs to know she's loved by a man! You've had over a year! If you don't tell her by the end of January that you love her and want to marry her, then I'm moving in. She'll be mine if she'll have me!" With that ultimatum, Thomas released Jonathan's reins and galloped to catch up with the others, leaving a stunned man in his dust.

CHAPTER TWENTY-SIX

Jonathan's detachment of men was sent to the border soon after arriving at Beaver Station. The following day, they captured two Confederate prisoners who gave them the alarming news that approximately six thousand men under General Marmaduke were, at that moment, headed to Springfield. Jonathan immediately sent Thomas and one other to ride north with the news.

The news of Marmaduke's approach reached Springfield late afternoon of January 7th. There were less than 1000 soldiers stationed in Springfield at the time. That number, combined with the 1000 hospitalized men and a few hundred recently discharged convalescents, was far too little to combat the force of 6000 Confederates under Marmaduke's command. General Brown wanted to withdraw from the city, but a few of his officers urged him to not abandon Springfield without a fight. Brown struggled with his decision throughout the night and finally, by morning, decided to stand his ground.

Quickly, he and his officers organized the forces available to them, including all hospital patients and convalescents capable of carrying guns. Runners were sent to nearby towns requesting reinforcements. Transients from a camp north of town and several private citizens also joined the quickly assembling forces, which now totaled about 2000 men.

Two twelve-pound howitzers and another mounted gun, a six-pounder, that had been left abandoned on the grounds of the Calvary Presbyterian Church, were quickly hauled to a blacksmith for repairs then moved into position at Fort No. 4 on South Street. Rations were moved to the forts or loaded on wagons headed north for Bolivar and plans were made to destroy the arsenal if the Union troops were forced to leave the city.

Citizens were in a frenzied panic. Some sought sanctuary at Fort No. 1, the largest of the forts that had been completed. Others, including the Scott household, moved to their cellars.

General Joseph Shelby led the main Confederate force under Marmaduke. Shelby and his men reached the town of Ozark late on January 7th, which he found already abandoned by Federal troops. He ordered that the fort and barracks be burned and all food and other supplies confiscated or destroyed. By midnight, he headed north toward Springfield.

At sunup on January 8th, Jonathan and Thomas with five of their men were sent to scout out the enemy's position. They saw Marmaduke's men approaching from the south. After estimating the number of troops, Jon sent a messenger back to General Brown with the news, while he and the rest of his men took up positions to continue observing Marmaduke, who seemed to be waiting for something or someone. Jon's messenger returned with the disturbing news that Gen. Shelby was in position to attack farther to the east.

As Jonathan and his men withdrew, shots were exchanged. They, along with all the other scouting parties, gradually made their way to Fort No. 4 where they took up positions in the fort and in the streets and buildings close by. General Brown, realizing the attack was coming from the south, ordered several homes south of the fort to be burned to the ground, allowing his soldiers a better view of the advancing enemy. Several times, Missouri State Militia, including Jonathan and his men, charged the Confederate lines but were driven back by the superior number and weapons of the south.

By one in the afternoon, the Battle of Springfield was fully underway. The big guns of the Confederates were unleashed on the forts and homes and even into the square. Repeatedly Federal forces charged and retreated, with the battle eventually becoming a fight moving among the very homes and yards of the citizens.

The Rebel forces soon took control of one large building and several houses close to Fort No. 4 and continued to occupy them for most of the day. Federal reinforcements were sent to Fort No. 4 and eventually the Confederates retreated west a few blocks.

Jonathan and his men were in the thick of battle, having been stationed between the fort and the buildings occupied by the Southern forces. As soon as they saw some of the Confederates begin to abandon a house they were firing at, Thomas hollered over his shoulder at Jonathan, "Cover me!" and ran across the street. To his horror, Jon saw blood spurt from Thomas' head as he fell to the ground. Without a second thought, he ran, grabbed his friend by the back of his collar, and dragged him behind a stone wall. Bullets whizzed by on every side and from every direction as he flipped Thomas over to examine the wound. Blood covered the right side of his head and continued to ooze as Jonathan probed. To his great relief, there was no puncture through the skull and although Thomas was unconscious, he was still breathing. For another hour, Jon stayed by his side and exchanged fire with the enemy. He maintained his position as the fighting gradually moved to the west then he, with the help of one of his men, picked Thomas up, slung him over his shoulder, and cautiously made his way to the fort where he left him with the other wounded.

With gritted teeth, Jonathan returned to the battle. To his dismay, he found that the Confederates had stopped just west of Market Street. Their heavy six-pounder was in position and was firing grape and canister into the midst of the Federal troops. Jonathan slid behind a house and made his way to the corner where he could fire at several rebels crawling on the ground from stump to tree to fence, advancing slowly but surely. Several of his men rejoined him, and together they made their way to the city cemetery. Both blue coats and gray could be seen hiding and shooting from behind gravestones. The noise was deafening: the continuous crack of rifles, the whistling of cannon shot, the shrieks and moans of the wounded.

Jonathan felt a sharp pain in his left arm, but adrenaline coursing through his system wouldn't allow him to stop. Taking aim with his Smith and Wesson revolver, pulling the trigger, ducking for cover, again and again, then dropping behind a gravestone, reloading over and over and over like a machine, he continued.

The Confederate forces seemed to dominate, even pushing as far north as Walnut between Market and Main Avenue. From there, they were driven back south to State Street by Colonel Sheppard and reinforcements from other parts of the city. At about five in the afternoon, with the sun about to set, Confederate General Shelby made one last, desperate attempt to take Fort No. 4 just south of the square. In a barrage of fire from both sides, they managed to get within one hundred yards of the fort but were held at bay until nightfall, when the Confederates retreated to take cover just a few blocks to the southwest. Later, under cover of darkness, they retreated farther south to the Phelps' farm to spend the night.

With the help of several of his men, Jonathan borrowed a wagon to transport his still-unconscious friend to his aunt Mildred. When they arrived, only Mildred, Eliza, George, and Jim had dared to come up from the cellars. They were sitting in the parlor with no lanterns lit, for fear of being seen by the enemy. Jon went ahead of his men and quickly announced their arrival as his men followed carrying Thomas on a stretcher. George ran to the door to let them in.

When Eliza saw the stretcher, she threw her hands over her face and staggered back against Jim. Her terrified gaze flew to Jon. With a strangled cry, she threw herself into his arms. He wrapped his right arm around her and held her tightly against his chest while he instructed the others to take Thomas down the hall to George and Sally's bedroom. Mildred called for Sally and quickly followed.

Jon dropped his face down to Eliza's head and whispered soothing sounds into her hair, "Shh...it's all right, Eliza. The fighting's over for today."

"Are they gone?" she asked, her face still pressed against his chest.

"For now."

"Where's Thomas?" she asked.

"He's here, Eliza," he answered slowly. "That was Thomas on the stretcher."

Her hand flew to her mouth but she didn't leave Jon's embrace.

"He has a head wound, but I think he'll recover. He's gonna need better care than the medics can give him though. That's why we brought him here."

As he talked, he led her down the hallway and through the door so they could see how Thomas was doing. Mildred and Sally were gently bathing dried, crusted blood from his swollen face. Thankfully, Thomas moaned and grimaced under the ministration of the two efficient women. Eliza stood at the foot of the bed and watched with a strange mixture of horror and relief.

Jon moved in closely and said, "Burns? Can you hear me?"

Thomas went completely still for a moment then groaned.

"You took a bullet to the head, ol' boy!" Jonathan continued, "but you're gonna be fine. Mildred and Sally will get you up and on your way in no time."

Thankfully, every time Jonathan spoke, Thomas got quiet and listened.

"The battle's over for today. For you, the fighting is over until you pull through. Stay here at Mildred's until I release you. That's an order. Do you hear me, Lieutenant?"

Thomas looked in the direction of Jon's voice and grunted then seemed to fall unconscious again. Jon stood to his feet and wiped a bandana across his face. "Someone will need to stay in the room with him for a while. Thank you, ladies."

He reached out his hand to Eliza and led her from the room and out onto the front porch where he dropped heavily into the swing. "I think I could sleep for a week, Liza girl."

He winced with pain and gingerly touched his left shoulder, where he discovered fresh blood.

"Jon! You're wounded!" Eliza gasped and sat next to him.

"Oh, yeah. I think I took a bullet." He glanced at it then flexed his fingers. "It hurts like the dickens, but all my fingers work, so it can't be too serious."

Eliza started to ease his shirt off while scolding, "I don't care how many fingers you can move. This still needs to be examined."

Jonathan watched her face and choked up at the sweetness he saw there. He continued to watch in awe as she gently pulled his sleeve off. *What a beautiful treasure she is.* Of course, Thomas saw her this way and loved her. He would have been a fool not to. This delicate, brave, headstrong beauty should not be taken for granted. Without a doubt, his love for her had blossomed into a full-blown, romantic attraction.

No! Not merely attraction. Way more. Far stronger than attraction. He loved her beyond any love he had ever dreamed of. Thomas' challenge to him just a day or two before had uncorked emotions in him that he had carefully bottled up.

Eliza lifted her eyes from his wound to his face. "Jon, are you all right? You look like you're about to faint."

Jon shook his head and grunted, "Yeah. I'm fine. Just tired. I need to get back to my men." He started to rise, but she pulled him back down.

"We need to probe for a bullet, clean this up, and get you bandaged before you leave." She turned toward the front door and hollered for George.

"Nobody's doing any probing but me," Jon said and removed her hand from his arm. By the time George walked through the door, Jon had felt around the wound and was satisfied that the bullet had just grazed him enough to cause a lot of bleeding, and that was all. George set to work cleaning and bandaging with Eliza watching intently, now and then looking up to find Jon's eyes on her.

Jim came out to join them and to get instructions from Jon about safety precautions for the household. Jon told them of the military situation and advised them to keep the women and children in the cellars until they knew the fighting was over. "I expect it will start again at daybreak. But this is war, and they may attack again tonight," he said. "Just pray. Please. We need it."

Jim excused himself to get food from the greenhouse. George went into the house to get a clean shirt for Jon. And Eliza moved to sit beside him again, this time next to his good arm. He chuckled and put his arm around her, pulling her in close to his side. She sighed and leaned against him.

"I'm frightened for you, Jon," she whispered.

He hugged her more tightly. "Don't be," he whispered against her hair. In spite of his fatigue, he longed to pull her into his arms, kiss her sweet lips, and declare his love. Thomas was right. She had no idea his love had grown into a fiercely possessive, passionate one. The powerful love of a man for his woman. She cuddled against him like a sister would to a big brother. She would be shocked to know the truth. Maybe even appalled at the idea.

Now wasn't the time. "I have to go to my men. There may be more wounded. And, if I'm to fight tomorrow, I'll need some sleep." He chuckled, trying to lighten the mood. She sat up and looked at him, tears streaming down her cheeks. He reached up and brushed them away. "I'll be fine. Don't worry, Eliza." She nodded and stood with him. "In the meantime, you stay in the cellar with the others. I need to know you're safe." Again, she nodded. He gave her a quick hug then went down the steps to his horse.

Eliza watched him ride away. She continued to stand at the porch railing, listening to the breeze in the trees and gazing at the full moon. Just before turning to go indoors, she heard movement to the side of the house. She cautiously walked to the end of the porch and listened. Relieved to hear Jim humming as he puttered inside the greenhouse, she quietly descended the steps and walked toward the backyard.

Again, she heard movement then the snap of a twig. She whirled around. "Who's there?" she demanded with a shaky voice. Silence filled the yard. She ran. Heavy footsteps came close behind. Then strong arms grabbed her and a hand covered her mouth. She was pulled roughly back toward the bushes, kicking and clawing every inch of the way. Hot breath blew in her ear as a very familiar voice hissed, "Tell me where you hid the gold, and I'll never bother you again." She worked her mouth to the side and bit into flesh as hard as she could bite. He hollered, shoved her to the ground, and she screamed.

"Eliza! Where are you?" came Jim's frantic voice. She heard the bushes give way as her assailant fled. And in the next second, Jim was standing over her ready to do battle with a shovel.

CHAPTER TWENTY-SEVEN

Jim held the shovel over his head and listened as heavy footsteps crashed through the bushes and through the fence into the alley. He reached down and hauled Eliza to her feet, never taking his eyes off the direction her assailant ran. "Are you all right, Miz Liza?" he asked, breathing hard with fear.

"I'm fine, Jim. Quick! Let's get inside and lock the doors!"

They scrambled for the porch, Jim brandishing his weapon like a true warrior. Inside, they quickly locked the front door then ran to secure the back. Mildred and George emerged from the bedside of Thomas, dread etched on their faces. When Eliza told what had happened, both men ran to get rifles and positioned themselves at the front and back of the house. Eliza and Mildred went to upstairs bedrooms to stand watch. After a couple of hours, they agreed to take turns so they could try to sleep. Sally stayed by Thomas' side through the night.

At sunrise, Mildred, Eliza, and Sally cautiously went

into the kitchen to scrape together some breakfast for Thomas and the three very frightened families still hiding in the cellars. George and Jim stepped out onto the porch and listened for the sounds of battle.

"That snow we got this morning left a fine, white dusting over ever' thin' out there," George announced as he and Jim came back into the house. "Look out th' window, Liza. Look at them fat snowflakes a drifting down slow as can be. It's so peaceful." He stood at the window with the curtains drawn back so Eliza could see also. "The silence out there is almost eerie. I'm not sure what's goin' on with the fightin'."

Jim joined them at the window. "I walked around th' house trying to find footprints in the snow but didn't see a thing." He paused. "Are you sure it was Henry?"

"There's no doubt in my mind. I'd know that voice anywhere."

"That rascal is persistent." George dropped the curtain and faced the other two. "He'll be back, ya know."

After Eliza finished delivering food to the rest of the household, she quietly approached Jim in the kitchen. The others were busy elsewhere, so she had a moment to ask for his advice. "Why do you suppose Henry is so desperate to locate Abe's gold? It seems to me that the gold is his legally, so why does he feel the need to resort to violence to get his hands on it? Why doesn't he go to Abe's lawyer?"

"I've been wonderin' the same thing, Miz Liza. Maybe the gold's not his, and he knows it."

"I'm sure Abe has a will somewhere. Do you know who he used as a lawyer?"

"That's not somethin' I paid a whole lot of attention to. Sorry."

"Do you know someone that might know?"

"Hmmm... Maybe Preacher Hobbs, down at the Methodist Church. That is, if he's still around. He was a good friend of Abe's. Used to drop by to see him almost every week."

"There hasn't been a service there since the beginning of the war. The church is being used as the armory. Do you know where he lives?"

At that moment, they heard boots on the porch and Jon's voice greeting the household. They ran to greet him and were stopped in their tracks by the big grin spread across his tired, dirty face.

"They left! The Confederates crawled out of bed and just rode right on out of town. We went after them, but they refused to fight!"

Eliza ran into his outstretched arms. George and Jim slapped him on the back and cheered, and the women ran to tell the frightened mothers it was time to get their children out of the dark, damp cellars.

"How's your arm?" Eliza asked.

"It's fine. How's Thomas?" he answered as he made his way down the hall with Eliza neatly tucked under his good arm.

After standing over the bed for several minutes watching Thomas sleep soundly, Jon turned to Mildred and asked, "Do you have a spare bed or sofa or floor where I could lie down and sleep, dear lady? I might be out for a few days."

"The parlor is yours, my dear boy. Would you like something to eat first?"

"Just water, please," he slurred as he released Eliza and made a beeline for the sofa in the parlor.

Almost twenty-four hours later, Jon emerged from the parlor and ate a hearty breakfast. He visited Thomas' bedside and was disturbed to see that he was still unconscious. Sally told him that he had stirred and muttered unintelligibly several times, but that was all. Jon told George to get a doctor if one was available. He then rose to go visit his other wounded men, most of whom were in the hospital at the courthouse. But, just before he walked out, he was reminded of Thomas' challenge to declare his intentions to Eliza by the end of the month.

Drat it, he thought as he dragged his hand through his hair. He hated to be forced into something this important. He paused at the door then realized how filthy he was. "Another day. But soon, Eliza. Very soon," he muttered under his breath just before he closed the door and went down the steps.

He returned every day to check on Thomas and used that as his excuse to see Eliza. Now that he had openly admitted his feelings for her to Thomas, a dam seemed to have broken inside. The sight of her was almost too precious to bear.

Eliza noticed the difference, and she basked in it. For too long, she had been puzzled by their relationship. Jonathan had said just enough to make her hope his feelings went beyond brotherly. But as soon as she dared to dream about the possibilities, he would dash her hopes with his absence or his distant moods. Now, every time he walked into the house and laid eyes on her, she could read something new. Something very sweet and very intense. It made her heart soar.

A week after the Battle of Springfield, Thomas woke from his coma. Sally ran screaming through the house announcing the news to all that could hear her. After allowing a few into the room to greet him, she shooed them all away so he could "get him some sleep!"

That evening, Jonathan arrived to hear the good news. He pulled Eliza into his arms and led her to Thomas' bedside where they settled down for a lengthy visit, in spite of Sally's protests.

"So, where have you been all week, Lieutenant? We've missed you."

Thomas grinned briefly then squinted at Eliza. "Not sure, Captain. You tell me."

Jonathan reached out and grabbed his hand. "It doesn't matter. It's just good to have you back, Burns."

Thomas chuckled and touched his wound. "I'm not sure I'm fully back. My head's killing me."

"It will take time to recover. In the meantime, stay here and do what Sally says. That's an order. You understand?"

"Yes, sir. For now, I have no desire to go anywhere." He gazed intently at Eliza. "I'm not sure if this was a dream or it really happened. I recall a conversation you and I had recently about this pretty lady I see by your side."

Jonathan looked uneasily at Eliza and back at Thomas. "It must have been a dream."

Thomas squinted at Jonathan for a long time then laughed. "Nope! It really happened. It was on the road to Beaver Station, a day or two before Springfield was attacked."

Jonathan stood to his feet and drew Eliza up along with him. He walked her to the door. "You'll have to excuse us for a moment, Eliza. This is private business." He gently guided her out the door and closed it behind her. Returning to the chair next to Thomas, he sat and studied his friend's face.

Thomas met his eyes and waited. "You really love her, don't you?"

Jonathan was surprised at his tears. "Yes. With everything that is in me, I hopelessly love that dear girl."

"And?"

"Yes, darn it! I'm asking her to be my wife! But I won't be forced!"

"I don't want to force you, Jon. I just want her to know the depth of your feelings. And your intentions. For her sake, Jon. You can't keep her wondering."

Jonathan rubbed his hand over his chin in frustration. "I understand. But my timing will be my own, not yours."

Thomas nodded then said, "So...I heard through a reliable source that you risked your life to drag me off the street and into the fort."

Jonathan nodded. "That's what an officer is supposed to do for his men."

"Well, I suppose since you probably saved my life, I could back off on my deadline."

"Your deadline?"

"Yeah. By the end of this month, if you haven't taken care of business with Eliza, I'm moving in to stake a claim."

"That's generous of you."

"You should be grateful. I'm giving you more time."

Jonathan clenched his jaw in irritation. He crossed his arms over his chest and leaned back.

"Yeah," Thomas continued. "How about I give you until the end of next January. That's a little over a year. If you don't take care of the job by then, you're hopeless, and Eliza will need to be rescued."

Jonathan laughed and leaned in close to the bed. "I'm sure she'll not need rescuing by you or anyone else, Lieutenant. But I'll have to correct something I said earlier."

"What's that?"

"I said my timing will be my own. But I pray instead that the timing will be God's, not mine."

"God's?" Thomas snorted. "I doubt he has much of an opinion on this."

"Of that, I'm sure you're wrong. In fact, I believe you're

still with us and doing well because of God and all the prayers that have been said for you."

"Believe what you want. I won't argue with you."

"Good," Jonathan said as he stood to go. "Nor I with you. But I will keep praying for you." They clasped hands before he left. "Until tomorrow, Thomas." Jonathan walked through the door and encountered Sally standing in the hall, impatiently tapping her foot.

Over the next few weeks, Jonathan visited almost every day. One sunny, warm day in late January, he asked Eliza to take a ride with him. He had borrowed a buggy from a livery close to the square. "I want to show you my farm," he said as the team of horses trotted east down Walnut Street.

"Is it safe to leave town?" she asked.

"I wouldn't take you there if I didn't think it was safe." He chuckled. "I'm surprised at your concerns for safety after some of the places you've gone in the past year and a half."

Eliza squirmed uncomfortably under his gaze. "Things have changed."

"Meaning?"

She looked directly into his eyes and answered, "Meaning, that at first, I really didn't care if I lived or died. My grief over Pa was suffocating me."

Jonathan was slow to respond to that revelation. "That was the reason you chose to do what you did, wasn't it, Eliza?"

"Yes. I thought you knew that, Jon. I tried to make you understand."

"I remember. It's hard for me to grasp that you were that depressed."

"I was also angry, very angry. My anger and desire for revenge actually seemed to help me."

Jonathan put an arm around her and pulled her close.

She rested her head on his chest and sighed. "Things have changed now that I have Christ in me. All of life looks different through the lens of His presence and His love. I have so much to live for now!"

Jonathan's heart swelled with love and tenderness. He pressed a kiss to the top of her head and drove south. They rode in happy silence through the streets of Springfield and on into the open countryside. Just before reaching Ozark, Jonathan turned right onto a long narrow road. "My place is the only place on this road. In fact, I own the land on both sides."

Eliza sat up tall and looked around at the gently rolling land. Soon, a house and several barns came into view. Jonathan pulled up and stopped in front of a small, abandoned house with a big front porch. A barn with a broken-down fence around the barnyard sat off to the right. Four other buildings and several giant oaks surrounded the yard. Behind the house ran a wide, bubbling, tree-lined stream.

"Jonathan! I love it! This is yours?"

He reached up and helped her down. "This is mine. What's left of it anyway. I sold most of my horses and cattle before the war, while I had a chance. The rest were stolen. Minus one cow that I butchered and gave to Mildred. When the war's done, I plan to rebuild this place."

Eliza walked to the porch. Surprisingly there was still a rocking chair there. She leaned against the railing and looked at the view. "Did you build this? Or was it already here?"

"I built it. With a lot of help from my ranch hands, of course. They stayed over there in that building," he said as he pointed to a bunkhouse just to the right of the driveway. He stood at the bottom of the porch steps and watched her.

"You chose your site wisely," Eliza said as she stared dreamily at the view. The house sat on a slight rise with a view of the land to the south which fell away in beautiful dips and valleys. "You can see for miles from here!" she exclaimed. Behind the stream, the land gradually rose up into forestland. Jonathan moved up the steps and took her hands in his. She shyly raised her eyes to meet his. "I brought you here to tell you something, Eliza. Something very important." He looked away for a moment. "This shouldn't be so difficult for me, but for some reason it is."

Eliza reached up, cupped his chin, and very gently said, "Tell me, Jon."

Jonathan could almost drown in those warm eyes. He swallowed a lump that was quickly forming. "I love you, Eliza. I love you with every fiber of my being. I've always loved you, but this is entirely different. Would you allow me to court you? No more of this friend business. I want you to be my girl, Eliza. My woman. Gosh darn it, Eliza! I want to kiss you so bad right now!"

Eliza threw her head back and laughed with joy. Before she could take a breath, he enveloped her in his strong arms and pulled her close for a kiss. A very long kiss. Eliza stood on her tiptoes, wrapped her arms around his head, and pressed in closer as the kiss deepened in intensity.

When the kiss ended, Jonathan held her face between his hands and gazed down at her. "I can't make any promises to you, Eliza, as long as this war continues, except there will be no one else but you. My dream is that someday, God willing, when the war ends, this will be our home together. Does that suit you, dear girl?"

Tears filled her eyes and spilled onto her cheeks. "Oh yes!" she breathed. "That suits me just fine!"

CHAPTER TWENTY-EIGHT

For the next several months, Jonathan courted Eliza. They managed to slip away frequently from the Scott household to take long walks. At times, they would take buggy rides in the countryside just outside of town.

The people of Springfield enjoyed the security of knowing that an attack by the enemy was unlikely. In February, Jonathan and most of his men joined a newly organized militia force called the Provisional Enrolled Missouri Militia (PEMM) that allowed soldiers of the Enrolled Missouri Militia freedom to stay near home, tend to their crops, and be available to assist in civilian duties and to be called to active military service in case of emergency. Jonathan's primary job in the PEMM was to continue hunting down Confederate guerrillas throughout southwest Missouri. Thomas' recovery was slow. He was not able to return to active duty until the end of February.

As much as possible during wartime, life seemed to return to normal. Businesses thrived, supplies came freely to the stores, people prepared and later planted gardens.

Neighbors strolled through the streets and called on one another. And more people dared to venture out to attend church. Mildred and Eliza often walked the short distance to Calvary Presbyterian Church on South Jefferson where Reverend Frederic Wines had been the pastor since the year before.

In spite of the relative calm, the city was experiencing a new sort of heartbreak. Swarms of war refugees from the southern part of the state flooded the streets and moved into abandoned houses, many with broken windows and no heat. Others moved into shacks or barns and outbuildings. Reverend Wines had been personally appointed by President Lincoln to be the Union Army's post chaplain in Springfield. Through his efforts and with the help of many of the women of Springfield, the refugees were fed and somewhat clothed. Donations of money to buy food came from many private individuals and from the War Relief Fund of St. Louis. Mildred and Eliza joined a ladies' group to sew and distribute clothing. Most of the women and children had no shoes, so Eliza and several other young women went door to door to ask for any extra shoes people might have on hand.

By the middle of May, the urgency of caring for the refugees had lessened. Many of the refugees who had been slaves continued to travel northwest into Kansas, not daring to believe Lincoln's Emancipation Proclamation would be honored in Missouri, a former slave state. Under the direction of the PEMM, many of the abandoned houses were made as weather-proof as possible and wood for fireplaces was cut and delivered to the neediest.

In the midst of all this activity, Eliza never forgot her resolve to find Abe Goodman's will. In spite of her asking around town, no one seemed to know where Reverend Hobbs lived. One Sunday, as Eliza listened to Reverend Wines' sermon, she thought possibly he would know the whereabouts of a fellow preacher. Sure enough, when she mentioned his name, Wines' eyes lit up with recognition. "Reverend Hobbs? Why sure, I know him. He's a good man."

"Do you know where he lives?" Eliza asked.

"Actually, no. I've never been to his home. He doesn't live in town. I'm quite certain he lives a ways south of here."

"Did you know Abe Goodman, the banker?"

"Yes. I knew Abe. I heard he died."

"I need to locate Mr. Goodman's lawyer, and I thought Reverend Hobbs would know who that was since he was close to him."

"Didn't Abe have a farm south of here? Perhaps they were neighbors."

Reverend Wines reached his hand out to greet a woman waiting patiently next to Eliza. Eliza turned to leave, not terribly encouraged by the little bit of information the Reverend had offered. "Wait a moment, Miss Long. I believe I can give you the name of a man who worked in Mr. Goodman's bank. I'll bet he'll know who his lawyer was." He had his eye on a couple who approached to greet him. After visiting with them and several others, he winked at Eliza. "I just found someone who knows the man I mentioned. His name is Andrew Simmons, and he and his wife live on Jefferson just north of here, in a white house with blue shutters. They are elderly and only attend services on rare occasions. Hopefully, he'll be able to help you."

Mildred was waiting at the door for Eliza. "What did Reverend Wines have to say to you? It seemed important," she asked.

Not willing to raise suspicion, Eliza quickly constructed an answer that was partly true. "I've been trying to find Abe Goodman's lawyer. I need to learn what his intentions for Jim were. Does he go to Henry? I need to find out for Jim's peace of mind."

"Jim's been emancipated, Eliza. He doesn't belong to anyone."

Realizing her blunder, she tried to recover. "I realize that, but many people in Missouri don't recognize Lincoln's proclamation. Jim is really afraid of Henry. It would help him immensely if I could see Abe's will."

Mildred was silent as they walked. "There's more to this, isn't there, Eliza?"

Eliza looked at her wise friend and nodded. "Yes, there is. But don't ask me to talk about it yet. Someday, I promise you, I'll reveal it all."

"Please tell me you haven't gone back to your spying job."

Eliza laughed and slipped her arm through Mildred's. "Don't worry, dear Mildred. I haven't gone back to that and never will."

The following morning, Eliza and Jim left to take a stroll north up Jefferson Avenue. It was a warm, sunny day without a cloud in the sky. They passed many houses of many different colors before they came to a weather-beaten white one with blue shutters. In spite of its looking abandoned, they approached the front door and knocked. Hearing scuffling noises from within, they waited patiently for what seemed a very long time. Finally, the door cracked open an inch, and a very short, petite woman peered out at them.

"What do you want?" came a quivery, very suspicious-sounding voice.

"I'm so sorry to bother you, ma'am," said Eliza in a friendly, soothing tone. "We're looking for a Mr. Andrew Simmons."

"What do you want with him?"

"We're friends of Abe Goodman. Reverend Wines told me Mr. Simmons used to work at Mr. Goodman's bank."

"That's true. He did." The door opened a few more

inches. "What do you want with Mr. Simmons?"

"Reverend Wines thought that perhaps Mr. Simmons would know the name of Mr. Goodman's lawyer."

"He most likely would, but he died the day after Christmas. God rest his soul." The door cracked open even wider.

"I'm so sorry to hear that," Eliza said. "Are you Mrs. Simmons?"

"Yes, I am," she said with pride, yet Eliza detected a quaver as she said it.

"This is none of my business, Mrs. Simmons, but do you live here alone?"

Mrs. Simmons chin rose. "Yes. What of it?"

"Do you have plenty of food? Do you have family that lives nearby?"

The lady's eyes softened. The door came all the way open. "Do you have time for tea and biscuits, my dear?"

"Yes. I would love that. Thank you."

Jim took a seat on the porch and waited. Mrs. Simmons bustled about and hummed. "My, my. You just sit right there, dear. It's been too long since I've had the privilege of being a hostess. Last time was long before my dear husband's death."

Over the course of an hour, Eliza heard story after story about the Simmons' long and happy life together. Just before Eliza excused herself, she asked if perhaps Mrs. Simmons knew the name of Abe's lawyer.

As expected, Mrs. Simmons said, "No." But unexpectedly, Mrs. Simmons eyes twinkled with delight as she laid her hand on Eliza's arm and said, "I'll bet I can find it though. Andrew kept a very detailed diary. He wrote about every detail of our lives as well as every detail that he knew about Mr. Goodman's life. Mr. Abe Goodman was a kind, generous man and a true friend to Andrew. Anyone who was a friend of his is a friend of ours. It will take some time to dig through his diaries, but if you're willing to come for tea again tomorrow, I'm sure by then I'll have the name of Mr. Goodman's lawyer."

Elated at this news, she and Jim walked back and waited until the next day. Sure enough, a very excited Mrs. Simmons served tea then shared her information as if it were buried treasure. And to Eliza, it was. Before she left, Eliza asked if she could return next week with two other very special ladies, Miss Mildred Scott and Miss Elin Johnson. Mrs. Simmons agreed with great delight.

As Eliza and Jim walked toward home, they opened the slip of paper on which, *Mr. Todd Franklin* was written in neat block letters.

"I recognize that name," Jim said. "I even remember what he looks like. He came to the farm a few times. I just didn't know he was the lawyer."

It was early enough in the day to go to the courthouse and try to locate Mr. Franklin. They were told that Mr. Franklin did indeed still live and practice in Springfield. The man behind the desk offered to send a message asking him to call on them at Mildred's house as soon as he could. "Unfortunately, he only drops in here about once a month."

"If you would be so kind as to give us his address, we could see him sooner. This is a matter of a disputed will, and the sooner we discover the truth, the sooner we can escape the negative communication we are receiving from some family members," Eliza told him.

The clerk studied her for a moment then dug in his drawer for the address. He scribbled it on a piece of paper and handed it to them. Eliza wanted to crawl across the desk and hug him.

The next morning, the two were off again, this time west of the square on College Street. Before they left, Mildred stood at the door and stopped them. George came up to stand next to her.

"I'm not sure what you two are up to. You've been

leaving together a lot lately and you're being very secretive about it."

"I'll follow them if that would make you happy," George offered with a twinkle in his eyes.

"No. That would be wrong. I'm sure they'll tell us when they're ready." She looked pointedly at Eliza. "I'm just frightened for you, girl, after knowing what you were involved in before," she said with a sigh. Then she addressed George. "You, too, for that matter, mister!"

George ducked his head and apologized for the umpteenth time. Mildred patted his shoulder and walked to the parlor, shaking her head and muttering to herself.

Eliza raised her eyes at George and shrugged.

"You two be careful out there," George warned them as they headed down the steps. "The war ain't over yet, ya know."

Mr. Franklin appeared at the door after the first knock. "Why, hello there. I believe you and I may have met before," he said as he nodded at Jim.

"Yessah." Jim nodded and smiled shyly. "I worked for Mr. Goodman, and this here is his good friend, Miz Eliza Long."

"Nice to meet you, Miss Long. Please come in. To what do I owe the pleasure of this visit?"

Eliza instantly liked this young, robust man. Before they could sit down in the parlor, Mrs. Franklin breezed in with a welcoming smile and an offer to get them some refreshment.

"First of all, may I express my condolences on the passing of Mr. Goodman. He was a truly good man and will be missed by this community."

"Thank you, sir," Jim answered. And then it dawned on Eliza that Jim had been welcomed into their home and was now sitting in their parlor being treated like a gentleman. Other than Mildred, Eliza didn't know many people like this. Her opinion of the Franklins rose dramatically.

"And, Miss Long, might you be related to Daniel Long?"

Eliza gasped. "Yes. You...you knew my father?"

"Yes, indeed I did. And again, may I express my condolences."

Eliza felt an unexpected lump form in her throat. "How did you know him? We were relatively new to Springfield."

"He was actually a client of mine. I was expecting to hear from you at some point, although not this soon."

"B-but, why?"

"He was a man of some means and was determined to not go into this war without drawing up a will."

Eliza chuckled. "I had no idea. We came here about Abe's will, not my pa's. What a surprise."

"Well, to be honest, Abe's will and your pa's are somewhat connected. I'm sorry, but none of this involves you, Jim, so I think you should excuse yourself unless Miss Long wants you to stay."

"No, please. I want him here. I trust him completely. And it actually does involve him, that is if he's still considered property of the Goodman estate."

"Lincoln's Emancipation Proclamation took care of that," Mr. Franklin said.

Eliza looked at Jim with kind eyes. "We were hoping that would be the case, but will it be honored if we lose the war?"

"We won't lose," he answered with confidence.

"And how are the two wills connected?" Eliza asked.

"The details escape me, but I'll tell you what I'm certain of. Tomorrow, I'll start digging through my files to find the actual wills. It may take days, if not weeks though. I'm dealing with quite a load of lawsuits at the moment. When I find the wills, I'll get back to you. Where are you living?"

Eliza told him then leaned forward and eagerly asked, "Tell us! What do you know about the wills?"

"Well, as you probably already know, your father and Mr. Goodman were very close friends and had been for years. My understanding was that the two of them and Mr. Goodman's brother traveled west to look for gold and were quite successful. Abe's brother died, leaving his property, which included some of the gold, to his son, Henry, who you might know. Abe had no children, and no heirs other than Henry, but for some reason was reluctant to leave it all to him. So, he left a portion of it to your father who, as Abe put it, was as close as a brother. How much he willed to your father, I'm not sure. And if your father died before Abe did, then it probably would all go to Henry. Do you know what day your father died? I know Abe died a day or two after the battle at Wilson's Creek."

"He died from wounds he received there, but I'm not sure of the day," Eliza said.

"That's something I can find out for you. When I pull all this information together, I'll call on you."

With that, he rose, shook their hands, and saw them to the door. Eliza was moved and intrigued by the possibilities. When they arrived back at Mildred's, they quickly separated and busied themselves with their routine tasks. Eliza then excused herself to visit Elin. Jim went to the greenhouse.

About a month later, in the middle of June, Mildred and Eliza watched a black buggy pull up in front of the house. A man in a suit walked confidently down the walk and up the porch steps. Mildred went to the door to receive him. He introduced himself as Daniel Long's lawyer and asked to meet with Eliza. Her heart started beating so fast she could barely contain herself.

"Mr. Franklin! Please come in. May we use the parlor, please, Mildred?"

"Of course."

"And could someone please go get Jim? This involves

him as well."

Mr. Franklin put up a hand. "Please, if you don't mind, Miss Long, I'd like to drive you and Jim out to Abe Goodman's farm. It would simpler for me to deliver my news out there."

Puzzled, but having complete trust in Mr. Franklin, they both got into the buggy and was off before Mildred could ask any questions.

After a mission to check out reports of a small guerrilla band harassing people west of Springfield, Jonathan made his way to his aunt's. He'd sent the other troops on ahead with Thomas because he had some serious thinking to do and didn't want the interruptions.

Eliza was on his mind constantly. The thought of waiting to marry her until the end of the war seemed illogical to him now. This war could go on for another decade for all he knew. The one thing he was sure of, it was getting harder and harder to leave her behind at his aunt's house. He longed to be with her, be alone with her. As it was, they were constantly in the company of a household of people. Frustrated with his feelings, he stopped his horse and looked heavenward.

"God, you've got to help me. I can't go on like this. I want her to be mine in every sense of the word. Is that selfish of me, Lord?" He ran his fingers through his hair in frustration. "Of course it is," he scolded himself. But then a new thought dropped into his head. What if Eliza was longing for the same thing? He was supposedly the logical one who had imposed the end of the war as the time for marriage. He'd never bothered asking her opinion. Dare he ask her today?

He continued to ride and pray. By the time he got to the edge of town, he had his answer. The peace that finally came to him was actually surprising. He planned to go straight to Mildred's, take Eliza for a long walk away from everyone, and ask her to be his bride. Not when the war ended but soon, very soon. He'd let her set the time, but he prayed fervently that it wouldn't be long from now.

He was bothered when he saw Thomas on the porch visiting with George and Mildred. This was something he preferred doing without their interference. Or without their knowledge, at least until Eliza gave him her answer and they had set a date.

"If you're here to see Eliza, I'm afraid you're out of luck," Thomas said.

"Where is she?"

Mildred took Jon's arm and led him inside where they could talk privately. "I believe she and Jim are on their way to Abe Goodman's place with a lawyer."

Jonathan was befuddled. "What? Are you sure? What in the world for?"

"I really don't know. Eliza's been trying to find a particular lawyer for a couple of months now. And for the past several weeks, she and Jim have been very secretive. I'm a little worried, Jon."

"She's never mentioned any of this to me. This doesn't make sense."

"I know. I'm sorry."

"Was it Abe Goodman's lawyer?" Jonathan asked.

"That's who she told me she was looking for back in May. But this lawyer said he was Daniel Long's lawyer."

"Really?" Jonathan scratched his head in wonder. "George knows how to get to Abe's farm, doesn't he?"

"I believe he and Jim went there several times a couple of years ago to try to salvage what food they could find."

Jonathan stepped out onto the porch and told George to saddle up and ride with him.

"Do you want company?" Thomas asked.

"Not this time, Burns. Sorry."

George wasted no time, and soon the two of them galloped away.

Mr. Franklin needed no directions to find his way to Abe Goodman's large spread. He pulled up in front of the house and assisted Eliza down from his buggy. She twirled around in wonder. The view from the house was breathtaking. In front of her stretched a wide valley with a glistening river flowing through it. She could just imagine what it had looked like before the war; with horses and cattle dotting the fields and pastures on either side of the river.

"So, why exactly did you bring us here. My curiosity is killing me."

"I wanted you to see this so that what I tell you will make sense." Mr. Franklin turned to Jim. "Jim, are you aware of how much land Abe owned? Could you show us both approximately where his borders are?"

"Yes, sir. I know exactly where the borders are. It'll take some time to walk it though."

"No need to do that. Just stand here and give us an idea of what he owned."

Jim gestured behind the house. "The property goes way back into those woods as far as the next road. And it includes pretty much everything you can see down there in that valley, all the way across the river and a little way into the woods way over there on the other side of the valley."

"Do you know how many acres he owned?"

"Yes, sir. A little over four hundred, sir."

"And, of course, this house and all these barns," Mr. Franklin added.

"Yes, sir."

Jim squirmed and stared at his feet. Eliza squinted at the young lawyer and asked, "What are you leading up to, Mr.

Franklin?"

"Eliza Long, all of this"—Mr. Franklin gestured across the expanse of land—"all of this is now yours."

Eliza just stared at him. Jim's head snapped up, eyes huge.

Mr. Franklin laughed, as if he was thoroughly enjoying his job at the moment. "That's why I brought you here. So, you can see with your own eyes what you've inherited."

"I...I don't understand," Eliza stuttered. "I need to go sit down." She staggered slightly, and Mr. Franklin lunged to catch her.

"I'm sorry, Miss Long." He helped her to the porch steps where she sat with a thud. "I didn't mean to shock you. I'm not sure how else I could have delivered such good news."

Eliza stared at him. "Tell me again. I'm not sure I heard you correctly."

"This property is yours, Miss Long. All 400 acres with the house and all the outbuildings."

"But why?" she asked, still unwilling to accept his words.

Abe Goodman's will states that at his death, all of his belongings go to Daniel Long if Daniel Long is still living. If not, then all of his belongings go to his nephew, Henry Goodman. When Abe died, your pa was still alive. The records show that your father died two days after Abe, giving him legal possession of all of Abe's property. Your father's will stated that, at his death, all of his property goes to his only child, Eliza Long."

Jim's face was unreadable. She stood and looked again at the huge expanse of land spread before her. "I can't believe it." She turned toward Mr. Franklin. "Are you sure of this?"

He laughed. "Yes, I'm sure, Eliza. Very sure. This is such a unique case and could possibly be contested, so I read the two wills over and over again as well as had another lawyer and a judge examine them. That's why it took me so long to get back to you. The three of us also investigated very carefully the records of the time of death for both Abe and your father. All three of us are certain there is no other possible way to interpret those wills and the death records. You can rest assured this will hold up in the Greene County courts."

Finally, Eliza smiled. "I still can't believe this."

"There's more," Mr. Franklin said.

"More?" both Jim and Eliza asked.

"Abe's gold is also yours."

Eliza's eyes flew to Jim's.

Franklin continued. "After the battle at Wilson's Creek, Abe sent his gold out of town with a few different people. I have a list of their names in my safe at home. He planned to contact them all at the end of the war and get his gold back. The list was for me in case he died."

"Have you seen it?" Eliza asked almost in a whisper.

"No. It's in a sealed envelope, not to be opened until the war is over and it's safe to put the gold back in a bank. The list is yours now if you want it. Or you can wait. It's safe. It also includes names of other people who owned the gold. Most but not all of it is Abe's. Some of it belonged to your father."

Eliza sat back down on the step and shook her head in disbelief.

"Can you handle more good news?" Mr. Franklin tentatively asked.

Eliza shook her head. "I don't know. This has got to be a dream."

"Do you remember when your father sold his farm in Fair Grove?"

"Yes."

"Well, just before the war hit Springfield, your father made some quick business decisions. He sold his farm then sold all his horses and livestock to the US military while they were still paying top dollar. He used that money combined with some of his gold and bought two hundred acres of prime land so he could start farming again at the end of the war. The two hundred acres he bought are adjacent to this land, along the river to the east. He wanted to finish out his days next to his friend Abe."

Eliza stood and walked several steps toward the beautiful valley with the river winding through it. "Six hundred acres? This is mine? This big house? Those barns? It's all mine?"

"Yes, Eliza Long. It's all yours."

"Jim? Did you hear that?"

Jim smiled a smile bigger than Eliza had ever seen on his face. "Yes, Miz Liza. I heard that. I sure did." Then he laughed. It was one of the purest, sweetest sounds she'd heard in years. He took his hat off and slapped his leg with it and laughed some more. Then Eliza joined him. She turned to see her valley again and whooped with joy, spreading her arms wide and twirling around.

"If this is a dream, please don't wake me up," she squealed and laughed some more. Soon, Mr. Franklin joined in. Tears started flowing and, against her better judgment, Eliza pulled both men into an embrace. She quickly released them and through her laughter, apologized, "I'm sorry! I just can't help myself. This is way too good to be true!" She laughed and hugged Mr. Franklin again. "Thank you, Mr. Franklin! Thank you, so much!"

Mr. Franklin watched with tears of joy. "Oh, how I wished I'd brought my wife to witness this. We all need more happiness these days, and she would have delighted in watching the delivery of such good news."

"Jim! Show me around! I want to see inside the house and every barn! Where did you live? It doesn't matter. You can pick whatever building you want. Did you grow up here, Jim?" Eliza chattered on as she walked into the house, dragging Jim with her.

Just as Eliza and Jim came out of the house, she heard the pounding of hooves coming down the drive. In a swirl of dust, two riders drew their horses to a halt several yards from the house. Jonathan! She ran to greet him with her skirts drawn up and gripped in her hands.

"Jon! Jon! What are you doing here?" Her heart pounded with joy at seeing him and with the anticipation of sharing her amazing news.

Jonathan dismounted and gathered her in his arms.

"Oh, Jon! You're not going to believe this! I have the most unbelievable, most wonderful news to tell you!"

He set her back from him and cupped her face between his large hands. "Can it wait, dear Eliza? I have something pretty important I need to ask you, and I need to do it now before I chicken out."

Seeing his intense gaze, she sobered immediately. "Yes, Jon. It can wait."

Jonathan looked up at George and motioned for him to leave them. Then he gazed back into her face. "Eliza, I've given this a lot of thought, and I've prayed about it over and over again. Eliza, will you marry me? Now, Eliza? Well, not right this minute," he chuckled, "but soon? Let's not wait for this dratted war to end. I'm not going to let it dictate something as important as this to me."

Eliza tried to speak past the lump in her throat but couldn't. She tried to nod, but his hands held her head too firmly.

"If you say no, I'll wait for you, Eliza, but I can't promise I'll do it patiently. I want you to be my wife now, Eliza, if you'll have me."

"Yes!" she sobbed. Then she laughed. "Yes! I'll have you, Jonathan Monroe! I'd marry you right now on this very spot if we had a justice of the peace to do the job!"

Jonathan's jaw dropped. "Are you serious?"

Eliza threw her head back and laughed again. "Of course I would! And why not?"

Jonathan picked her up, twirled her around then lowered his head and captured her in the sweetest kiss they had ever shared.

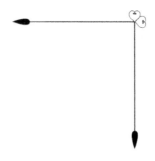

EPILOGUE

On April 10th, 1865, news reached Springfield that the war was officially over. A huge celebration took place throughout the city with a 200-gun salute being fired from the forts.

By then, Jonathan and Eliza Monroe had been married almost two years. Their wedding had taken place in Mildred's backyard a week after Jonathan's proposal. Elin Johnson was one of the honored guests. When she heard of their coming wedding, she almost begged them to live in her house. She was getting old and feeble and needed to have a family live with her. They accepted. Soon, Jon and Eliza added a third member to their family, with the birth of little Daniel, just eleven months after they said their vows.

Jonathan rebuilt the two gates in both Elin's backyard and Mildred's backyard so his pregnant wife could easily exit their yard and walk down the alley to visit the Scott household. Eliza often thought what a very different experience it was walking that alley compared to all the times she had walked it as a spy.

Mildred bought a small house down the street for former

slaves Jessica and Sarah and their eight children. She found jobs for both women doing housework and laundry for several families, making enough money to feed and clothe their children. Lucy and her two children were invited to stay with Mildred, much to the delight of George and Sally.

And Jim went wherever Eliza went.

In the two years after their wedding, Jon and Eliza made big plans for their future. As expected, Jonathan had as much trouble as Eliza in believing the news about Abe's will. Over time, they both agreed to sell Jonathan's land and make their home on the 600 acres Eliza had inherited. Living there during the war was out of the question though.

The whereabouts of most of the gold was still in question, as well as its owners. They saved that information for the near future, knowing Mr. Franklin held the answers in a sealed envelope in his safe. They all agreed to keep it hidden until the war was over and the banks were safe again.

Word reached them that Henry knew he was going to be charged with desertion and probably hanged, so he fled to Mexico with many other Confederate soldiers.

At least, that's what they were told…

ABOUT THE AUTHOR

Ava MacKinney formerly taught American history and Art. She is a lover of the outdoors, artist, history buff, blogger (thecrazycrookedpath.com), mother to five, grandmother to nine and wife to her amazing husband, Steve. They enjoy life on their small farm in the Ozarks, surrounded by dogs, cats and endless wildlife. Raised on a sheep farm in the mountains of Vermont, her parents gave her free reign to explore and to dream. Today she delights in dreaming up stories filled with adventure, romance, and spiritual growth.

If you'd like to follow Ava on Instagram, go to @avamackinney

Facebook, The Crazy Crooked Path.

Website: thecrazycrookedpath.com

AUTHOR NOTE

The Civil War in the Ozarks was complicated and often brutal. I loved researching this place and time as I wrote *Eliza Long*. All of the troop movements and battles that are mentioned in this book are historically accurate, with the exception of the activity of Jonathan and his men.

The accounts of the Battle of Wilson's Creek in August of 1861, Zagonyi's Charge in October of 1861, the building of several forts throughout Springfield, the Battle of Springfield in January of 1862, and many other military activities were thoroughly researched.

All of the messages carried by Francis, a fictional character, included information about actual military movements.

Several officers mentioned were also based on fact, including Generals Sterling Price, Nathaniel Lyon, John Fremont, Benjamin McCulloch, Samuel Curtis, Egbert Brown, James Totten, John Sappington Marmaduke and Major Charles Zagonyi.

If you enjoyed Eliza Long…

You will also enjoy the next two stories in this series. I hope you look forward to reading them as much as I enjoyed writing them.

Maddy Malone (Book 2)

Maddy dreads the day her neighbor, Silas, will return home from war to claim his two little children. Two children that have worked their way into her heart after four long years. Yet she knows they need their pa.

How can she maneuver through the days ahead as she tries to release them into the care of their father? How can she avoid the unwanted attention from her other neighbor, Sam Potter, who is determined to marry her and add her acreage to his?

As Silas rebuilds his neglected farm, he becomes more and more aware of Maddy's dire and dangerous predicament. He wants to help her but isn't sure how. In a bold and desperate move, Maddy backs him into a corner.

Megan O'Mally (Book 3)

Megan, desperate to flee scandalous rumors, joins her sister's family on a wagon train headed to Oregon. Her encounters with fellow travelers challenge her and help her receive God's forgiveness.

The wagon master, Nick Webster, is the biggest challenge of all. Will they resolve their continuous conflicts and grow to trust each other? Especially when the rumors catch up to her?

Printed in Great Britain
by Amazon

45372276R00169